The Broken Token

Chris Nickson

CREME DE LA CRIME

... it is good to see a publisher investing in fresh work that... falls four-square within the genre's traditions.

– Martin Edwards, author of the highly acclaimed Harry Devlin Mysteries

Creme de la Crime... so far have not put a foot wrong.

– Reviewing the Evidence

First published in 2010
by Crème de la Crime
P O Box 523, Chesterfield, S40 9AT

Copyright © 2010 Chris Nickson

Typesetting by Yvette Warren
Cover design by Yvette Warren
Front cover image by Peter Roman
Map of 18th century Leeds by Linda Hornberg

ISBN 978-0-9560566-1-0
A CIP catalogue reference for this book is available
from the British Library

Printed and bound by CPI Cox and Wyman, Reading, RG1 8EX

www.cremedelacrime.com

About the author:
Chris Nickson has years of experience as a professional music journalist and 30+ non-fiction books to his credit, though *The Broken Token* is his first published novel. He lived for 30 years in the USA, but hails originally from Leeds where the novel is set.

For Graham

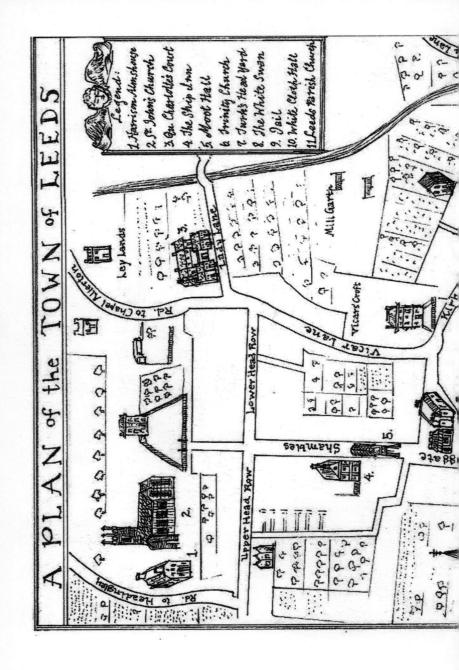

A PLAN of the TOWN of LEEDS

Legend:
1. Harrison Alms house
2. St. John's Church
3. Gen. Charlotte's Court
4. The Ship Inn
5. Moot Hall
6. Trinity Church
7. Turck's Head Yard
8. The White Swan
9. Jail
10. White Cloth Hall
11. Leeds Parish Church

Key Lands

Rd. to Chapel Allerton

Lady Lane

Mill Garth

Vicars Croft

Vicar Lane

Lower Head Row

Upper Head Row

Shambles

Kirk

Rd. to Headingley

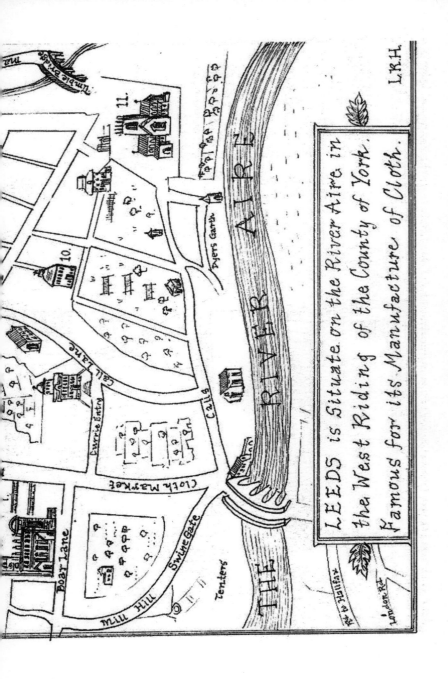

LEEDS is Situate on the River Aire in the West Riding of the County of York. Famous for its Manufacture of Cloth.

L.R.H.

Here is a token of true love,
We'll break it into two,
You have my heart and half this ring
Until I find out you.

Riley the Fisherman, Traditional

1

Sometimes he thought he'd been Constable for too long. After fourteen years he believed there was nothing that could shock him any more. He'd seen all of man's inhumanity to man, not just once, but many times over, and he understood nothing was going to change the way people were. They'd continue to steal and kill whether he caught them or not. All too often he felt he was trying to stem a tide with a bucket. Why, he often wondered, did he persist?

His title certainly sounded grand enough: Richard Nottingham, Constable of the City of Leeds. But for all the fulsome words, it paid barely enough to keep his family in a modest house on Marsh Lane. And to earn it he had to suffer the whims and demands of the Mayor and the aldermen, all of them grown fat and florid off the wool trade. They expected him and his men to solve all the city's crimes. By the year of Our Lord 1731, that was almost impossible.

He pushed the fringe off his forehead and stretched in his chair. It was ten o'clock on a September night and the raucous noise from the White Swan Tavern next door to the jail filled the air. He'd been working for fifteen hours and he was ready to go home.

He locked the building and walked down Kirkgate, past the shadowed, brooding bulk of the parish church and through York Bar before crossing Timble Bridge to reach Marsh Lane. It took no more than ten minutes, but it felt like an hour as the niggling events of the day played again in his mind. One carter grievously assaulting another over the right of way on Briggate, a drunk tumbling into the River Aire and drowning at Dyers Garth, money and meat stolen from a butcher in the Shambles while his back was turned, and a robbery turned bloody on the Upper Head Row, both thief and victim close to death. Then there was a slippery cutpurse with three victims so far. Plenty of work for today and tomorrow, and for all the days to come. It had been that way from the time, years before, when he'd started as one of the Constable's men, and worked his way up to deputy and finally Constable.

There was never any shortage of work for the morrow. The poor would always hurt the poor, then die themselves as they performed the hangman's dance. The rich, though, were never guilty, no matter what they did – and he'd seen them commit crimes others wouldn't dream about. The wall of property and influence they built around themselves kept the law firmly at bay. He'd tried hammering at it a few times, but one man couldn't bring down an edifice, even for justice.

As he opened his door the dim light of a candle greeted him, and he smiled to see Mary still awake, her face bent over a book. He knew what it would be – *Pilgrim's Progress*, the volume she read every autumn to prepare her soul for the long, bleak months of winter. She raised her head and he bent quickly to kiss her.

"I was beginning to wonder if I should go to bed," she said with a gentle smile.

"It's been a long day," Nottingham apologised, shaking his head wearily. "And more of the same tomorrow, by the look of it."

She stood, the plain fustian of her homespun dress sliding soundlessly as she rose, and he put his arms around her. There was a tranquillity about her features, not quite beautiful but content, and an ease and grace with which she moved. He felt safer with her close, with her warmth and love flowing into him. They'd been married over twenty years now, wed when he still had no idea of his future, and they were just living day to day in a room they shared with her parents.

And even that had seemed wondrous to him then, after growing up in damp, stinking cellars or sleeping rough. He'd known what it was like to be poor in Leeds, leading gangs of children to scavenge for rotten vegetables at the market so they could eat, cutting purses, doing anything he had to in order to survive until the next morning. He'd managed it, but so many hadn't.

Now he and Mary had an entire house of their own, and two daughters who were growing all too quickly. There was food on the table and coal on the hearth, as long as they weren't greedy. And he had Mary. He was grateful to her for giving him her love. And in turn he loved her.

The fire had died, but there was still a vestige of its warmth in the room. He settled gratefully into his chair as she brought him bread and cheese and a cup of ale.

"How are the girls?" he asked as he began to eat, realising how hungry he was. When had he eaten last – had it been something in the middle of the day?

"Rose's man called for her again this evening," Mary answered, beaming with pleasure. Now almost nineteen, Rose was ready for marriage. "I like him, Richard, I think he'd do well by her."

"We'll see," he answered noncommittally, although he knew the pair were a good match.

"He's scared of you," she informed him with a laugh.

"Good." He gave her a sly smile and a wink. "That way he'll not be taking advantage of her. And what about Emily? What did the Queen Bee do today?"

"The usual. Flounced around the house after school, expecting to be waited on hand and foot," Mary said with exasperation, rolling her eyes. At fifteen, Emily seemed to believe that her father's office elevated her to the gentry, and she expected to be treated that way by everyone, including her own family. Nottingham grimaced. With her attitude the lass will get a shock soon enough, he thought, one that'll bring her crashing back to earth.

He finished the food, picking the crumbs off the plate. But as he swallowed the last of them, a wave of tiredness seemed to envelop him. He needed sleep. He needed his bed.

He undressed, taking off the stained coat he always wore for work, the smell of wool filling his nostrils as he hung it on a nail driven into the wall. Its style was old and unfashionable, the cuffs reaching back almost to the elbow and the lapels broad as a desk, but it served its purpose, keeping him warm and reasonably dry. His shoes and hose were covered in mud from the courts and alleys where he'd walked all day and much of the evening. The once-elegant pattern on the long waistcoat had faded and rubbed over the years, and his linen shirt had been mended almost everywhere.

Before he slipped into bed Nottingham tied his hair back. As a young man he'd been so proud of his thick, straight blond locks that he'd refused to wear a wig. Instead, he grew it long, letting it flow on to his shoulders, the fringe all too often flopping into his eyes. Now it was thinner, so pale it was almost colourless, but the vanity had become habit; he still refused to follow the fashion of the day by cutting it short and donning a periwig.

Under the chilly sheet and rough blanket, Mary curled against his back, and he lulled himself in the heat of her familiar body. He closed his eyes, his mind skipping between despair and contentment, and hoped not to dream.

2

The relentless banging pulled Nottingham groggily from sleep. Once he'd identified the sound he slid uneasily from the bed, reaching across automatically to grab the short, thick cudgel from his coat pocket. The pearly light outside showed barely dawn and the floor was bitterly cold under his feet. A thin wind out of the west whistled through gaps in the window frame.

Wrapping a threadbare old cloak around himself, he wrenched the door open before the pounding roused the entire street. Standing before him, flushed and still panting, was John Sedgwick, the lanky, eager young man he'd made his deputy two years before.

"We've got a murder, boss," he announced breathlessly. "Two bodies."

"Two?" Nottingham asked, his mind coming rapidly awake as the air touched his face. "Where?"

"Queen Charlotte's Yard, behind the workhouse."

The Constable sighed. This was no way to start the day. He began issuing the necessary orders.

"Right," he commanded. "Make sure someone's looking after the body. Then go and wake the coroner. Ask him to meet me there."

Sedgwick gave a wry grin. "He's going to love that at this time of the morning."

Nottingham smiled darkly. Edward Brogden, the coroner, was a fastidious little man who also served as the city's Sergeant-at-Mace, preening in his self-importance, his wardrobe and the money his father had left him. He despised the poor, always ready to declaim that they were only in that state because they refused to work hard and better themselves.

But the law insisted he view every suspicious death, so Nottingham was going to take him to a filthy street where he'd complain constantly, cover his nose to try vainly to keep out the overpowering stench of life and death, then leave as soon as he was able. It was going to be a grim pleasure.

"The bugger'll live."

Sedgwick gave a wheezing laugh, and strode away with his long, powerful lope. Richard Nottingham dressed in the clothes he'd worn the day before, grabbed the dry heel of a loaf for his breakfast, and left the house soundlessly, to walk back into town.

There was a faint crispness under the dawn air, a sense of seasons beginning to change. Another month would probably see the first frost of the year. Wisps of smoke were already rising from a few chimneys on Vicar Lane as servants lit the early fires in the grand houses, and in the distance he could hear the muted sound of weavers setting up their trestles for the Tuesday coloured cloth market on Briggate.

Nottingham had lived on Briggate once, in a grand house near the top end where it met the Head Row. He still passed it every day. He'd been just eight when his father had discovered that his wife had taken a lover. He didn't understand it at the time, but he remembered the furore, his father yelling madly at his mother to get her body from his house and take her bastard son with her. Afterwards came the confusion of where to go, how to live… and then the hunger that governed their lives.

He still remembered his father faintly, although he'd done everything he could to push the man from his mind. Charles Nottingham had been a gentleman of high pretension and loud airs, a drinker and gambler who often stayed out all night – or all week, if the whim took him – with little regard for his wife and child. In his cups his temper would rise; he'd beat the servants, and even thrash his son. And when it finally suited him to be outraged by his wife's behaviour, he'd thrown out his family, even though she'd brought all the money to the marriage. But she had no rights; they all rested with him. Someone had told him that his father had left the city not long after, gone with his new mistress to join rich London society. In the sour tenements of Leeds, the boy and his mother had enjoyed no such choice.

He passed the grim face of the workhouse, took a deep breath and entered the maze of small alleys off Lady Lane.

Queen Charlotte's Yard was a majestic name for the row of hovels cramped on top of each other behind a thin archway that led off another small, ruined street. The houses struggled out of the mud as if they'd exhausted their strength, one, sometimes two, decrepit storeys tall, places of plunging, desperate poverty. The kind of places he knew all too clearly, where damp streams coursed down the walls and sewage backed up on to the floors after a heavy rain.

A small crowd had gathered, brought together by the dire spectacle of death. Nottingham forced his way between them, and they shrank away as they recognised his face. The Constable was authority, he was the city, and his presence never brought good news for them.

The bodies had been pushed face down against one of the houses, then roughly covered in rubbish and excrement so only the limbs showed. It was a man and a woman, the male on top in a splayed parody of animal fornication. Nottingham reached down and touched the woman's small hand for a moment, her flesh clammy and unyielding against his fingers. Dead a few hours, he decided. He'd wait for the coroner before uncovering them.

"Who found these two?" Nottingham raised his voice and looked around the people.

A scrawny man with long, matted hair shuffled forward. He had a pale face under a unkempt beard, his coat torn, dark breeches baggy over his thin thighs. Mould was growing in the seams of his coat, and dust, like beggars' velvet, lay on the nap.

"I did, sir," he answered, his eyes lowered deferentially.

"What's your name?"

"John, sir, John Chapman."

"You live here, John?" the Constable queried kindly.

"Over there." He looked up, showing ruined teeth, and indicated a house where the glass had been broken from all the windows and the door hung perilously loose. "With my brother and his family. I'm a potman at the Talbot Inn. I was leaving for work this morning and saw them there."

"What did you do then?"

"I went and found one of your men," he explained carefully. "He told me to come back here and wait for you."

"Did you hear anything last night?" Nottingham wondered. He knew it was a pointless question, but he had to ask it. "A fight, shouting?"

"No more than usual," Chapman demurred, and glanced quickly around the other faces in the crowd. "This isn't a quiet place at night, sir."

Voices murmured assent.

"But none of you heard anything like murder?" Nottingham asked them.

They all shook their heads, as he knew they would. There was no sense in asking more.

Sedgwick strode through the archway, followed by the coroner. Brogden picked his way daintily through the filth and puddles. He'd taken the time to dress in clean hose and breeches and there was a shine to his shoes. As expected, he had

8

a scented handkerchief clamped to his nose. Nottingham greeted him noncommittally and turned to the bodies.

"I'll need them uncovered," Brodgen ordered brusquely, distaste in his voice. The Constable nodded to Sedgwick, who pulled and turned the male corpse.

Nottingham knew him immediately. Just three days earlier his men had helped rescue him from a mob by the Market Cross at the top of Briggate. Daniel Morton, his name was, a dissenting preacher from Oxford who'd been invited to Leeds by one of the merchant families intent on saving the wicked souls of the poor. But from the way the poor had reacted on Saturday, they had no desire to be saved. Now Morton's expensive grey broadcloth coat had been ruined by bloodstains across the chest where a knife had ripped wounds and taken his life.

Then with a grunt Sedgwick heaved the woman over, and Nottingham felt his heart lurch. Hers was a face he knew far better than the preacher's. For a while she'd been almost as close as family to him. Now she was here, violently dead, humiliated, and beyond his protection.

"Christ."

The word tore quietly from his mouth, although no one seemed to hear. He bunched his fists in his coat pockets and turned away as Brogden bent to look at the corpses. Nottingham bit down on his lip and offered a silent prayer for her soul.

She'd been Pamela Watson when he first knew her, barely thirteen when she came to work for him as the serving girl. His daughters had been young and boisterous then, and Mary, struggling desperately to recover from pneumonia, had needed plenty of help looking after them.

Pamela had come on the recommendation of her grandmother, Meg, a seamstress who'd raised the girl after her mother died. She'd soon learned the ways of the place and made herself invaluable, always cheery and good-natured, even when the children were fractious.

She ended up staying for four years, sharing every hour of their lives, until she'd become like a third daughter. When she met Tom Malham, a farm labourer from Chapeltown, it had been Nottingham who had vetted him and approved the match. And when she left for a new life with him, there had been a hole in their house for a long time.

So he couldn't understand why she was here, stabbed and bloodied and left with the rubbish, beside a minister who'd only arrived in the city four days before.

He studied her face again, but there was no mistake; it was Pamela, beyond doubt. There had been no peace in her when she died; her lips were pushed back in a cruel rictus of pain. She was clothed in a tattered dress of cheap homespun, ripped at the hem and mended many times, her legs and feet bare, the skin already pale and waxy. A broken scrap of blue ribbon hung round her neck, as if someone had torn something off it.

"Definite murder, the pair of them," Brogden announced, doing his duty and dragging the Constable sharply from his thoughts. The coroner replaced the handkerchief over his nose and Nottingham caught the heavy smell of lavender.

"From his appearance, the man must have been of a little substance," the coroner continued unnecessarily. "That coat and breeches didn't come cheap. The woman was probably a servant or a whore, though. A bit old for the tastes of most men, I'd have thought."

"I know who they were." There was a coldness in Nottingham's tone that caused Brogden to glance warily at him for a moment.

"I'll bid you good day, then," he said, and tried to find a reasonably dry track out of the yard. Nottingham watched him leave, then turned to Sedgwick.

"You stay here and watch no one tries to strip this pair clean. I'll send some men to bring them to the jail. After that I want you to talk to everyone you can find in the court." His deputy nodded, and Nottingham continued, "You can trust Brogden to miss the obvious. These two weren't murdered here, there's not enough blood. So they were brought here, and it couldn't have happened silently. Someone must have seen or heard something."

"I'll find out, boss."

They wouldn't talk to him but they might open up to Sedgwick, he thought. The man looked more like one of them, his shoes barely holding together and his coat the product of many better years before it ever came into his possession. They wouldn't fear him the way they did the Constable. Nottingham might have come up the hard way himself, from Constable's man to deputy to Constable, but now his authority scared people.

"When you've finished, come back and tell me what you've found."

He just hoped the man could come up with something solid. Meanwhile, he had to go and break word of two deaths.

3

The chantry chapel bell on Leeds Bridge had tolled the end of the cloth market, and now other traders were setting out their wares on Briggate. Men were putting up chairs and saucepans, knives and spoons, selling everything that any house might need, from the finest quality to roughly mended tinker goods. Isaac the Jew, the only one of his tribe in the city, had a trestle filled with old clothes, from rags to the cast-offs of the rich. Up by the Market Cross others displayed the quality of their poultry, with chickens, ducks and geese locked in small wooden cages, their frightened racket drowning out any hope of talk.

Nottingham walked by it all, scarcely noticing the chatter and gossip of the sellers as his mind raced. Unbidden, the picture of Pamela's face as she lay there came into his mind.

A whore, just as his own mother had been. It made no sense to him. His mother had had little choice, cast out with no money and a young son after her husband learned of her love affair. With no skills and a reputation as a fallen woman, no one would employ her. Her body was all she had to make money. It had been hard, living hand to mouth, especially as she grew older and less desirable. Nottingham had helped, working when he could, stealing if the opportunity rose, but it was little enough. He'd watched his mother grow weaker, hating her life and herself, until she let death claim her. But Pamela… as far as he knew, she was still happily married and living in the country. How could she have died in Leeds, dressed like a pauper, with a man she could barely have met?

He had to find Meg, her grandmother, and tell her, to try to discover what had brought Pamela back to the city, and when.

He knew perfectly well what his first duty should be. He ought to be going to the merchant's house to inform him that his minister guest had been murdered. Then he should be using all his men to find Morton's killer. In the eyes of Leeds Corporation, the men who ran the city, Pamela's death would count for nothing.

But this time he couldn't look through their eyes.

The last he'd heard of Meg, she'd found a place in Harrison's almshouses, a series of neat cottages behind St John's Church. She'd be seventy now, if she was even still alive. When he knew her she'd been an optimistic, industrious soul, sewing every hour she could manage to provide for herself and her granddaughter. But she'd never missed a Sunday in church, both morning service and evensong, singing the hymns with a heartfelt joy and belief.

Nottingham couldn't stop the thoughts skittering through his mind like blown leaves. If Pamela had come back to Leeds, why in God's name hadn't she come to him? They didn't need a servant any more, that was true, now the girls were older and helping around the house. But he'd have found her a position with a decent family.

He kicked a stone and watched it rattle down the Head Row as he crossed and made his way through the grounds of St John's, taking the winding path between the gravestones laid flat on the earth. Nearby, girls from the charity school sat outside and learned politely under the eyes of a teacher. A teasing sun played down, tempting with the faint promise of warmth that might come later in the day. The almshouses stood together in a small terrace, sheltered by the back wall of the churchyard. They were homes for the lucky pious few among the poor who could find places there, where they could live out their days with a secure pension, free from the terrible spectre of the workhouse.

He walked curiously to the first of the houses, its stonework carefully pointed, the window glass clear and shining, door freshly painted, and knocked. There was a long pause before it was answered by an ancient woman, bent so low with arthritis that she had to cock her head to look up at him.

"Good day, Mistress," Nottingham said politely. "I'm looking for Meg. She used to live here."

The woman breathed in gently, gave a smile that turned her wrinkled face beatific, and pointed down the row.

"She still does. Fourth door, just down there. The one with the window box. She'll enjoy having a visitor, she doesn't get many."

"Thank you," he replied, bowed courteously to her and made his way down. There was a tranquillity about the place, just far enough from the city proper to seem removed, although merchants were beginning to build their mansions on nearby streets, and the sound of the boys over at the Free School carried across the field.

There was indeed a window box at the fourth cottage, and blooms had been coaxed out of the late flowers. If his errand hadn't been so grim, this would have been a good place to sit and think and visit awhile. For a second he wondered why he hadn't come to see Meg before.

But he knew the answer to that. There was always so much to do. If he wasn't working, he wanted to spend time with his family. There were barely enough hours to sleep, let alone think of himself.

Nottingham brought his fist down lightly on the door, suddenly aware of his tatterdemalion appearance, the coat with its frayed cuffs, stained with dirt and blood, the old breeches and mended hose.

He could hear her slow footsteps on the flagstone floor,

still unsure how to break the news. Pamela had been her only remaining family.

Then she was before him, the door swinging wide. Time had been kind, letting her face settle in wide laughing lines around her face and eyes. Her thin grey hair was carefully gathered under a mob cap. She stared up at him blankly for a moment before suddenly recognising his face.

"Richard!" she said with a genuinely pleased smile. "You're the last person I expected to come calling on me today." The youthful lightness in her voice made it sound as if her life was one long social round. "Come on inside," she beckoned him, "you look tired."

She bustled him into a tidy room. A chair and stool sat in front of the fireplace, although the grate was empty. There was a worn table under the window and a bed in the far corner. It was small, but Nottingham could see she had everything she needed.

Meg eased herself into the chair and gestured to the stool.

"Sit yourself down, Richard. And then you'd better tell me why you're here. From your face it's not good news."

He lowered himself awkwardly, still with no idea how to tell her.

"Is it something to do with Pamela?" she asked, and he nodded mutely in reply.

"You've come to tell me she's dead, haven't you?" The words were stark, all the joy suddenly stripped away.

He looked up and faced her, his heart as empty as hers.

"I have, Meg, yes. I'm sorry."

She was silent for a long time, then raised her right hand, knuckles gnarled into ungainly shapes, the fingers thick.

"Sewed all my life to make a living, until I couldn't do it any more."

"I know," he told her.

"I saw her settled with you, then married to Tom." Meg shook her head. "What's wrong with life, Richard?"

"What do you mean?" He gazed at her quizzically, trying to find the meaning beyond her words.

"I'm still alive and she's gone." She cocked her head at the walls around them. "I'm happy enough here, but..." Her words trailed off and he could see her eyes glisten as the tears began to form. "How did she die?"

He reached out and tenderly placed his hand on her arm. "She was murdered, Meg." He knew it would hurt, but he had to offer her the truth. She deserved his honesty.

Nottingham could hear her praying under her breath, her eyes closed. He left his hand where it was, keeping her anchored to the world. Finally she focused on him again.

"Thank you," she told him.

"I'm so sorry," was all he could manage. To his ears it sounded empty, forlorn.

"She had two miscarriages with Tom, did you know that?" Meg told him, drifting away on bitter memories. "And a still-born son that almost killed her."

"I had no idea," he said sadly, shaking his head. They'd had no word after she married.

"She survived all that. It was God's will, it had to be. I thought she was safe then, even if she couldn't have babbies. And now you're telling me He saved her just so someone could murder her." She sounded as bleak as a mid-winter night.

"Why was she even back in Leeds, Meg?" He asked the question that had been nagging at him since he'd seen Pamela's body.

Her sigh came from a place deep inside.

"Tom died, a year or so ago."

He shook his head.

"I didn't know. And she returned after that?"

Meg nodded.

"The landlord turned her out. He needed the cottage for a labourer, not a widow."

"Then why didn't she come to me?" he wondered imploringly. "I'd have helped her find a post."

"Oh, I know you would. I told her to go and see you." Her hands tugged and pulled at the old material of her dress. "But she'd developed some strange ideas out there, lad. She felt she daren't be a burden to anyone."

"A burden?" Nottingham said, astonished and confused by the idea. "How could she have been? We loved her."

"I know. We all loved her." The woman sighed again, and age settled heavily on her face. "But she wasn't going to listen to me. She wasn't going to listen to anyone, come to that. She'd never really talk about what happened there, but she'd changed. She was… harder, I suppose you'd say."

"From the look of things, she'd become a whore," he informed Meg cautiously.

The old woman nodded again, sadly.

"Oh aye, I know all about that. We argued about it enough. She didn't want to, but once she'd made her decision, she refused to have any regrets. Claimed it was the only way she could make a living. She tried to get work as a servant, but she didn't have any references, and no one wanted her when there were girls of twelve and thirteen available." She looked into the Constable's face. "Selling her body didn't stop her being a good woman, Richard. She was here every week, you know, bringing me a little money, whatever she could afford. It wasn't much, but she gave it gladly, and it made my life a little easier."

"When did you last see her?" Nottingham asked.

Meg thought back, counting through the long days. "Let me see… Thursday, it'd be. She brought me a little piece of ribbon she'd bought at the market. It's still over there, on the table. I told her I didn't need any ribbons at my age, but she said it'd make me feel like a girl again." Meg gave a brief, tight smile that flickered off her face as soon as it arrived. "And she was right, well, for a minute or two, anyway."

With difficulty she pushed herself out of the chair and crossed slowly to the window, picking a small length of bright blue ribbon off the table and rubbing it with her fingertips. He remembered the torn blue ribbon at the corpse's neck.

"Did she still wear that old token I gave her?" Nottingham asked.

"Every time I saw her," Meg replied with a nod, a warm glint of memory in her eyes for a second. "She always loved that, Richard."

It was one of the very few items his mother had refused to part with, even at her poorest; her half of a lovers' token. A penny, cut jaggedly in two, with a hole drilled in the metal so it could be worn around the neck. It was used at a parting, a vow of love, even a wedding gift, and a promise to return, however long the time might be. The halves would come together again one day, and the broken tokens would become a single whole.

For his mother it had remained broken. He didn't know who gave it to her. Vaguely he recalled a man who'd visited for a while, but there'd been no lover who came back to save her. Nottingham had been the only one at her bedside in the end. Yet she'd worn it around her neck faithfully until she died.

He wasn't even sure why he'd kept it; the thing had done her no good. By itself the token meant nothing to him. There were other, happier memories that didn't involve her waiting and hoping in vain for someone who'd never intended to return.

But Pamela had been taken by the coin when she first saw it.

18

He'd explained about broken tokens, and the romantic idea of parted lovers reunited had brought a bright gleam to her young face. So for her birthday one year he'd given it to her.

Then he looked at Meg and he could feel the hurt twisting up inside her, joining all the other pains of her long life – the loss of her husband and daughter. Losing her granddaughter might be the cruellest blow of all.

"Did she seem strange?" he asked eventually. "Was anything troubling her?"

"No more than usual." Meg sounded distracted, distant. "She'd stopped being a carefree soul by the time she came back here, Richard. Half the time she looked like she had the weight of the world pressing on her."

"Had anyone hurt her or threatened her?"

"Of course people had hurt her." Sour flintiness crept into Meg's voice. "For God's sake, she was a whore! Men used her and hit her. She was usually bruised or cut when I saw her. But she was still my Pamela. I could still see the little girl in there."

"I know," he said softly, and realised he'd seen it too, even in the silent scream of a dead face.

"I can't afford to bury her," the old woman told him.

"I'll take care of that," Nottingham assured her patiently. "I'll take care of everything. And I'll make sure you're there."

"Thank you." She looked at him with sad warmth. "And thank you for coming to tell me yourself."

"I couldn't do anything less," he admitted.

"Do you think you can find the man who did it?" Meg asked, and he could hear the hope in her, barely daring to rise. After a lifetime of disappointments he sensed she was scared to even make the request. He waited a moment before answering.

"I don't know, Meg," Nottingham replied truthfully. "But I'm going to try."

"And I'm going to weep like an old woman after that door closes. Please, Richard, come and see me again. Just bring me better news next time."

4

John Sedgwick gazed around the hovels of Queen Charlotte's Court. Looking up he could see the pale blue of the sky and the faded lemon colour of the sun, but the light barely seemed to penetrate between the buildings to offer hope here.

Now the bodies had been taken to the jail, people had shuffled back to their homes and the small street seemed suddenly bare. The doors were closed and unblinking in front of him.

The yard was like the one where he had a room with his wife and their baby son, like the place off Kirkgate where he'd grown up, like so many other courts crammed into every free space between streets and behind houses. It was all most people could afford. But one day he'd have better.

When the time eventually came for Nottingham to quit his post, he hoped the Corporation would make him Constable. He was twenty-five now, old enough for the responsibility. He'd been the Constable's man for seven years and deputy for the last two, doing more than his share of the dirty work and the investigations. He didn't read or write, but he knew he could learn those things, and he possessed a good memory. He knew the boss had faith in him and his abilities. In the meantime he worked long hours, every day of the week, just as Nottingham himself had once had to do. It was the way things went.

Sedgwick's long legs took him over to the first door. He knocked on the thin wood. There was no answer and he moved along, working methodically. He felt comfortable with people like these, flirting with the women and joking with the men, cajoling them gently into opening up. That empathy was his skill, the small, subtle prods that released thoughts and images.

This morning, though, all his charm seemed to fail him. No one admitted to knowing anything. He knew there'd have been noise until late, the roaring drunks, the fights that let off frustration at having nothing. That was the music of their lives here. But anything more they'd have ignored, either from fear or just because it was so different.

He continued around the court. A few people offered snippets that might help, but he could tell there was no substance to them. Only one old man offered anything of value, and even that was vague, a sort of stifled scream and blow he believed he'd heard in the middle of the night that roused him briefly from his rest.

"What time was it?" Sedgwick asked.

"I haven't a bloody clue," the man admitted, idly scratching a wild thatch of hair. "It were pitch dark, that's all I know. I went back to sleep."

Sedgwick sighed silently. It was almost nothing, but it was a place to start, and from there he'd be able to find more.

He'd come back and try again in the evening. Persistence paid off; he'd discovered that in the past. The Constable had once called him a terrier, and he liked the image, knowing how true it was. Once he caught the right scent he followed it, digging and worrying at things until he uncovered the truth.

He hadn't given much thought to the bodies. They were dead, beyond help. He remembered the preacher from Saturday, of course, another tosspot full of words and promises for the hereafter. Sedgwick had no patience for sermons. He'd watched how his father worked himself into the grave, dying young as he tried to keep his family clothed and fed. No god he wanted to believe in would have let that happen. The curate might have talked about a better place when he tossed a sod on the coffin, but what better place for his father than alive, with the people who loved him? Given his druthers, Sedgwick would have left this preacher to the fists and let him take his chances in the here and now. But he'd had his orders, so he'd hustled the man away. Roughly.

The girl had been unfamiliar. He'd realised immediately that the Constable knew her though, and that she meant something special to him. At first he thought she might have been an old lover, but he dismissed that. To his knowledge Nottingham didn't stray; if he did he was very discreet. And if he'd wanted a whore there were plenty of younger, prettier girls who'd willingly oblige a man of his rank.

He'd wait. If Nottingham wanted to tell him, he would. Meanwhile, there were other, more urgent answers that he needed.

5

The market was in full spate as Nottingham walked back down Briggate. Servants gossiped as they crowded around the improvised stalls, and mistresses were halted by the cries of the sellers with their boastful promises of the best goods at the cheapest prices.

When he was a boy the twice-weekly market had been a treasure trove. At the end of the day, while the traders packed up, he and other lads would scavenge, picking up all the rotting pieces of fruit and vegetables no one wanted to buy. It looked like a childish game, but it was all done with deadly seriousness. It meant survival. The food tasted bad, but it filled the belly and staved off aching hunger for another night or two. It had kept Nottingham and his mother clinging to life through a few bad winters.

Children still did it; if anything, there seemed to be more of them now. He could pick them out easily, dressed in clothes that were dirty rags, their eyes darting everywhere as they tried to remain invisible. Some of them would grow up to be cutpurses. A few would grow up and have jobs and families. But most of them, he knew full well, wouldn't live long enough to find out.

Just below the Moot Hall, the building where the business of the city was transacted, he turned into a gap between two houses that opened into a cleanswept flagstone court. A series of small, neat stone buildings were set around it, surprisingly quiet after the raucous bustle of the street. He opened the closest door and walked in.

Two clerks were working, the only sound in the room the

careful scratching of quills on paper. One of the men glanced up as light came into the room, eyes squinting as if he were emerging from a dream.

"I'm looking for Mr Rawlinson," Nottingham announced.

"He'll be in t' warehouse," the man answered, obviously eager to rest for a moment. "I'll take thee back there, sir."

"I'll go back myself."

The warehouse stood at the rear of the court, built against a thick wall. It had no windows, and the stout wooden door, now open, was usually firmly double-locked to protect Rawlinson's valuable inventory from thieves.

He was a merchant, making a good living buying cloth at the market then reselling it to the Continent. The wool trade was Leeds's prosperity and its reputation, and Leo Rawlinson was one of the men who kept the tide of money rolling in.

Nottingham had little more than a nodding acquaintance with him, but as far as he knew the man was honest enough – as honest as any man in business could afford to be. There'd never been any gossip about his character. He took his family to service every Sunday at Holy Trinity Church on Boar Lane and lived on the other side of the River Aire in a large new house he'd had built the year before on Meadow Lane.

The Constable knocked on the open door but didn't enter. This was a merchant's premises; he'd wait for an invitation.

Instead the man came out. He was short and running heavily to fat, his face blotchy red and jowly under a freshly-powdered wig. Rawlinson's coat was of expensive pale broad-cloth, only the best, fashionably cut without being ostentatious, the lapels carefully pressed flat against his chest, cuffs fastened with discreet gold buttons.

"Mr Nottingham," he acknowledged with a small, imperious nod. "What can I do for you?"

"I believe you've had a Mr Morton staying with you, sir."

A fleeting look of astonishment and annoyance crossed Rawlinson's eyes.

"I do," he admitted cautiously, "but what business is it of yours?"

"Everything that happens in Leeds is my business, sir." Nottingham allowed himself a short smile to accompany the formal politeness.

"Happen it is," the merchant conceded grudgingly. "But if you know the answer, why are you asking the question?"

"You can vouch for the man?"

"Of course I can," Rawlinson said dismissively. "Daniel Morton is a man of strong Christian convictions. My wife and I invited him here from Oxford to preach."

Nottingham gave a sage nod.

"I know, sir. I had to stop a crowd injuring him on Saturday at the Market Cross."

Rawlinson stiffened, his pride bristling. "I was very disappointed by that. I hoped those without privilege might have welcomed his words."

"I wouldn't know, sir." It was the blandest answer the Constable could manage.

"What's this about?" the merchant asked suspiciously. "Has there been more trouble? Has someone else attacked him?"

"Yes, they have." Nottingham paused. "I'm afraid he's dead, sir. Someone killed him last night."

The colour fled from Rawlinson's face. He seemed to deflate, all the substance vanishing from his body, and he reached out to steady himself against the stone of the building. He was a man who inhabited a world where violent death didn't exist, and where tragedies came from God, not man.

"How?" he asked once he'd regained a little composure, and then, "Where?"

"He was murdered, over by the workhouse," Nottingham

explained briefly. "I'm sorry, Mr Rawlinson."

There was incomprehension and pain on the merchant's face. It was all beyond his understanding.

"Would you like me to escort you home?"

"No, no," he answered unsteadily. "I'll stay here."

A long silence lingered between them before Rawlinson wondered in a wounded voice, "But why would anyone want to murder Daniel?"

"I don't know that yet, sir," Nottingham answered soberly. "We only found the bodies this morning."

"Bodies?" The merchant looked up in surprise. "There was more than one?"

"There was a woman with him, a prostitute."

Honest puzzlement crossed Rawlinson's face.

"A prostitute? And she was murdered too?"

"Yes."

"My God." The words seemed to hiss out of the man.

The Constable waited before pressing on.

"I'm afraid I'll need to ask you about Mr Morton, sir." He knew the merchant would rather be alone, but the more he knew now, the sooner he could resolve the killings.

"Yes. Yes, of course." Rawlinson sounded like a man suddenly distracted by images of mortality.

"When did you see him last?"

"Yesterday evening, I suppose," he answered. Nottingham could see the man piecing events together and trying to draw omens from them. "He was with us for supper about eight. He said he was going for a stroll afterwards."

"And you'd no idea he hadn't returned?"

The merchant shook his head, looking dazed.

"We retire early, Mr, Nottingham… and then I was at the cloth market by dawn. I assumed he was still in his bed then."

"Had he received any specific threats that you knew of, sir?"

Rawlinson barked a grim laugh.

"Oh aye, there were plenty of those. More than he told me, probably. But he said they weren't going to stop him spreading God's word. I admire that." He stopped and corrected himself. "Admired."

"How long had he been here?"

"Since Friday." The merchant sighed. "My wife and I met him when we were visiting friends in Oxford. We heard him preach and we were both very moved." He glanced up at Nottingham. "I take it you're a Christian man?"

The Constable inclined his head slightly and smiled, hoping that would suffice. He believed, and attended church, but the last thing he wanted now was to discuss religion.

"Daniel was part of a very young group called Methodists," Rawlinson explained. "We heard him preach three times while we were there, and he truly had a gift from God." He smiled at the memory. "He could touch people in their souls. This city needs someone like that."

"So you invited him here?"

"We did." The merchant pulled a large white handkerchief of fine linen from his breeches and wiped his face. From being a man of heft and privilege, he now looked as if the slightest breath of wind would tumble him. "I felt privileged when he accepted. But you know what happened here when he preached."

"Yes, sir," the Constable agreed. It had been an ugly scene, as close to a riot as he'd seen in Leeds in several years. He still had the bruises.

"Daniel said the people didn't want to listen, and the church here didn't want a voice that might be louder and stronger than theirs," Rawlinson continued. "The Reverend Cookson went to hear him speak, did you know that? He had the nerve to come to my house afterwards and tell me Daniel had to go, and that several merchants and aldermen agreed with him. He claimed Daniel was fomenting revolution."

So Daniel Morton was despised not only by the poor he'd come to save, but by their masters too, Nottingham thought with growing curiosity. That made for precious few friends in the city.

"And was he talking revolution?"

"Don't be so daft!" the merchant exclaimed with a withering look. "God's love is hardly revolutionary, Constable."

"I suppose not." He hadn't had chance to listen to Morton's words on Saturday; he'd been too intent on keeping the man safe. But plenty of people had found no love in what the man had said.

"If there's any consolation," Rawlinson said with a wintry bleakness in his tone, "it's that he's with God now. He was a devout man. I don't know why or how he ended up next to a prostitute, but I'm certain it wasn't for the reasons most people will gladly assume."

"I only hope I'll be able to find out," Nottingham answered with heartfelt sincerity.

6

It was only a short distance back to the jail on Kirkgate, not far enough to let his thoughts wander. The bodies would already be there, waiting on thick stone slabs in the back room they kept as a mortuary, and he needed to look more closely at them.

It wasn't a prospect he ever relished. Murder in all its forms was common enough, and he saw the results. The souls might have gone to a better place, but too often it was obvious that the bodies had done all they could to cling to life. Nottingham found no pleasure in examining the wounds or the effect of poisons, and cataloguing the pain on the faces.

This would be harder than most. Usually the bodies were anonymous, just names on a sheet of paper or faces he'd seen before. This time he had to look at Pamela, to go past the memories and see beyond the girl he'd watched grow into a woman and find anything that might help him discover the person who'd killed her.

Nottingham felt the chill of the room as he entered, his candle throwing large shadows on the walls as he set it down on the table. He decided to concentrate on Morton's body first, trying to keep his mind off Pamela, and yanked the sheet off the corpse. The dead man's face had strong features, and his hair had recently been shaved to stubble under a costly wig. When the Constable turned the wrists, he saw Morton's hands were those of a gentleman, soft and clean and unused to labour. Slowly, Nottingham unbuttoned the corpse's long waistcoat and shirt, noting the two cuts on the chest, teasing the material away from the dried blood, working gently and patiently until he revealed skin.

He judged the blade must have been an inch across and finely sharpened. As far as he could tell, it must have been long, too, driven deep into the body between the ribs. He spent several silent minutes poring over the wounds and imagining the angle of the blows. Not a professional killing, he concluded; that would have only needed a single cut. Yet at the same time, it didn't look like the crazed work of a madman. That wasn't much help, but it was better than nothing at all.

The Constable turned his attention to Morton's pockets. There was a notebook in his coat, almost new, with a few lines for sermons scribbled in it, and the letter from Rawlinson, written the month before, folded and refolded several times, inviting him to Leeds to preach. A handkerchief, well used, as if Morton had been suffering from a cold. The waistcoat only held a few small coins and a gold watch, still ticking, inscribed *To Daniel, from your loving father* on the back. So robbery hadn't been a motive.

He had to steel himself to move across to Pamela and pull down the shroud that covered her. In death she looked younger, more brittle. One of the men must have found an old, faded shawl in the court and folded it across her belly; the scrap of blue ribbon had been laid on top of it. He remembered Mary giving her that shawl years before, one spring night when she looked chilled. She'd kept it all this time, or maybe she'd never been able to afford a new one. Her dress had been mended so many times that in places it seemed more yarn than material.

She'd been stabbed twice, too. Like Morton, the blows had been to her chest. Even without pulling down the bodice of her dress, Nottingham could judge that the same knife had killed them both. One of them must have cried out, he thought, idly stroking his chin. Someone must have heard something.

Cuts and bruises covered her arms, some fading, others more recent. What interested him was a livid mark on her face, by the cheekbone. It hadn't had time to bloom, but the blow had obviously been vicious. He could almost feel it and see her head snapping backwards. It would have been enough to leave her stunned, gasping and vulnerable.

Pamela's small hands were bunched into fists, and he pried them open carefully. Her fingers were rough and red, the nails cracked and bitten, the palms heavily calloused. No one would have mistaken her for a lady.

Her hands were empty, and he understood the fists were her last small act of defiance against her murderer. There was no sign of the token he had given her. Had she lost it in the struggle, or had the murderer taken it? If so, why? He leaned back against the wall, gazing at the two bodies. Someone had put them together, thrown them away among the rubbish. But the way they'd been placed, in a harsh, deliberate parody of coupling, meant that whoever did it had wanted people to believe them together.

Perhaps they had been, Nottingham wondered. Morton would hardly the first preacher to succumb to sins of the flesh. In his time he'd known several whose words and deeds hardly matched, and Pamela couldn't have afforded to be choosy about her men. Rawlinson had insisted his guest was a devout Christian man, but keeping secrets was easy. An evening stroll could quickly turn into a hunt for a woman.

Yet why kill them? What had they done, what had they seen?

Nottingham sighed and ran a hand through his hair.

Maybe someone had wanted Morton dead, and Pamela had been killed because she was in the wrong place. Or, he thought, turning the idea upside down, Pamela had been the victim, and Morton had been the innocent.

But it was too early for theories. He needed evidence.

7

Nottingham was finishing his daily report for the Mayor when Sedgwick returned. He knew it was pointless, but as he wrote he still attempted to play down the double murder, trying not to give it too much weight among the other events. The cutpurse had struck three more times, including a lady's reticule. Still no one had seen or felt a thing. But however much he tried to hide it among other crimes, he knew the pressure to solve the preacher's killing would arrive soon enough. Rawlinson would talk to the Mayor and the notes and questions would flow fast.

He put the quill down and stretched.

"Find anything, John?" he asked wearily. With his long legs, the lad always looked awkward, never seemed completely at home in his tall body with its pox-scarred face. But there was intelligence in his eyes and a warm smile that invited confidences.

"Bugger all," Sedgwick replied, shaking his head in frustration. "The only glimmer I got was a man at the other end of the yard who heard a noise."

"Anything worthwhile?"

"He said he might have heard a short scream, sort of stifled, then a blow." Sedgwick shrugged and kept his eyes on the Constable.

And he wouldn't have got up to look, the Constable knew. People didn't want to see, because to see was to be involved, and he didn't blame them. Most lives had trouble enough without seeking more.

"He was the only one who heard anything?"

"So far. I'm going back later and find the people who weren't there this morning."

"You were at the Market Cross last Saturday, weren't you?" Nottingham asked.

Sedgwick grinned. "Oh aye. The way that preacher was acting I wasn't even sure he wanted to get out. He seemed to enjoy the attention, if you ask me."

"Why do you think they went for him?" the Constable pondered. He hadn't understood their reaction. Maybe it had been a factor or motive for murder.

"Why?" Sedgwick looked astonished at the question. "Well, look at it, boss. They hear enough about God as it is, right?" Nottingham nodded. "You're poor and someone tells you that your lot in life is to suffer but you'll have your reward in heaven. Now, that's meant to make you feel better about not having anything while you're here, but it's all nothing." He glanced at the Constable, who was concentrating fiercely on his words. "Heaven isn't helping when there's no jobs and you can't pay the rent, is it?" He felt himself begin to redden with anger but didn't stop. "All it does is keep the rich richer. Then this bugger comes along, and he's obviously got money, too. He starts spouting on about how we're all equal in the eyes of God, when most of us know we have nothing. But he still wants us all to pray for our salvation. How would you feel?"

"So someone spotted him last night and decided to send him off to God?" Nottingham speculated. It was possible.

"Happen so," Sedgwick agreed, his fury spent. "He was with a whore, after all."

The Constable shifted in his seat. He had to tell the deputy about Pamela.

"There's something you'd better know, John. That whore was once our servant."

"Oh?" Sedgwick raised his eyebrows. The gesture tilted a

small knife scar beside his mouth and gave him a ghoulish smile. "Did you have to turn her out?"

Nottingham gazed at him levelly. "She left nine years ago to marry a farm labourer. Evidently she came back to Leeds a year back, after he died."

Sedgwick lowered his eyes. That explained a lot, he thought.

"Sorry, boss," he apologised hurriedly, "I didn't mean any disrespect. Do you think she's important in this?"

"I don't know," the Constable admitted with a baffled shake of his head. For now he knew very little. "But we're going to find out. She used to be called Pamela Watson, then she was Pamela Malham out in Chapel Allerton. See what you can find about her," he ordered briskly.

"Yes, sir."

"I talked to Rawlinson earlier. He said the preacher went out for a walk after supper last night. I want to know who saw him, where and when." Nottingham paused, looking worried. "The Mayor's going to want the person who killed the preacher. Leeds has to look respectable and safe. And I want the bastard who killed Pamela."

He needed to know more about Daniel Morton. Nothing the preacher had told Rawlinson could be taken at face value; words could be twisted into so many fabulous shapes. So in his best hand Nottingham composed a letter to the Constable of Oxford, asking for any information about Morton's background and character, then dispatched it to leave with a coach the following morning.

With the state of the roads it could be a fortnight before he heard anything. Hopefully he'd have the killings solved long before he received word, but it would all contribute to building a picture. With no immediate leads he'd snatch at every scrap of knowledge he could gather.

Nottingham sat back in his chair, concentrating, fingers steepled in front of his mouth. He barely noticed the afternoon tumult of the street outside, the carters cursing at each other as they angled for room on Kirkgate, the clatter of horses' hooves, the constant bristle of conversation and the cries of vendors as they tried to sell out their wares for the day.

He was groping in the dark at the moment; he needed a way into the maze of this mystery. All he had were the bodies of two apparently unconnected people who'd been murdered together. He needed something… anything.

Finally he stood up. He headed down Briggate in firm, concentrated strides. Just before Leeds Bridge he turned on to Swinegate, walking past the King's Mill with its wheels still loudly and busily grinding corn into flour, then along a row of cramped, dilapidated cottages and artisan dwellings that looked on the verge of toppling over. A cobbler had his goods displayed in the wide front window of a house, the sound of his hammer against the last echoing across the street as he worked. Heat escaped like a thick sheet from the blacksmith's forge, while next door a stable reeked of horse dung as an ostler's boy shovelled the steaming mess on to a larger pile against the wall. Servants shopped late for their mistresses, talking and laughing loudly as they passed, enjoying the brief respite from the grind of their chores. Another frontage was piled with chandlers' goods – coiled ropes, canvas duck, and all manner of items for the barges that plied the Aire. Outside the door, two women, both haggard and old before their time, chatted earnestly as their children played in the dirt, close to the puddles and mud where people had slopped the contents of the chamber pots into the street that morning. Somewhere in an upstairs room a baby was yelling, its cries going unheeded.

Without stopping to knock or announce himself,

Nottingham slipped through a small door into a house that reeked foully of sweat and excrement. Thin light came through a dirty window, showing a pair of boys, neither of them more than five, their faces grimed almost black, playing on the filthy floor. A woman of indeterminate age sat on a chair in the corner, her eyes closed, oblivious to the world, an empty cup of gin on the table beside her.

He followed the passage through to the kitchen, a tumble-down affair that had been added to the house sometime in the past hundred years and never cleaned since the day it was built. The man he was seeking would be there, enjoying the sun through the window and the heat of the cooking fire.

Amos Worthy was leaning against a wall, eyeing a girl who stood in the centre of the room. She kept glancing up at him nervously, her face blushing red from his gaze, scarcely a day over thirteen. Seeing her, Nottingham thought of Emily, safe and sheltered at home. This lass had probably just arrived from one of the villages, hungry and in need of the only work she could find in the city.

Worthy was a procurer, one who ran many of the prostitutes in Leeds. By rights he should have been before the Assizes many times over, convicted and hanged or transported to America. But several of the city's aldermen used his whores; he provided them with girls and in return they kept him safe from the law. His finger was firm on the pulse of the city's crime.

Worthy turned his head, saw the Constable, and casually instructed the girl to come back later that evening, watching as she scuttled away.

Although he had to be well into his sixties, Worthy still cut a powerful figure. He was an inch or two taller than Nottingham, with a stiff, straight back and a barrel chest. His nose had been broken and badly reset so often that it curved awkwardly and unevenly across his face.

Two of the Constable's men had once worked for Worthy, and told with awe how the man always relished a fight, first into the conflict with fists and boots flailing and last to leave, his cheeks flushed with blood and battle lust. His vicious reputation went beyond men; Worthy was also ruthless with his girls. If one didn't do as she was told, he beat her bloody with his own hands. A repeat offence brought cuts from the razor he kept in his waistcoat pocket. If there was ever a third instance, the girl simply disappeared.

"Mr Nottingham," he said lazily. "A pleasure to see you here."

There was no trepidation in his eyes, merely a mocking smile. Worthy was a rich man, even if he spent little of his wealth on his clothes or his surroundings, and even less on his girls. Yet no matter how full his coffers or however many favours the people who ran Leeds owed him, his profession and low birth made him socially unacceptable. However important he was, the order of things kept him at arm's length – but within easy reach.

"I'm sure you heard about the murders last night," Nottingham began bluntly.

"Always unfortunate when people are killed," Worthy agreed, calmly picking at a tooth with his thumbnail. "Especially when one of them is a guest in our city. But it's nothing to do with me, Constable."

He grinned, holding up a tiny piece of food for inspection before wiping it on his greasy coat.

"You deal in girls," Nottingham pointed out. "She was a prostitute."

Worthy shrugged carelessly. "Another girl. You know there's no shortage of them." He fixed the Constable with a pointed gaze. "If she'd been one of mine you'd have heard about it by now." He made it sound like a threat.

"Did you know her?"

"Of her." He chose his words carefully. "She came to me last year, but I turned her away. She was too old for the tastes of my customers. They prefer someone… younger."

"Like the girl who was just here," Nottingham said, keeping his tone deliberately even.

"Exactly, Constable," Worthy smiled sharply, showing jagged teeth. "Pretty little thing, ain't she? Still got her youth, and maybe even her maidenhead, too. She'll be good for three or four years yet… as long she does what I tell her."

The Constable let Worthy's bait dangle between them for a few heartbeats. Then he calmly asked, "Can you tell me anything about the girl who was killed?"

The procurer considered the question before answering.

"I used to see her at the Ship sometimes. I don't think anyone ran her, I'd have heard if they did. But for the little she'd earn, it would be a waste of time. I couldn't even tell you her name."

"Pamela." The Constable supplied the name firmly.

Worthy nodded as if he'd learned an interesting new fact.

"One way or another, they all die." He paused before adding, "You should know that all too well, Mr Nottingham."

The Constable stared hard at Worthy, wondering at the meaning beneath the words. He desperately wanted to smash the smugness from Worthy's face, but knew better than to do it. He breathed in and out slowly and said, "I'd be interested in knowing if she had any friends, or any regular customers, anyone who knew her."

"You know me, always of service." This time the grin was wolfish. "If I find anyone, I'll let you know."

8

Nottingham had scarcely returned to the jail before a messenger arrived, summoning him to an audience with the Mayor. He'd expected it, and sooner rather than later, but he'd still hoped for a small reprieve, at least until tomorrow, when he might have known a little more about the murders.

Edward Kenion had only been sworn into office ten days before, and this would be their first official meeting. Kenion would be eager to establish his authority as Mayor, and that meant he would want a quick solution to the preacher's murder to gain the confidence of the merchants and the Corporation.

Grimly, Nottingham ran a hand through his hair, and vainly tried to brush the worst of the dirt off his old coat before walking over to the Moot Hall.

The elaborate two-storey building stood like an island in the middle of Briggate, forcing traffic to flow around it. In the cellar lay a dank, secure jail for prisoners committed to the Quarter Sessions for serious crimes, a place to pass the days until sentence of transportation or the noose. The ground floor was given over to the Shambles, the city's butchers' shops. Around them the paving stones were permanently discoloured by blood, and a small pack of salivating dogs circled hungrily all day, fighting as they hunted for offal and scraps.

Upstairs, however, it was a different world. Everything was quiet and luxurious. The wood was polished to a deep, lustrous brown, and the rooms had thick Turkey carpets to hush the footfalls. The business of the city was carried out and the future of its citizens decided in meetings and unreported conversations. The windows, appropriately, looked down on the bustle of Leeds.

Kenion was waiting for him, not yet quite at home in the Mayor's chamber. He'd hold the position until next September, then another alderman would take over for the following twelve months. Nottingham had seen them come and go, some venal, a few good, most just taking it as their reward for faithful service.

To his eyes Kenion appeared nondescript, a man of average height, with a pale, astonished face and hook nose, neither thin nor fat, a fellow who seemed to disappear into his wig and clothes. But that anonymity only made him all the more dangerous, the Constable decided. He'd want to make his mark if he could. What happened now would set the tone between them for the next year, and they both knew it.

"Sit down." Kenion gestured at a chair, and Nottingham folded himself into it. The Mayor remained standing.

"I've had Alderman Rawlinson here," he began slowly.

"About Mr Morton's death, of course," the Constable said smoothly, hoping he could put the Mayor on the back foot. "A terrible business."

"Yes." Kenion seemed a little nonplussed and Nottingham continued to take the initiative.

"I understand how devastated he must feel," Nottingham glided on. "Mr Rawlinson was in shock when I broke the news to him this morning. After all, he invited the man here to perform good works. Then Morton was abused while preaching, and finally murdered."

"What are you doing to find the culprit?" Kenion asked briskly, trying to retake control of the discussion.

"Everything we can." Nottingham held out his hands, palms up. "We don't know much yet. But I've got men searching for the place where the murders took place, before the bodies were moved to the yard. And I have people trying to trace Mr Morton's movements last night."

The Mayor nodded in approval.

"Good, good."

Nottingham hesitated deliberately before continuing.

"I understand the vicar and some of the aldermen didn't approve of Mr Morton, sir."

Kenion looked up sharply, a blush rising from his neck.

"I believe there had been a few words," he admitted in a quiet voice.

"I'll need to find out more about that." It was an opportunity to press, and he was going to take it.

"You don't seriously think they could have had anything to do with it, do you?" Kenion sounded appalled at the mere idea.

"I don't know. But if I don't follow up all the possibilities I'm hardly doing my duty to the city," Nottingham pointed out.

"Of course," the Mayor agreed after a moment's awkward consideration. "But you realise this is a crime that has to be solved. And I want it solved quickly."

"I understand." The Constable rose from his seat, bowed to the Mayor, and left. "I want it solved too."

There'd been no mention of Pamela, he thought without surprise.

Outside, he breathed deeply. It had gone well, all things considered, and had been mercifully brief. Thank God Kenion was still new and uncertain of his power. That would pass soon enough, and he'd become as demanding as everyone else who'd ever worn the chain of office.

Nottingham wove his way across the road, between the carts clogging the street, negotiating a path among clumps of stinking horse and cow dung that hadn't been cleaned up yet, then walked purposefully back down Kirkgate, past the graceful weight of the White Cloth Hall where the Tuesday afternoon buying and selling was already in session, to the parish church.

He'd known it all his life, but its size still gave him pause, a huge grandeur against the sky, the spire reaching towards heaven. When he was young he'd truly believed it was the house of God, that He lived there, unseen but all-knowing. It had been a good thing for a child to believe, but he'd grown out of it quickly enough. He still loved the building, though, its stone blackened by the city's soot, and he hoped that the words and hymns there went directly to God's ears.

The tall, thick oak doors stood open, but he didn't enter. Instead he followed a small path around the side of the building and knocked on a smaller door beside the transept.

It was opened by a man about his own height in a cassock of richly-dyed black wool, a short wig perched squarely atop a head with deep-set, suspicious eyes and strong, handsome features. The new curate, Nottingham surmised. He'd heard one had been appointed, but not that he'd already arrived. He looked to be in his early twenties, and had a haughty scowl on his face. A younger son with money and connections, Nottingham thought, serving a brief apprenticeship here. Soon he'd probably be appointed to his own expansive living.

"I'd like to see Reverend Cookson."

The curate cast a dismissive eye over Nottingham's clothes, making a swift judgement.

"I'm afraid that won't be possible," he said, failing to keep the sneer from his voice. Nottingham looked directly at the man.

"My name's Richard Nottingham. I'm the Constable of Leeds."

"Oh?" It was apparent that the curate didn't believe him.

"I'm here on official business," the Constable stated firmly.

"A matter of murder."

The man pursed his lips, weighing whether the visitor was telling the truth.

"The Reverend isn't here," he admitted finally, and Nottingham felt his fuse start to run short.

"And did he happen to confide in you where he was going?" he asked acidly, wanting to humiliate the curate for his assumptions. "Or when he'd be back?"

The other man lowered his eyes for a moment.

"No." He barely concealed the anger in the word.

"No, I don't imagine he did," the Constable said with satisfaction. "Tell him I called, and that I'll be back tomorrow. I need to see him."

"Yes."

"What's your name?"

"Crandall," the curate replied haughtily. The door closed silently on well-oiled hinges and Nottingham was left with the empty quiet of the churchyard, broken only by the small twittering of sparrows in an oak tree.

There was little more he could do today. Sedgwick was unlikely to have anything to report before morning, and if he turned up anything important, he'd come to the house. The lad would be a good Constable some day.

He made his way across Timble Bridge; the beck below was not much more than a trickle after the long, dry days of summer. Away from the heart of the city there was stillness in the air, and he relished the absence of noise assaulting his ears. God willing, he'd have peace tonight. But first he had to tell Mary about Pamela, and that wouldn't be easy.

She emerged from the kitchen, thick smudges of flour on her apron, hands and face, surprised and happy to see him so early, and guiltily Nottingham realised he was rarely home before dark.

He embraced her, closing his eyes to smell her hair and feel her cheek against his shoulder. Only when she started to pull away did he realise he'd been holding her longer than usual.

"You were off with the lark this morning. It must have been important," Mary said finally, giving him a curious look.

"When isn't it?" he laughed, trying to make light of the situation.

"They expect far too much of you," she told him seriously as he followed her into the kitchen.

"Well, this time they were right." He poured a cup of ale from the jug on the table. "A double murder," he said solemnly.

"Oh God, Richard."

She was a Constable's wife, but even after all these years she'd never come to terms with the violence that was part of his work. He rarely told her about the crimes; if she knew even a fraction of the truth she'd be horrified. But this time he knew he had no choice.

"One of the victims was Pamela," he said softly.

She stopped and turned to stare at him, her eyes suddenly wide in utter disbelief.

"Pamela?" she asked. "Our Pamela? Pamela Watson?"

He nodded, with no idea what else to say.

"Oh, dear Jesus," Mary cried, and he pulled her close again, stroking the back of her neck beneath the mob cap as if he was comforting a child. Suddenly she pushed him back.

"It can't be her," she announced with sudden confidence. "She married that labourer in Chapel Allerton, you remember that. She doesn't even live in Leeds any more!"

He looked down at her sadly.

"He died, love." Nottingham spoke in little more than a whisper, watching tenderly as the final shred of hope died in her. "Seems she came back about a year ago and didn't tell us.

It's her, it's definitely her."

The tears came then, flowing silently at first, then she started to wail. He knew Mary had felt especially close to Pamela, spending every day with her. They'd been mistress and servant, but the bond had gone far beyond that. They'd known each other's lives and secrets. Now all he could do was hold his wife until the crying stopped. He didn't say anything more.

Finally, wiping her eyes with the back of her hand, she sat at the table and drank deeply from his untouched cup. The track of a last tear wound its way like a slow river through the flour on her cheek.

"How?" she asked shakily.

He reached over and took her hand. It seemed small in his, and he squeezed it lightly before shaking his head, indicating he wasn't going to tell her and knowing she'd guess.

"Have you found whoever did it?"

"No," he admitted. "And right now I don't even know where to begin. I went to see her grandmother – you remember Meg? I promised her we'd take care of the funeral."

"Of course we will." She tightened her grip on his fingers as if she was holding on to life. "You're going to find her killer, aren't you?"

He loved the full, simple faith she had in him.

"I hope so," was the closest he dare come to a promise. "I'll do everything I can."

Mary stood slowly and walked to the window, clasping her hands together tightly and looking out to the fields in the distance. For a long time she remained silent, letting her thoughts and memories fly. He watched her, trying to imagine what she was feeling. The minutes seemed to stretch until she eventually wondered, "What are we going to tell the girls? They'll both remember her, especially Rose. She was seven when Pamela left."

"Maybe it's best just to tell them she died," he suggested. How did you tell the young about murder, he thought. "They don't need more than that."

Mary nodded her agreement sadly.

"Where are they, anyway?" he asked.

She turned back to him, trying to cover her sorrow with a wan smile.

"Rose took little Michael from next door down to the river to play so the Earnshaws can finish their cloth." Their neighbours were weavers, and the clack of their loom could usually be heard for all daylight hours along the street. "She's good with children. She'll make a fine mother herself one day soon."

He understood his wife's need to talk about everyday things right now, to ground herself in life and run away from death. But her statement caught at him. He'd always thought of his daughters as little girls, but they weren't any more. They were almost grown. Time was rushing on, not only outside but within himself, too.

"And what about Emily? Where's she?"

"She announced she was going over to Caroline's after school." Like her sister before her, Emily attended the local dame school, at Mary's insistence. She believed girls needed reading and writing as much as boys. But where Rose had loved to learn, Emily went sullenly, paying little attention to her lessons. She was clever, there was no doubt of that, but she believed herself too advanced and grown up for the basic education the little school provided. Nottingham had seen her reading adult books which he would hesitate to approach himself.

"Announced?" He found his voice rising sharply. "That lass has got far too many airs and graces."

They both loved the girls, but all too often despaired of their younger daughter. For the last year Mary had insisted Emily would eventually grow out of her moods, but if anything they'd become worse. Punishments had no effect on her. With her sharp tongue and impertinent ways, Nottingham fretted that she'd end up wearing a scold's bridle one market day, on display outside the Moot Hall.

"I'd better get back to work," Mary said, to herself as much as to him, seeking something to do. "I still have to finish kneading the dough for tomorrow's bread."

Her hands began to move rhythmically in the bowl. Nottingham knew there were more things she wanted to say, but they weren't going to come out now. That had been her manner for as long as he'd known her. Sometimes it infuriated him, knowing she was keeping words and feelings carefully locked inside. But they'd emerge eventually. It had taken him a few years after their marriage to understand that. Once he did, he knew it was one of the reasons he loved her. She was someone who needed to approach the world in her own time and in her own way, after consideration and thought.

But in their bed she'd always been passionate, working with her body rather than her mind. Even after twenty years she was still like that, as playful as the young girl he'd courted and tumbled in the woods by the old manor house. Sometimes her urgency astonished him, her need to be touched, to simply be. And it always made him respond and transported him. If the girls or the neighbours heard them, he didn't care. She was his wife, the woman he loved. He had no apologies to make.

9

Sedgwick doubted he'd be finished before midnight. It wasn't a job he'd trust to any of the men; they were fine for keeping the peace, but none of them could use their brains. He'd started south of the river, canvassing the inns to see if Morton had been in any of them the previous night, without any luck. Then he'd crossed back over Leeds Bridge to cast his net wider. The landlord at the Old King's Head thought he remembered someone in good grey broadcloth, but he wasn't certain. So far no one else had come up with even an inkling of recognition.

When he was finished he'd return to Queen Charlotte's Court to question the people he hadn't seen that morning. It was going be another exhausting day, and he knew that when he finally returned to his room his shrewish wife would accuse him of being out drinking and whoring. She'd been uneasy when he began this job, but in the two years since he'd become deputy it had grown worse; at any excuse she'd begin shouting until her voice was raw. Then things would be fine, at least until the next night, when she'd start all over again.

Even her own father had advised him not to go through with the marriage.

"Her mother were bad enough, God rest her soul," the man had said miserably as they shared a jug in the Talbot. "But Annie's ten times bloody worse. Do thisen a favour and steer clear of her, and I say that though she's me own blood."

But he had been seventeen, and youth and lust won out over sense; he'd been paying the price ever since. His job meant long hours, some of them spent in taverns with tipsters and

50

criminals. And if he'd been out whoring a couple of times, it was simply because he needed a little warmth. Since the birth of their boy James, two and a half years ago, Annie's embraces had been cold, her tongue even sharper than before. A man needed something to keep him going, and whatever it was, Sedgwick wasn't receiving it from his wife.

He slipped into the passageway that led from Briggate to the Ship, hoping they might still have some food he could eat as he asked his questions. Nottingham would be at home by now, sitting with his family, and Sedgwick envied him the calmness of his house. Not only the space, but the serenity that seemed to fill the place, as if the troubles of the world couldn't touch it.

The food was all gone so he was left hungry, but at least there was a tankard in his hand as he chatted to the landlord, a ramshackle, wiry man in his fifties with muscled arms and wild, dark hair that grew in a bushy mass from his head.

"You heard about the preacher who was killed?" Sedgwick asked.

"Oh aye." Walter Shipton wiped his hands on his leather apron and spat on the sawdust floor. "Whole town's heard about that by now, lad. The preacher with his feet of clay and the whore." He shook his head.

"Was he in here last night?" Sedgwick asked.

"Ee, lad, not that I recall," he answered slowly. "It were a quiet night, so like as not I'd have noticed him. You found out what he was doing with her, anyway?"

Sedgwick laughed to himself. If the landlord couldn't imagine what a man did with a whore, it wasn't his place to educate him.

"Shame about her, though," Shipton continued, drawing himself a small pot of ale and tasting it appreciatively.

"How do you mean?"

51

"She were a nice lass," he said thoughtfully. "Bit strange, but nice, you know."

"You knew her?" Suddenly Sedgwick was very interested.

"She were in here most nights, did a lot of her business from over there." He nodded at a corner. "No trouble, mind, she'd just sit, and the men would come to her if they wanted her. They'd go off and, you know, then she'd be back."

Pleased at finally discovering something useful, Sedgwick drained his mug and pushed it forward for a refill. It wasn't food, but it was the next best thing.

"How long had she been coming in?"

"A year, mebbe?" Shipton creased his brow, emphasising the drinker's broken veins in his ruddy cheeks. "Aye, around that, I suppose. Bit less, mebbe." He leaned forward conspiratorially across the counter and added in a whisper, "She give me a tumble once, in t'back when the wife were gone. Called it my commission." He chuckled wheezily at the memory. "By Christ, lad, she were a good tup, too, passionate like. I thought she'd be the death of me that day. Made me feel twenty again, she did."

Sedgwick shared the other man's smile for a moment before pushing on.

"Was she in last night?"

"Last night? Let me think." He called over the serving girl, a harried rail of a lass who looked the Constable's man up and down briefly before giving Shipton her attention. "Was Pamela in last night, do you recall?"

"Early on," she replied without any hesitation, rolling her eyes when he looked confused. "You remember. You had to throw old George out for shouting the odds like he always does when he's drunk as a lord. She helped you get him through the door. I didn't see her later, though."

"Aye, that's right." Shipton brightened. "Must have been about nine. George Carver had had a few too many and he was trying to pick a fight with some 'prentice lads. Always wants a brawl when he's drunk, does George. I had to get him out for his own safety, else they'd have bloodied up my floor with him. Course, he didn't want to go, ranting and raving. Pamela started talking to him while I was trying to push him out and he ended up going meek as owt."

"Did she leave with him?" Sedgwick asked carefully. He was alert now, on the scent.

"'Ee, I don't know, I weren't looking by then, once the bother were over." He glanced at the serving girl who shrugged noncommittally.

"Do you know where she lived?"

"Somewhere close, I reckon, but I couldn't tell you where. Never asked. It didn't seem to matter." He took a long drink and drained the pot. " 'Appen someone'll know. I can ask for you, if you like, there'll be more in later."

Sedgwick nodded his appreciation.

"Did she have a pimp?" he wondered. The landlord might know.

"Pamela?" Shipton shook his head firmly. "Nay, not one like her. Too old, and not enough business to warrant one bothering with her."

Sedgwick finished his ale and left, satisfied with the bit of business. He'd found out a little. In the doorway he almost collided with a familiar face trying to slide in for a quiet drink.

Adam Suttler was the most talented forger in Leeds, an educated man with the ability to copy anything faithfully, but no sense of judgement. Twice Nottingham and Sedgwick had stopped him before he became too foolish. Changing a will to favour a younger son could have found him on the gallows. So could his alteration of a merchant's bill of lading to the continent, allowing thieves to make off with some bales of cloth. On both occasions the paper evidence had handily been destroyed, saving Suttler from capital justice. They'd visited his rooms at the top of a winding stair, surprisingly airy and clean, and put the fear of God into Adam with threats and promises as his wife and daughter had scuttled into the other room.

Sedgwick wasn't naïve enough to think he'd returned to the straight and narrow – apart from working as a clerk or a scrivener, what could Suttler do? – but at least they hadn't heard much of him in the last year.

"Evening, Adam," the deputy said breezily. "Staying out of trouble?"

"Of course, Mr Sedgwick," Suttler answered uneasily. It was a lie, and they both knew it, but for the moment they accepted it as the truth.

"You heard about the murders."

Suttler shook his head sadly. "A terrible business. I saw him preach on Saturday, very inspiring."

He might be a criminal, but the forger was also a thoughtful, religious man, in church without fail every Sunday. Still, the deputy supposed, what he did was no worse than some of the merchants, and they were always ready to bow their heads piously.

"A lot of people didn't like what he said," Sedgwick pointed out.

"True," said Suttler, bobbing his head in agreement. "But perhaps they chose not to hear."

"Did you see him at all after Saturday?"

"I didn't," he said with regret. "I'd have liked to talk to him."

"You go and enjoy your ale," Sedgwick told him. "And keep out of trouble, Adam. Next time we might not be able to save you."

With a shy, embarrassed smile, Suttler ducked into the tavern.

Oh well, the deputy thought. Even if there was nothing to be gained from Suttler, the information about Pamela and George Carver was worthwhile. Now all he needed was a little more luck at Queen Charlotte's Court to make it a good night.

But it seemed as if fortune had just been teasing him. By ten he'd discovered nothing new. His long legs ached from walking and standing, and his knuckles were sore from rapping on doors. At least he'd been able to find many of the dwellers in the court at home. Yet however much he tried to joke and charm information from them, there was little to be had. A couple believed they might have heard something in the middle of the night, but they weren't certain. Most, it seemed, had been dead to the world. And perhaps they'd earned that, he thought. Working too many hours for too little money, with hardly any food in their bellies, sleep was their only escape from drudgery, the only place where all things and all people could be equal. When simply living was an act of concentration, how could he blame them for not noticing the deaths of people they didn't even know?

Still, he continued to go methodically around the court, knowing he wouldn't be satisfied until he'd done everything possible. In the attic of a building that should have been razed twenty years before, its stairs rickety and rotted beyond danger, he found an impossibly young mother, with her husband and tiny baby. She looked barely thirteen, her eyes not yet lost in desperation, wearing a dress that had likely been fourth- or fifth-hand when she found it two or three years earlier. Her man barely seemed older himself, a walking jumble of rags tied to his body with string.

"We heard summat, didn't we, Will?" she told Sedgwick. "I were up with the baby – he's got the croup, I think – and there was this noise."

Sedgwick smiled down at her.

"What kind of noise, luv?"

"I wasn't sure at first. Like someone was dragging something heavy. You remember, Will, I woke you?"

The lad nodded.

"What time was that?"

The girl looked confused.

"Time? I couldn't tell you that, mister. It were dark, and it felt lonely, so it must have been the middle of the night. You know how everything feels far away then? Except him, of course," she added, rocking the child in her arms.

"Did you look out?" Sedgwick asked. The room's sole window opened on to the court.

The girl shook her head.

"Not at first. I mean, the noise stopped, so I didn't think much more of it, and I had to deal with the babbie. But when it started again, I did."

He looked at her pinched face, alert now.

"Started again? You mean there was more? How much later was that?"

She considered her answer.

"Not long. I don't know, I'd just got him settled and fed, and I was going to go back to sleep when I heard it."

"And what did you see?"

"There wasn't much of a moon, so I couldn't really make it out proper. But it looked like someone pulling something, I thought it were a sack of rubbish or summat. I thought it was an odd time, but folk are strange, aren't they?" she asked with an almost childlike sense of wonder at the world.

"They are, yes." He smiled kindly at her. "Did you see or hear anything else?"

"Not really." She frowned as she tried to recall. "A bit more noise from down there, and that's it. I didn't really see anyone, not enough to make them out or owt. Once it went quiet again, that was it."

"Was it a man or woman you saw?"

The girl shook her head.

"I didn't really notice. Just a shape."

"Thank you." Sedgwick noticed that the boy she called Will had barely glanced up throughout the conversation, a sullen expression on his face.

"Will Littlefield," he said, and the youth turned sharply. "You do right by this lass of yours, or I'll be back."

"You know him?" the girl asked, taken aback.

"Oh aye," Sedgwick replied. "Been friends a long time, haven't we, Will? Just haven't seen much of him recently, and you might say that's a good thing for everyone."

He bowed to the girl and left.

Not a bad night after all, he said to himself as he strolled back down Briggate towards home. It might even make the bollocking he'd get from his wife worthwhile.

10

Telling the girls about Pamela's death hadn't been as bad as he'd feared, Nottingham reflected the next morning. Rose, with her feelings always close to the surface, had sobbed, comforted by her mother, but Emily, always self-absorbed, had been stoic.

As he poured water from the ewer into the basin and cleaned his teeth with a piece of sponge, he could hear them all in the kitchen. Mary was issuing her quiet instructions, Rose was trying too hard to inject some gaiety into her voice, to sound lively and happy, while Emily's brooding presence was evident in her silence.

The subject of death was carefully avoided as they broke their fast with porridge and small ale. But the conversation remained stilted, almost as if Pamela's ghost was in the room with them. As soon as he'd eaten Nottingham pulled on his coat and left, eager to escape the close atmosphere of the house.

Sedgwick was waiting at the jail, dark circles underlining his eyes. He'd arrived home long after the clock struck midnight and had been back by six, listening to the reports of the two men who made up the night watch. He was a good young worker, the Constable thought, there was no doubt of that.

Nottingham sat and listened carefully as his assistant explained what he'd discovered the previous night.

"Good," he nodded appreciatively. "I talked to Amos Worthy yesterday, and he told me Pamela was often at the Ship. Now we need to find where she lived. I'll take care of that. Have we found the killing ground yet?"

"Not yet. But from what that lass said, it can't be far away. I've got a couple of men searching; we should have it this morning."

"You keep on looking for anyone who might have seen Morton the night before last. The bugger was somewhere before he was killed."

"What about George Carver?" Sedgwick wondered.

The Constable rubbed his chin. Carver was a local legend. He'd been a successful merchant once, selling cloth to the Continent. Somehow the business had slipped away from him and he'd lost everything, his family, his house, whatever money he'd had. No one knew how he earned a living now, but he was in the inns every night, drinking. Pleasant, even charming, company when sober, once he was drunk he turned belligerent and violent, going out of his way to pick fights. He was under five feet six, his body bloated by years of alcohol; all too often he was the one who ended up bloody and unconscious. He'd spent plenty of nights in the cells, as much for his own protection as for the trouble he caused. It was hard to picture him as any kind of murderer, let alone killing in cold blood. But stranger things had happened.

"If anyone saw him with Morton, we'll bring him in," he decided.

Sedgwick nodded, then said, "By the way, the cutpurse hit again last night. Twice."

Nottingham sighed slowly and pushed a hand through his hair.

"Jesus God, how many times is that? Are you sure it's the same one?" Anger rippled through him. He didn't need this on top of the murders.

"Got to be, boss. No one saw or felt anything. One of the victims this time was a merchant."

Nottingham swore.

"He'll be complaining to the Mayor. That's all we need right now."

"He's a clever bugger, whoever he is," Sedgwick said, shaking his head in admiration. "Slick, too."

The Constable rubbed his face. Already it seemed as if this was going to be a very long day.

"You know it'll be sheer good luck if we get him, don't you?" He sighed again. "Still, we'd better show willing and put someone on it. Who can we spare?"

Sedgwick pursed thin lips and thought for a moment. Including the two night walkers, they had a total of six men. It wasn't enough, and they both knew it. Nottingham kept trying for more money from the Corporation, but they weren't prepared to pay. Safety was good, as long as it came cheap.

"There's Wilkins," he suggested. "He's not the sharpest lad, but he's willing."

"He'll do," Nottingham agreed. "Tell him to spend the day walking around and keeping his eyes open."

"He'll be doing it within the hour."

The Constable sat back in his chair, framing his thoughts.

"We need to find out *why* Pamela and Morton were murdered, John. It looks like it had something to do with sex, but they were both fully dressed." He shrugged helplessly. "It could be someone trying to confuse us, or I could have got it all wrong. What do you think?"

Sedgwick chewed the inside of his cheek as he considered his reply.

"It must have something to do with sex," he agreed with conviction. "It has to. He'd not have gone to all the trouble otherwise, dragging the bodies around like that to make his point."

"Go on." Nottingham was giving his full attention, intrigued by where this might lead.

"Whoever did it can't be right in t' head. Laying them out like that, it's a sick thing to do."

"True," the Constable agreed.

"They weren't robbed," Sedgwick continued, counting the points on his fingers, "so we can forget that."

"So how do we find the killer?" Nottingham asked him bluntly.

"If we knew that, he'd be in the cells now, boss."

A slow silence filled the room.

"I agree the murderer's probably mad in some way," Nottingham said finally, "but that just makes him more dangerous."

The deputy digested the thought.

"We'd better find him soon, John."

After Sedgwick had left, Nottingham sat quietly. In his head he went through every step he'd taken so far, wondering if he'd missed or ignored anything that could hint at the murderer's identity. Most people killed from passion or from drink, quite often the pair of them together. This was something very different, however, coming from the mind, not the heart. Usually it took no more than a day to find a killer. But this time he could throw all his men into it and still not come up with a result. And the other business of the city – the cutpurses, the thefts, the violence – wouldn't stop just because he had to concentrate on this. Finally, exasperated, he shook his head, closed the door behind himself and began walking back to the parish church.

This time the new curate didn't ask his name, simply looked at him resentfully and escorted him into the vestry. The Reverend Cookson was at his desk, poring over a Bible and making notes – doubtless for one of his interminable sermons, Nottingham thought. He glanced up as the Constable entered, laid down his quill, and straightened the expensive powdered wig that was already perfectly perched on his head.

"I heard you were looking for me yesterday, Constable."

"I was," Nottingham confirmed. Unable to resist the dig, he added, "Your curate seemed to doubt my identity."

Cookson had the grace to offer a slightly embarrassed smile, showing discoloured teeth in a large mouth.

"You'll have to forgive Mr Crandall. He only arrived a short while ago and doesn't know Leeds or its people yet. I think he's more used to parochial ways."

The Reverend had a rich, mellifluous voice, used to filling the nave with its rolling cadences on a Sunday, its sound almost too big for such a small room. Although he wasn't a merchant, Cookson's position made him one of the most important men in the city, well paid as a shepherd of souls, his influence extending into every walk of life. Tall and thin, he had the self-satisfied, smug look that Nottingham despised. For all that he was supposedly a man of God, Cookson was also a fighter, always eager to slyly grab a little more power or consolidate what he already had.

"Now, what can I do for you, Constable?" he asked.

"You'll have heard what happened to the visiting preacher?"

"I did." The vicar sat back and crossed his arms. "A terrible business when someone serving God is murdered," he said, but there was no great sympathy in his tone. "Do you know who killed him?"

"Not yet, no," Nottingham replied straightforwardly, his eyes fixed on the other man. "From what I've heard, I gather you didn't approve of what he was saying."

Cookson raised an eyebrow. "Are you trying to imply I might be a suspect in this death?"

Nottingham weighed his answer carefully.

"I rarely imply things, Reverend. If I have something to say

I come right out and say it."

Cookson examined the words for hidden meanings or barbs, then nodded.

"You're right, of course. It was impossible to approve of someone who wanted to upset the social order in the name of religion."

"And what was it he said that was so upsetting?"

"People like the late Mr Morton aim their words like missiles, Constable. They end up making the poor discontent with their lot, and that's a dangerous thing, as you well know." He searched Nottingham's face for a reaction. Seeing none, he continued, "When you have a man talking like that, it's sowing the seeds of rebellion and revolution, and that's asking for trouble in a place like Leeds. The Jacobins up in Scotland would love to see confusion down here so they could march in."

"Then perhaps you feel his death was a good thing?"

Cookson shook his head in vigorous denial, but the Constable could see the truth in his eyes.

"I never said that, Mr Nottingham. Every death, particularly one so violent, is a tragedy. But you saw the reaction he provoked on Saturday – and that was from the very people he was supposed to comfort! We can't have more scenes like that. It was almost a riot, man!"

And he was right, Nottingham knew. If they hadn't hustled Morton away quickly, it would have been ugly.

"I'd planned to ask that the Mayor ban Mr Morton from speaking in public, for the safety of Leeds," Cookson stated. "Then, of course, it became unnecessary."

"I believe there were several merchants who agreed with you?"

The vicar look astonished at the question. "More than several – the majority, I'd imagine. The idea underlying Morton's words is one that challenges the entire social order.

We may be equal in the eyes of God, but here on earth we all have our separate roles to fulfil. Some lead, others follow, and that's the way it's always been. To suggest to the followers that maybe the whole idea is wrong is rather like letting a young child play with a lit candle. It's irresponsible."

And dangerous to those in power, Nottingham thought cynically. Yet it didn't fully address Saturday's events.

"But as you said, the people he came to help didn't want to hear him, either. Why do you think that was?" he asked.

"The nature of man is essentially conservative, Constable, surely you've noticed that in your work?" The Reverend gave a short, broken smile. "People like the familiar, the routine of the church. The followers are content to follow, it's what they know, they're comfortable with it. But if people like Morton repeat their message often enough, at some point people will start to question things. Once that happens, the future becomes a lot less certain."

"Mr Morton's future became very certain," Nottingham said flatly.

"Just because I didn't want him preaching, that doesn't mean I wanted him dead." Anger bristled like lightning across Cookson's face.

"I never said it did, sir," the Constable replied softly, defusing the tension. "There's one other matter I'd like to bring up with you."

"What's that?"

"The girl who was with him."

"A prostitute, from what I've heard," the Reverend dismissed her.

"That's right. She needs to be buried."

Cookson looked up questioningly.

"Surely a pauper's grave is adequate?"

"I'm paying for the funeral," Nottingham announced without explanation.

The vicar looked as if he was about to say something, then stopped and nodded.

"Very well," he agreed gracelessly. "Have her brought over and I'll have someone take care of it."

He hadn't expected more from Cookson. The Reverend was a wily man, one who hoarded power, spending it only when absolutely necessary. He relished his position in the city, so well established that he had no need to flaunt it. Nottingham didn't care if he delegated Pamela's funeral as long as she received a decent burial, and he felt no qualms on his insistence.

The whores were plying their trade outside the taverns on Briggate. With no market, the street seemed almost quiet, the thick trudge of cartwheels on cobbles and the yells of drivers the main backdrop. The air smelt of dung and smoke and offal, the smell of Leeds that Nottingham had known all his life.

Just past the Ship, where a passage opened like a crack in the wall to a teeming court, he stopped to talk to a prostitute who was idly watching the passing men. Polly had a proud face. At twenty she'd been doing this for seven years, but there was still a mischievous spark in her eyes. The life hadn't beaten her down yet.

He stood so that his shadow fell across her face, and she turned, suddenly aware of his presence.

"Mr Nottingham," she said with a smile that looked surprisingly happy. "Out for some morning fun wi' a lass?" Her wink was so deliberately outrageous that he couldn't help but grin at her.

"Doubt my missus would like that too much, Pol." His voice became serious. "I'm looking for a little help."

"Go on, then," the girl replied. She pulled a threadbare

shawl tighter around her shoulders as a light breeze began to funnel down from the north.

"You heard about the girl who was murdered the other night?"

Polly's expression saddened.

"Show me someone who doesn't know about that by now, poor bloody cow. It's been all over the place since yesterday morning. What's so special about her, then?"

"She was our maid once, a long time ago."

He saw the initial disbelief in her eyes and kept staring at her until her expression softened again.

"Pamela, wasn't it?" she said, and he nodded. "I used to see her. Quiet girl, you'd hardly know she was there. You've got to put yourself forward in this game if you're going to make any money."

"Do you know where she lived?"

She shook her head. "I'm sorry, luv, I don't." She shrugged. "No reason, you see. Do you want me to ask around?"

"Please, yes." He brought a penny from his breeches pocket. "If you find out, send a boy to find me." He was about to walk off when her voice stopped him.

"Mr Nottingham? I didn't know her, but I'm sure your Pamela were a good lass."

He smiled sadly.

"She was, Polly. She was that."

He talked to several contacts, whores, touts and con men, before walking back to the jail. He'd have the information soon, he knew. Pamela might have had very few friends, but people knew her face, and someone would know where she lived. All he needed was a little patience.

Back at his desk he wrote a note to Rawlinson, releasing Morton's body, and arranged for an undertaker to prepare Pamela's corpse and carry it to the church.

More than twenty four hours had gone by since the murder and he was no further along than when he'd first seen the bodies. By his calculations he had another day before the Mayor would demand results. He needed some bloody answers.

11

It took two full hours before a boy ran breathlessly into the jail to give him Pamela's address, longer than he'd expected in a city of seven thousand people. He threw the lad a farthing before striding out up Kirkgate and crossing Briggate in the shadow of the Moot Hall.

The place was a step up from Queen Charlotte's Court, but only a small one. Unpaved, it stank of night soil the residents had thrown out. Long ago, Nottingham mused, this would have been part of the garden of a grand house. Now the only thing it grew was people, bunched together like weeds in a neglected, overgrown lot. He'd spent half his childhood living in places like this.

If anyone had ever cared for these buildings, that time had been far in the past. A couple seemed to be collapsing in on themselves, propped up by scavenged pieces of wood. The others seemed little better, held together by a mixture of faith and despair.

The boy had told him the front door of the house he wanted was white, but that was a generous term. What remained was a grimy, tired grey, and the wood was so warped that opening it became a battle.

Downstairs in the cellar, he'd been told, the third door, and he went, the smell of unwashed bodies, illness and hopelessness around him. He knew places like this all too well. You could leave them but they never left you, sticking inside the body and the mind forever, like an itching burr, and squeezing out hope. Nothing good could ever happen in this kind of place.

He tried the handle of the third door, surprised when it opened; most residents of places like this had precious little but locked up what they had. Anything Pamela had owned would be the property of others by now.

He came face to face with a burly man nearly as tall as himself. His blue eyes were filled with wildness, and a bushy, uncombed beard cascaded on to his chest.

"Who are you, eh?" It wasn't so much a question as an accusation, the words delivered in a long slur as his alcohol breath filled the room. A nearly-empty jug of gin sat on the floor next to a straw-filled pallet, the room's only furniture. Nails had been hammered into the walls, and an old coat, worn through at the elbows, hung on one.

The man came closer.

"I said, who the fuck are you?"

Nottingham raised his palms in conciliation and smiled cautiously.

"I think I have the wrong room."

In the face of an apology the man seemed to deflate.

"Unless the bastard's let it to you, too."

"How long have you been here?" the Constable asked, suddenly suspicious.

"Since last night." He gestured expansively, legs wobbling. "All mine, until next week when I can't pay his rent."

"And where's the man who runs the house?"

"Upstairs." The man paused, scrambling down to his knees to drink greedily from the gin as if it were nectar. "Top two floors." He paused again. "The king's palace," he added enigmatically.

Nottingham backed out of the room and climbed the stairs quickly, past the fractious squall of hungry babies and silences as deep as death. Where they ended the solid door looked no cleaner or brighter than the rest of the place. He knocked loudly, hearing shuffling steps on the other side. A moment later the haunted eyes of a very young maid looked at him.

Her dress had been exquisite once, the stitching small, even and fine, but over the years all the colour had been washed from it. Far too big, it hung loosely on her tiny body, trailing dangerously on the ground and covering thin, childlike wrists. The neckline was high, but not high enough to cover the fading bruises.

"I'd like to see your master," he said.

She curtseyed briefly, then led him into a small, spare parlour where she lit a candle on the mantelpiece. The floor was polished wood, with two uncomfortable chairs on either side of an empty grate which was blackleaded to a shine. No pictures hung on the walls, and there were no windows to let in the day. It was a strange, disquieting room, so different from the life below.

He didn't have long to wait there. Within two minutes a short man bustled in, an ingratiating smile on his face. Like the maid's dress, his wig had been quality some twenty years earlier. Now its style, draping down on to his shoulders, looked ridiculous and old-fashioned. The linen shirt had been mended many times, and a bony elbow protruded awkwardly from a fresh rent. His dark breeches flapped against a pair of skinny thighs, and the white stockings had discoloured to ivory.

"Welcome, sir, welcome." The man gestured at a chair, but Nottingham didn't move. He stared impassively down at the man, trying to judge his age. Fifty? Sixty? Older? It was impossible to be certain. There were lines on his face, but it was as if he defied time. The flesh around his eyes was puffy, as if he'd just been woken.

"Do you know who I am?"

"Of course I do, sir." The man smiled, showing a mouth

almost empty of teeth. Seventy, Nottingham finally decided. "It'd be a poor man who didn't recognise the city's Constable."

"And you are?" the Constable asked.

"Mr King, sir." He gestured expansively and gave a hearty, toneless laugh. "Welcome to the king's palace."

That explained it, Nottingham thought. An old, poor joke. He was surprised he'd never heard of the man before, although the city had many landlords like this.

"You had a whore living in a cellar room, I believe. A girl named Pamela?"

King nodded tentatively. "There was a girl of that name," he admitted warily, "but I don't know what she did. As long as they pay the rent, that's all I care about."

"You know she was murdered, of course." Nottingham said.

"How couldn't I know?" King tried to shrug, but the gesture looked like a tic. "It's been the talk of the town."

"And so you let her room." He let the words fall out like an accusation.

"I'm a landlord." King answered earnestly. "Empty rooms don't bring in money, Mr Nottingham, surely you understand that."

The Constable moved a pace closer. His voice stayed even. "You own a few places, Mr King?"

"Two in this court, two in another," the man replied with a smile.

"Queen Charlotte's Court?" Nottingham asked, suddenly curious.

King shook his head seriously. "I like a place where a man can make a living from his rents. There's nothing for an honest landlord over there."

There was very little honesty here, either, Nottingham thought. The place felt like a house of the dead. He shivered slightly.

"What about Pamela's belongings, Mr King? Might I ask what you did with them?"

"I had the girl bring them up here, of course." He glanced up slyly and lowered his voice. "Mind you, I had to make sure she hadn't taken anything for herself, thieving little bitch. She'd leave me with nothing if she could."

"I'd like them, if I may."

"Of course," King agreed readily, but the disappointment was apparent in his face. Nottingham knew the man had expected to keep everything for himself, just as he probably stole from most of his tenants. "I'll have her bring them." Opening the door, he yelled, "Cissy! Bring that girl's things from last night."

They were wrapped in a small parcel, just a few items. He doubted it was everything she'd owned; King would have picked it through and kept anything of the merest value. He tucked it under his arm and the landlord looked on, eyes anxious now. It would be pointless asking him about Pamela. She'd been nothing more than a few coppers each week to him.

"Thank you, Mr King. I'll leave you in peace now." Just before he reached the door, Nottingham turned. "I'm surprised we've never met before," he added.

"But I'm an honest man, sir," King replied, trying to sound nonchalant. "Honesty and the law rarely need each other."

The Constable nodded for a moment.

"Maybe you're right," he agreed. "But I'm sure we'll be seeing each other again. I'll bid you good day."

At the jail he unwrapped the ancient, musty cloth that held Pamela's possessions. There was a wooden comb with several of its teeth missing, a crude, smudged drawing of a man Nottingham thought might have been her husband, a clay candle holder and a small doll made of rags that he recalled her bringing when she'd arrived as a servant. It was so little to speak of a life, these things that defined her, that she'd carried around and held dear.

But there was no token, and he was certain now it must have been torn from the ribbon around her neck, although he couldn't see why. It had no value, and its only significance was to his family. Pamela had sworn to treasure it and keep it safe forever. And maybe she had; it was impossible to know now. Her forever had ended too soon. Whoever killed her had taken the broken token. It was one more thing Nottingham would make him pay for.

Next door to the jail, the White Swan offered good ale and a decent stew for his dinner. He was sopping up the gravy with a piece of bread when Sedgwick flopped noisily on to the bench opposite him and poured a mug of ale.

"Anything?" Nottingham asked.

"Looks like we've found where they were killed," the deputy said, sounding satisfied. "The other side of the work-house. It's overgrown there. The weeds have been trampled down and there's a dark patch that could well be blood."

But Nottingham found himself troubled by the questions that raised.

"So why move them?" he asked. "If he'd left them, it could have been a while before they were discovered."

"I was thinking that myself," Sedgwick answered, and put forward an idea. "He wanted them found, boss. Why else would he go to the trouble of putting them like that? I walked it, and it'd take a fair effort to get two bodies there. He had a reason."

"And why in Queen Charlotte's Court?"

Sedgwick offer a straightforward explanation.

"Well, coming from the other side, it's the first place you get to. And no one there's going to pay much attention to noise in the middle of the night. They're used to it. So he wouldn't be disturbed."

Nottingham drank, pushed the fringe off his forehead and nodded. It made as much sense as anything in this.

"You're probably right. Good work, John."

Sedgwick smiled at the praise.

"What did you find on the preacher?" the Constable asked.

"Bugger all. I tell you, it's like the man vanished after he left Rawlinson's house until he ended up dead." He shook his head. "I've asked everywhere, but no one remembers seeing him."

"We need to find out where he was. People like him don't just disappear in the city." Nottingham felt frustrated, as if every turn led to a dead end. "I found where Pamela lived. Her room's already been rented, so there was nothing there to help. Have you heard of a landlord named King?"

"Oh aye, old Ezekiel King. She had one of his places, did she? Poor lass. We had a room from him when I was a lad. Never pays for owt because he has light fingers when it comes to his tenants. I doubt he's bought a piece of clothing in thirty years. That bastard's so tight he can make a farthing scream for mercy. If there's a bigger miser in the city, I don't want to meet him."

"Just keep an eye on him from time to time, will you? Let him know I haven't forgotten our little chat this morning."

Sedgwick grinned.

"My pleasure, boss. You never know, I might even find my dad's old hose on his legs."

12

The bodies had been taken from the jail, and a note from Cookson curtly announced that Pamela's funeral would take place the following morning at nine. Nottingham sent a boy up to inform Meg and tell her that he'd call in ample time.

By nightfall they'd learned nothing more. Sedgwick was going around the inns once again, still trying to find someone who might have seen Morton on the night he died. As he walked home, the streets quieter now the working day was long over, Nottingham reflected on his deputy's eagerness. He was ready to do anything; all he lacked was the education. Nottingham remembered having that energy himself, in the days when he'd started working for the Constable, and when he was courting Mary. But thinking back it was as if he was looking at another man, a good man, maybe a better man than he was now.

Sometimes he could barely remember himself at twenty. At other times he didn't feel a day older, youthful and vital inside. That only lasted until he saw his reflection in a glass or looked at the girls. Even sullen Emily could spark with daunting energy at times.

He opened the door, expecting to hear Mary moving around in the kitchen and the girls in the room they shared. Instead the house was silent except for Emily, turning the page in a book, her face half-illuminated by the light on the table.

"Hello," Nottingham said gently.

She looked up, startled, obviously absorbed in the words she'd been reading. He glanced at the title on the spine –

Robinson Crusoe by Daniel Defoe – and understood why she'd been so captured by the words. "Where's everyone?"

"Mama and Rose are visiting Mrs Middleton." She was an elderly widow who lived alone down the street.

"And what about you?"

Emily shrugged. "I just wanted a little time to myself, that's all." She closed the book and stood up, her gown rustling softly.

Nottingham was struck by how mature she looked, how poised, more a woman than a girl now. She carried an air about her, he thought, a kind of lingering sadness mixed with ill-formed bitterness, and he didn't understand where it came from. Emily began to walk to her room.

"We've been at odds a bit, you and me," he began tentatively, and she turned to face him, a small smile on her lips. "I don't like it, you know."

"Neither do I," she replied sadly.

"Well, I'm pleased to hear that," he laughed, relieved and surprised at her reaction. "I was beginning to think you hated us all."

"Sometimes I do," Emily said with the blunt, weary truthfulness of youth. She came back and sat on the chair, facing him. Her eyes were glistening as if tears were beginning to form. Nottingham reached across the table and put his hand of top of hers.

"We don't like to see you unhappy." It was the truth. He wanted everything for her. He just wondered if she could see that.

"Sometimes I just feel there has to be more to life than this." She waved her hand around the house. "Do you know what I mean, Papa?"

"I'm not sure I do," he answered honestly. All this seemed ample to him, everything he could have dreamed of and more.

"Well…" Emily took the time to be exact with her thoughts. "What's going to happen to me? Maybe I'll make a respectable marriage, the second son of a merchant or a farmer, perhaps? Or if not I'll probably end up as governess to some awful child. That's the way it works, isn't it?"

"Something like that," he agreed. At least she had a candid view of life, he thought.

"And if I marry I'll have children and grow older and that will be my life."

"But a life lived in comfort," he pointed out.

"Comfort, charm and genteel surroundings." She uttered the words as if they were vile.

"They're a lot better than starving, believe you me," Nottingham told her with complete conviction.

"I'm sure they are, Papa." She caught the look in his eye and added, "Really, I do believe you. But what will I have done with my life in all that? Where will I be?"

"You'll be at the centre of a family. People will love you and you'll love them."

"And I'll take care of the household accounts, play with my children and supervise menus with the cook."

"What's wrong with that?" he asked in bewilderment. To most women he'd known, even to Mary, a life like that would seem to be paradise. But paradise, he knew, could be lost.

"Nothing's *wrong* with it," Emily said cautiously. "It's fine if that's what you want." She tapped the book cover. "Do you know how many times I've read this?"

He shook his head, wondering why she'd changed the subject.

"Five. It's my very favourite book. Do you want to know why?"

"Of course." He was genuinely curious.

"Because he gets to build his own life. There's no one to say he should be doing this or that and something needs to be done at such a time. He's on a desert island but he's free."

"It's just a book, Emily," he told her.

"But books have ideas, Papa." Her fists were clenched so tight that her knuckles were white. "When I'm reading it I'm on that island and I'm free, too. He gets to feel, he gets to *be*, and I want that!" A small tear leaked from her eye and she brushed it away with a quick, embarrassed gesture.

"You're young still," Nottingham started, but she cut him off.

"I'll feel differently when I'm older? Maybe I will." Her face was flushed with pinpoints of colour and she ran a hand through her hair in a gesture that reminded him eerily of himself. "All I know is that I'm young now and this doesn't seem enough. I want love, I want some passion in my life."

"And you'll have it, I promise you," he tried to reassure her. They'd never talked like this before. For the first time he started to believe he might understand her, and he felt closer to her than he had since she was tiny, in apron strings. "Things like that happen in their own time, Emily."

"But that doesn't help me now, does it?" she asked plaintively.

"No," he admitted quietly, "it doesn't."

So now he knew why she hurt, but he had no idea what to do about it. She was right about her future, that was the way society worked, and there was no respectable place for women outside that – unless you were rich and titled. He looked at her sympathetically, but couldn't find any honest, comforting words.

"I wish I'd been born a boy," Emily said finally.

Nottingham gave a small smile at her innocence.

"Because boys have freedom?"

She nodded sharply.

"I'll tell you something," Nottingham confided. "It only looks that way."

"What do you mean?" she wondered, her attention engaged.

"A man gets married, they have a child, often five or six," he explained. "Who do you think has to earn the money to feed that family? Who has to find a job that pays enough? Aye, it's the wife who's looking after the children all day, but it's the man who has to make the brass. That's responsibility, not freedom."

"But you can go where you like, when you like, stay out drinking until all hours…"

"True enough," he conceded. "And there are plenty who do. But let me ask you, would you want a husband who did that?"

"No, of course not," Emily answered. "I'd expect him to be more considerate."

"So then, if you were a man, you wouldn't be like that," Nottingham said after a moment. He was remembering his own father, a man who'd been anything but considerate to his wife and son.

"I suppose not," she agreed slowly.

"Drinking and whoring doesn't make someone a man," Nottingham said with quiet conviction, "and don't you ever forget it."

"But whores can become ladies. Moll Flanders – "

"You've read that?" he asked sharply.

"Yes – " Emily began, but before she could continue the door opened and Mary and Rose bustled in.

"I'm sorry we're late," Mary said in a merry voice. "We were talking and lost track of the time. Good Lord, we need more light in here. It's almost pitch black."

"That's all right," Nottingham told her. "Gave us time for a chat." And he winked at Emily.

Later, after the girls were in bed, Nottingham and his wife sat by the dying fire. He was dozing intermittently, jarring awake as his chin fell on his chest.

"So was it daggers drawn earlier with Emily?" Mary asked.

He shook his head. "Not at all. Not even a cross word," he answered happily. "We could have talked a lot longer."

She raised her eyebrows, not quite believing him.

"Then that's a change."

"She's just beginning to learn that the world is a smaller place than she'd hoped." He hesitated, then asked, "Do you ever feel like all this isn't enough?"

"All what?" said Mary, confused.

"This." He groped to put the idea into words. "Me, the girls, this house. Don't you ever feel your life should be more than that?"

"Ah," she replied with gentle understanding. "So that's the problem. I'm content with this, Richard. I always have been. It's easier now than when we started out, but I was happy then, too, you know." She reached over and took his hand, her fingers lightly stroking his palm. "But I knew what I wanted and I got it."

"Emily's different."

"I suppose she always has been." Mary sighed and started to lose herself in the past. "She was never one for playing with the other girls, do you remember that? She always seemed happiest on her own. And after she learnt to read, it was all we could do to pry her away from a book."

"True," he smiled. He couldn't remember all the times he'd found her reading in bed when she should have been sleeping.

"Rose is like me. She'll be quite content to settle down with her nice lad and have a family. But I don't know that Emily's ever going to be happy," Mary said with a tinge of sadness. "Not really happy. And I know that's a terrible thing to say about your own daughter, but it's true. I think deep down she knows it, too. That's why she's so angry. She just wasn't made for the world as it is."

Nottingham knew she wanted to talk about this, but he was uncomfortable. He felt at home with facts, even ideas, but emotions always left him uneasy and restless.

"So what do we do about her?" he asked, hoping his wife would have an answer.

"I honestly don't know, Richard," Mary replied with a help-lessness that reflected his own. "I wish I did."

"She told me something that worried me."

"What's that?"

"Did you know she'd read *Moll Flanders*?"

Mary laughed lightly, her eyes twinkling in the dim light.

"Of course I did, Richard. Who do you think lent it to her?"

The sun was shining, the sky clear and blue, with just the faintest breeze coming from the west. It was as if summer was enjoying its final gasp. Normally Nottingham would have enjoyed the weather, but now it seemed to be making a mockery of the day.

He'd borrowed a cart to take Meg to the church, and he was soberly dressed in his best coat and breeches, sweating under their weight as the grey woollen hose itched against his calves. The old woman was in the same dress she'd worn the last time he'd seen her – probably the only one she owned, he thought – leaning heavily against him for support as they walked very slowly on the path through the churchyard to the imposing wooden doors.

Mary and the girls were already inside, sitting in the front pew. Mary put her arms around Meg's hunched shoulders, whispering in her ear as the new curate began the service.

He spoke sonorously, letting the litany of the words flow

smoothly, much to Nottingham's surprise. He'd expected Crandall to rush through the funeral. Cookson would have given him the task, and Pamela was nothing to him. He glanced at the others; Meg's face was in her hands, Rose and Mary both looked down and Emily was gazing at the curate.

Outside, they followed the cheap coffin to the waiting grave in the far corner of the churchyard. The curate took his time, letting the power of the words flow into the listeners. Reluctantly, Nottingham had to admit that Crandall was a powerful, mesmerising speaker. He watched the curate pause, eyes moving around the mourners to gauge the effect of his voice, his glance lingering on Rose, and a little longer on Emily, before returning to the verses. Finally it was all done, the ashes to ashes and dust to dust, and Nottingham followed Meg in tossing a clod of dirt into the grave. Another life spent so fast, to be covered and forgotten as the days went by. At least Pamela had a proper burial, he thought, and remembered another whore in a pauper's grave.

As he walked away, Crandall called to him and took him aside.

"I wanted you to know I don't approve of this," he said in a low, angry voice.

"Of what, Mr Crandall?"

The curate's eyes were dark. He spoke quickly.

"Of burying a whore here. Of giving her a service in the church. Her profession was evil."

Nottingham answered slowly, coldly, and carefully.

"Then understand this for your pains. You did your duty for a woman who was brutally killed, a woman who'd once been the servant in my house, someone who was loved. Think on that. Then try remembering that Our Lord took in Mary Magdalene. Wasn't she supposed to have been a whore?"

He turned on his heel and walked away.

They rode back to Harrison's almshouses. Mary, Rose and Emily would stay with Meg for a little while. Nottingham would return the cart and get back to work; Thursday was already slipping away. Sometimes he wondered if death wasn't easier than life.

Sedgwick was waiting for him at the jail, nibbling the remains of a pie that was probably his dinner. He stood up quickly as Nottingham entered, crumbs falling from his cheap, worn waistcoat on to the floor.

"Sit down, John," the Constable said, pulling off his coat and draping it over the chair. He felt exhausted, drained by the funeral, his heart empty. "Did you find anything more yesterday?"

"Oh aye," Sedgwick grinned broadly. "I've finally got someone who saw Morton Monday night."

"Oh?" Suddenly Nottingham felt alert again, rubbing his hands together in anticipation. "Where was this?"

"The Talbot." The deputy let the name roll off his tongue.

The Constable raised his eyebrows in surprise. "I wonder why such an upstanding man of God was in a place like that," he said. "It's not filled with the holy spirit."

The Talbot was notorious in Leeds. It had a pit for cock fighting, and a reputation as a thieves' den, where violence was exchanged as common currency.

"Maybe he didn't know what it was like," Sedgwick suggested graciously.

"A couple of minutes inside should have told him all he needed to know," Nottingham dismissed the idea. "You've got a good witness?"

"A man called Martin Hooper. He was at the Market Cross on Saturday, saw Morton preach. Called him 'that bloody mouthy bastard.' No mistaking the identity." Sedgwick paused.

He'd been carefully hoarding the last piece of information. "And he says Morton was drinking with Carver."

"Carver?" Nottingham sat upright quickly. "What time was this?"

"He claims it was about ten."

"And we know Carver left the Ship around nine with Pamela," the Constable mused. "Did your witness say anything about her?"

Sedgwick shook his head.

"I asked him if there'd been a girl about. He just looked at me as if I was daft and said that of course there were bloody girls about, but he didn't remember one in particular."

Nottingham rubbed his knuckles over his chin. She might have been there, taken a shine to Morton's money, and the old drunk could have become jealous... it was possible.

"Let's have Carver in," he ordered abruptly. "I want to hear him explain this."

"I've already got a couple of the men on it," Sedgwick answered. "But I think we'll have better luck tonight once he goes out drinking."

The Constable nodded his agreement. Like some strange beast, Carver only seemed to emerge as the daylight faded.

"Just make sure you find him before he gets pissed, then. We don't need another fight."

13

Nottingham needed information on Carver, and he knew the best place to find it. The merchants, the business elite who brought money into Leeds through their woollen cloth dealings, effectively ran the place by controlling the Corporation. Most of them would be unwilling to talk about someone who'd once been one of their own, even as dissolute and broken a character as George Carver.

But there was one man who might help. Three years before, Tom Williamson had been named the city's Cloth Searcher. It was an ancient office, and largely ceremonial, although Williamson had taken it seriously. During his year long tenure he and Nottingham had become friends, quite easily and unconsciously straddling the social barrier that divided them. They didn't see too much of each other now, but the goodwill had remained.

It was early afternoon and that meant there was a fair chance Williamson would be at Garroway's Coffee House on the Head Row, enjoying a dish of tea. The merchants tended to gather there, conducting business in its informal surroundings, reading the *Leeds Mercury* and the London newspapers, or idly passing the time.

As Nottingham entered the building, he was struck by the smells, so exotic and rich. There was coffee, powerful and enticing, and underneath a deeper, more mysterious hint of chocolate. He'd tried them both, once, but didn't care for the taste of either, too alien to a palate that was used to small beer and ale. He'd tasted tea, too, and enjoyed that. But all these were luxuries, far beyond his meagre pocket.

Williamson was in the corner, shoulders hunched, engrossed in the backgammon board in front of him. In his mid-thirties and tall, the merchant had the most straightforward, honest face Nottingham had ever seen, which probably wasn't a great business asset, he thought wryly. And he was a poor liar. But from all the rumours, his business was thriving. Williamson's father had died the year before, and now Tom was running it himself, making sound decisions and prospering even more than before. He was plainly dressed, his breeches and coat of good quality, the waistcoat carefully tailored in length and cut, but sober, the buckles on his shoes dull metal rather than gold.

His roll finished, Williamson looked up and spotted the Constable, a smile curling his mouth upwards.

"Richard!" he greeted warmly. "What brings you to this den of iniquity on a lovely afternoon?"

Nottingham returned the smile, genuinely pleased to see the man. It had been too long. "I wanted a word with you, actually."

For a moment Williamson looked nonplussed, as if searching his memory for any wrongdoing. Satisfied, he said happily, "Well, have a seat, and we can talk while I thrash Mr Greenwood here."

"Better in private, if you don't mind."

"I see." Williamson gazed at his companions. "Looks as if luck's on your side today, Jeremiah." Picking up his immaculate tricorn hat off the bench he followed Nottingham outside.

"What's all the mystery about?" he asked as they began to stroll up the Head Row.

"I'm after a bit of information, Tom," Nottingham admitted bluntly.

The merchant tilted his head slightly in curiosity.

"Something a little delicate, obviously. Information on whom?"

"George Carver."

"Oh dear." Williamson wiped his mouth with the back of his hand. "Poor old George is in trouble again, is he? What do you want to know about him?"

"I know he lost his money, but I've never heard how it happened," Nottingham said. "As far as anyone can tell, he doesn't do a stroke of work, but he still has somewhere to live and the brass to go out drinking every night. I thought you might know something about that."

"It's not really a secret, I suppose," Williamson began readily. "It's just that it's never seemed like anything to talk about. I was just a lad when it happened, so I heard most of it from my father. It seems George found a new buyer in Holland – this was back when they were still a big market for us. Good references, everything you could want. Things went well. After a couple of shipments they placed a big order, asked for credit, and George extended it to them. I'm not sure exactly what happened, but they never paid."

"Very unfortunate," the Constable agreed, although it wasn't an uncommon business tale.

"If that had been all, he could probably have weathered it," Williamson continued. "Most of us keep a reserve for emergencies. But George liked to play cards, too, and he was a heavy gambler. Sometimes he won, sometimes he lost, but he was in the middle of a losing streak when all this happened."

"And everything collapsed around him?" Nottingham asked.

The merchant nodded. "The lot, even his family. Everyone thought he'd kill himself, but he didn't." He paused. "Well, not immediately. He seems to be teasing out his death in drink."

They'd walked a few yards before the Constable asked, "So how does he live now?"

"He has a pension."

Nottingham gazed quizzically at the other man. He'd never heard of such a thing before.

"Who from?"

"Us," Williamson explained. "We each put in a small sum every year, and he's given a weekly allowance. It's enough to put a roof over his head and keep him fed. And enough for drink too, obviously."

"So Mr Carver is still a man of independent means."

"More dependent means, I suppose," Williamson countered wryly. "What's he done?"

"You know the preacher who was murdered?"

"I heard about it," the merchant said. "But I suppose everyone did."

"It looks like Carver was the last one to see him alive."

Williamson stopped and stared in surprise. "Come on, Richard. You're not seriously suggesting Carver killed him. I know he can get rowdy, but he wouldn't murder anyone."

"No, I'm not suggesting anything," Nottingham replied evenly. "I just want to talk to him, and I thought it'd help if I knew more about him. Nothing more than that."

The merchant didn't appear convinced. "You obviously suspect him, or you wouldn't be asking me these questions."

Nottingham offered an eloquent shrug. There was a firmness in his voice as he spoke. "Right now he's what I've got, Tom. Someone killed two people and dumped their bodies like – well, you know how they were found. I can't just dismiss Carver because of who he is – or was. If he didn't do anything, he might well have seen something useful."

Williamson glumly nodded his understanding and acceptance. If the Constable needed Carver, the merchants wouldn't stand in his way.

"Did you go and hear Morton preach last Saturday?" Nottingham asked casually, although he knew it was a clumsy shift of topic.

"No." The merchant shook his head. "I've already got my faith. I'm not looking for another."

"A few of your colleagues were there with Reverend Cookson. They didn't seem to like what they heard."

Williamson smiled slyly. "A little more fishing, Richard?"

Nottingham laughed, but felt no embarrassment. "Let's say I'd like to know why they feel that way and what they might have been inclined to do about it."

"Murder?" Williamson looked genuinely shocked.

"As I told his Worship, I'd be remiss if I didn't investigate all the possibilities."

The merchant eyed his companion thoughtfully before speaking. "All right. I heard there were a few who thought his words were more than a little dangerous. But no one was talking about anything as extreme as killing."

"Who?" Nottingham wondered.

"I don't know, I wasn't there. But I heard Mr Dale and Alderman Goodison talking about it at the cloth market on Tuesday morning – before we heard Mr Morton was dead, you understand."

"And what did they have to say?"

"They felt he should be asked to leave Leeds, that his words might give the people ideas above their station. Thankfully," he added, "Mr Rawlinson wasn't about at the time." Williamson hesitated for a moment. "You know me well enough, Richard. I don't play with politics. That's all I heard and I'm quite content to leave it that way."

"I wouldn't ask for more," the Constable assured him.

"Of course you would, if you really believed you could get it."

Nottingham grinned.

"Maybe you're right, at that. But only if needs must, Tom."

Sedgwick found Carver in the Ship a little after seven. The timing was good; Carver had just finished his first drink, and a single mug of ale wasn't going to have any effect on his wits or his temper. Oblivion was still a couple of hours away.

"The Constable would like to talk to you, sir."

Carver glanced up. He smelt of stale sweat, and his thinning hair was lank and greasy. His coat, once exquisite, had been ruined by years of hard wear. Flecks of dried vomit coloured the once-elegant waistcoat and twine held the soles and uppers of his shoes together.

"Then you should tell him where I am, young man," he said with careful politeness.

"I think he'd rather have the conversation at the jail. Somewhere quieter and less public than this."

Carver raised an eyebrow. "And without the presence of alcohol?"

Amusement danced in Sedgwick's eyes. The old bugger wasn't as addled as everyone said. "That too."

Carver pushed himself away from the bar and picked up the remains of a hat.

"Very well. No doubt you'd only hound me if I refused."

"I would, sir. Trust me, it's much easier this way."

The desk separated Carver and Nottingham. The Constable was sitting back in his chair, arms folded, quietly assessing the other man. Sedgwick leaned casually against the door, watching and listening carefully.

"I believe you were out drinking on Monday night," Nottingham began.

Carver looked bemused. "As I'm sure the whole of Leeds can tell you, Constable, I'm out drinking every night. There was no reason Monday should have been different."

Nottingham kept an impassive face, his voice low. "Do you recall the landlord throwing you out of the Ship?"

"Did he?"

Nottingham watched carefully as Carver tried to place the incident.

"If he says so, I'm sure it's true."

"A young woman helped him," the Constable offered as a reminder.

"Ah." Carver brightened. "I remember her vaguely." He gestured at his appearance. "Women don't often speak to me, especially young women."

"Do you recall what she said?" Nottingham never took his eyes off the other man's face, looking for any sign he might be hiding the truth.

"No," he replied guilelessly. "Beyond the fact she was young and female, I don't think I could tell you a thing about her. No, wait," he said suddenly. "She had something blue around her neck." He closed his eyes for a moment. "A piece of ribbon, maybe?"

"Did she take you anywhere?"

"I haven't the faintest idea." Carver sounded genuinely baffled. "Does she say she did?"

"She can't say anything," Nottingham told him. "She was murdered later that night."

"I see." Worry creased Carver's forehead and he tried to concentrate.

"She was killed at the same time as a preacher."

"Is he the one everyone's been talking about?"

Nottingham nodded. "The strange thing is, someone told us you were with the preacher in the Talbot at ten that night."

"I was?" Now Carver looked bewildered and a little frightened. "They're sure it was me?"

"Certain," Sedgwick confirmed. "Why?"

"I don't usually go in there, that's all. But if they saw me, I must have been."

Nottingham and Sedgwick exchanged perturbed glances.

Sedgwick knew what his boss was thinking. It was too easy. Carver remembered nothing, and was trustingly willing to accept what everyone else claimed for him.

"Did you wake up the next day with blood on your clothes?" Nottingham asked.

"I don't know. I don't think so." Carver looked confused, then smiled innocently. "Look for yourself, Constable. These are the only clothes I own. Do you see any blood?"

Beyond the stains and the dirt it would be impossible to tell, Sedgwick thought. The man's coat resembled a midden. If it hadn't been so well made it would have fallen apart years before. But if there was blood on it, it certainly wasn't obvious.

"I wish I could be more help," Carver said, now sounding properly distressed. "I drink to forget, you see, and all too often it works perfectly."

"Obviously so," Nottingham said dryly.

"I know I'm a figure of fun. I know I'm kept around as a warning to others – *be careful or you'll end up like him*." Yet there was dignity in his words. He stared at the Constable, his blue eyes suddenly sharp. "But, you know, I don't really care. Maybe it sounds like madness, but I like my life."

"Why?" Sedgwick asked in astonishment. He could see little to enjoy in Carver's existence.

Carver turned in his chair. "No one's asking anything of me. I've got money enough for my wants, and God knows those have lessened over the years. If you had that, wouldn't you feel like a satisfied man?"

"But you also get in plenty of fights, Mr Carver," the Constable observed coolly.

"I do," he admitted with a touch of shame. "And lose them all, I'm told. But alcohol has a wonderful way of dulling the pain."

"If you can fight, you can commit murder," Sedgwick suggested ominously.

"And if I lose fights, I can be murdered," Carver countered, smiling. "Yet I'm still here."

"But two other people aren't," Nottingham said, briskly returning to the subject, "and you evidently saw them both that night."

The man pulled together the few shreds of his pride.

"Is that an accusation, Constable?"

"It might become one." Nottingham's threat hung in the air.

"You'd be able to help if you could remember more," Sedgwick told him.

"I might be able to help *you*," Carver said firmly. "Believe me, memories are no help to me at all."

"Do you own a knife?" Nottingham asked.

The man fumbled in one of the large pockets of his coat, eventually drawing out a small, worn blade.

"That's it. That's my weapon. Not too deadly, I'm afraid, unless you're a piece of twine."

"Murder isn't a laughing matter, Mr Carver." The Constable was beginning to sound frustrated, and Carver hung his head.

"I know, I'm sorry."

"Consider what we have. You were seen with both of the victims that night, and you can recall next to nothing about what happened. Try suffering the pain of memory to see if anything becomes clearer."

"And if I can't remember anything?"

"Then that might prove unfortunate," Nottingham pronounced, his eyes holding the merchant.

"They'd never hang me," Carver said hopefully.

"When scandal rears its head, friends have a habit of looking the other way. Think about that. You can go, Mr Carver."

After the door had closed Sedgwick rounded on the Constable, trying to contain his anger. "Why in God's name didn't you arrest him, boss?"

Nottingham looked up slowly and shook his head.

"I don't think he did it," he answered. He knew there was enough evidence to put Carver in a cell for now, but his gut told him it was wrong; the man was confused, even ridiculous – but not guilty of murder. "I can't make up my mind whether I despise him or feel sorry for him, but I believe he's innocent."

"He was seen with both of the victims," Sedgwick insisted, his face reddening. "And he's a clever bugger, for all the drink."

"Do you really think he's the killer, John?" the Constable asked quietly. "Are you absolutely sure?"

"Yes!" Sedgwick said insistently. "He fits. Why don't you believe it?"

Nottingham gazed at the deputy, so certain in his convictions, and wished he could share them. God knew he wanted this solved. But from the moment Carver had entered, the merchant had seemed so genuine in his confusion that it was impossible to think he was capable of the murders. Those had required decision and action, two things that were far beyond the old sot these days. About all he could manage was to drift through the remainder of his life.

"I just feel it," the Constable said bluntly, holding up his hand before Sedgwick could protest. "I was watching him, John, and there was nothing about him that made me think he was a murderer. Everything inside is telling me he's innocent." He desperately wanted to make Sedgwick understand, but he didn't have the words to properly express his thoughts. He couldn't even really explain it to himself; it was just instinct and experience yelling at him. "I know you think I'm wrong, but I know I'm not."

The deputy paced around the room, trying to work off his mood. Nottingham sympathised; there'd been times before when he'd tried to convince his superiors of someone's guilt, only to have older heads say no.

"What happens if someone else dies, and we find out Carver was responsible?" Sedgwick asked bluntly. "What will you do then? It'll be on your head."

"I know," the Constable acknowledged calmly. "And if he's a murderer, I'll arrest him, watch him hang, and live with being wrong for the rest of my life. But honestly, I don't believe he is."

In the meantime he'd pray he'd made the right decision in letting Carver go.

By the time he arrived home, Mary was putting the finishing touches to dinner, a pie of vegetables with a scant handful of meat to flavour it. He could hear the girls talking quietly in their room.

"Thank you for spending time with Meg after the funeral," he told his wife. "I would have, but..."

She nodded her understanding.

"How was she when you left?"

"Sad, bitter and lonely," Mary replied gently, shaking her head. "We did what we could."

"What about Emily?"

"She sat by the window and sulked most of the time."

Nottingham sighed. "I'd hoped we'd turned a corner when we talked yesterday," he said ruefully. "Obviously we didn't."

"She's not going to change overnight, Richard," Mary said patiently. "Give her a little time."

"You're right." He pulled her close and kissed her lightly.

"Have you found him?"

He didn't need to ask who she meant.

"No," he told her softly, stroking her hair. "Not yet."

He almost started to tell her about Carver, but stopped. Like Sedgwick, he knew he could never make her see why he'd let the man go, and he was too weary to discuss it. He wanted to sleep. Please God all this would be over soon, and life could return to its usual pace. And please God he'd made the right decision.

Then there was another knock in the middle of the night.

14

The dream had been vivid, although he couldn't remember it once he was awake. The hammering at the door was like Monday night all over again and immediately he knew what had happened. He pulled on a pair of breeches, took the cudgel from the bedside, and went to open the door.

Sedgwick was standing there, wild-eyed, hair streaming, his face flushed. "Another one," he announced.

He was always the one they told first.

Nottingham blinked, trying to clear the sleep from his eyes and force himself to full wakefulness. Another murder. Dear Christ, he thought with sudden panic, had he been wrong about Carver?

"Shit," he said. "Shit, shit, shit." His mind was racing. "Where? Who?"

"A man and a girl again," Sedgwick replied, breathless from running. "In Turk's Head Yard."

"Right, you know what to do. Get Brogden and I'll meet you there as soon as I can."

He dressed, pulling on waistcoat, stockings, coat and shoes, then set out at a fast walk through the darkness. By the time he'd cleared Timble Bridge his mind was focused. He prayed it might not be the same killer, a coincidence, but in his bones he knew it couldn't be anyone else.

Turk's Head Yard ran off Briggate, just a few yards down from the Moot Hall. Sedgwick had left a man with a torch to watch over the bodies, and he pulled at his forelock as Nottingham approached.

"Anyone been near them?"

"No one, sir. A few curious, like, but none of them wanted to get that close to the corpses."

"Right. Start asking around. I want to know if anyone heard anything at all, understood?"

"Yes, sir."

It was the same scenario as before, the girl sprawled face down, legs apart, with the man on top as if taking her from behind. He couldn't see their faces, but he could wait until the coroner had given them his cursory examination.

The Constable paused and looked around him. This yard was a far cleaner place than Queen Charlotte's Court; its houses were cramped together around the Turk's Head Inn, but carefully tended around a path of swept flagstones. It was the kind of place where artisans lived, joiners and masons, families with incomes and aspirations. For them a murder like this would be an affront. This time, he thought, it was possible that some houseproud folk had seen and heard something. For now, however, although he sensed they were awake, they were keeping behind their locked doors.

Sedgwick arrived with Brodgen. As the coroner bent to examine the bodies, Nottingham took his assistant aside.

"Who found them?"

"Our man there," Sedgwick answered. "He was doing his rounds and came down here. As soon as he saw them he came to find me at home, and I ran for you."

The Constable nodded and rubbed the stubble on his chin, looking at the shuttered windows around them.

"I want you to talk to everyone in the yard. Go house to house before it gets light. A place like this you'll probably find them all at home. It's small enough you should be able to cover it all. There must still have been someone awake at the Turk's Head. Someone must be able to tell us something."

"Right."

He was considering his next course of action when Brogden approached.

"From the look of them, I'd say another whore and a farmer," he said distastefully after a brief glance, his mouth pursing. Tonight his clothes looked dishevelled, hastily thrown on, and he'd left his wig at home. He bent over to give a rough examination of the corpses. "Killed by a knife, the same as the last two you dragged me out to see," the coroner described impatiently. "But it can't have been too long ago, they're still fairly warm."

"Anything else?" Nottingham asked.

Brogden rose and shook his head.

"Go ahead and look for yourself. They're dead, Constable, that's all you need me to say. And with that, I'm going back to my bed." He put the hat on his head and walked out of the court.

Nottingham detailed men to carry the bodies to the jail, then examined the ground once they'd gone. There was very little blood. Once again they hadn't been killed where they were found, although given the place, that didn't surprise him. Whores and their clients wouldn't dare use a respectable place like this for tupping.

But they hadn't been dead long, and it had only been an hour at most since they were discovered. They couldn't have been murdered far away. At first light he'd send men out combing the area. He realised that even if they found the site it might tell him nothing. Yet it was better than not knowing. Everything, or anything, could be important.

He sat at his desk, pinching the bridge of his nose and trying to summon up the will to face the corpses in the cold cell. It was barely dawn; a cloudy grey sky promised dull weather after yesterday's sun.

Finally he sighed and stood to do his duty.

He was almost scared to gaze at their faces in case he saw someone else he knew. But both of these were strangers.

Brogden had been right about the man. He was in his mid-thirties, as far as Nottingham could judge. The clothes were better than any labourer could afford, but still country cut and stitched at home, the seams awkward and uneven, the breeches tight around stout, muscled thighs. Blood had turned the material to a rust colour from a pair of deep stab wounds in the chest. The dead man had a florid face, reddened by exposure to the weather, and his hands were well calloused, nails cracked and short, with dirt ingrained into the skin.

The girl couldn't have been above eighteen. Even in life no one would have called her pretty; there were extensive pox marks on her cheeks and an old white scar on her chin. She'd been a scrawny reed of a thing with bones poking through her flesh: scarcely a decent meal in her life, he imagined. Her dress was a faded blue, cut low to expose most of her tiny breasts. She'd also received two cuts, one to her stomach and another between her ribs.

Who were they, he wondered. He'd doubtless learn the man's name soon enough, when a wife came looking for her errant husband. But the girl might remain anonymous forever. The chances of kin, or even someone who cared enough to find out where she'd gone, were small.

It chilled him to know there was someone in Leeds who'd do this to people. Not just once but again – and more, he was certain, if he had the chance. It had to be the work of a lunatic. No sane man would kill a couple in cold blood that way.

Nottingham looked at the bodies again, rubbing his chin as his mind worked through the possibilities. Unless there was some unlikely connection between this unknown farmer and Morton, someone was randomly killing whores and the men with them.

He closed his eyes for a moment and prayed it wasn't Carver.

The sound of the jail door roused him. Sedgwick was sitting at the desk, shaking his head to keep himself awake.

"What did you find?" the Constable asked.

"You mean besides the fact that hard work for godly souls means an undisturbed night's sleep?" Sedgwick responded bitterly. "I think they were more offended that people had been killed on their doorsteps than anything else."

"And were any of the good citizens able to give you information?"

"A couple admitted they heard noises, but 'the middle of the night' was as exact as they could be. And since their houses were locked up tight, they didn't look."

"What about the inn?"

"Closed early, not much trade. All in their beds and asleep."

"Whoever's doing this is either lucky or very canny," Nottingham pondered. "He picks his spots well, places where no one will care or no one wants to know."

"It's definitely the same man, then?"

"Has to be. Killed by a knife, same position." Could he have predicted and prevented this? he asked himself – although inside he knew he couldn't.

Sedgwick yawned and stretched slowly.

"It means the killer didn't single out Morton and Pamela," Nottingham continued. "He's murdering prostitutes and the men who've bought their services."

He looked pointedly at his deputy, and Sedgwick's eyes widened at the implications. "Once the pimps and procurers realise that they're all going to think the competition's doing it."

"Exactly," the Constable said glumly. "So they'll be killing each other and the whores will be terrified. And don't forget our friends on the Corporation," he added acidly. "They like their regular tumbles, too."

"What are we going to do?"

Nottingham sighed and shook his head.

"We'd better find him, John. As fast as we can." He hesitated, grateful Sedgwick hadn't mentioned the name yet, then said, "I'm going to discover where Carver was last night."

He'd sent Sedgwick home for a few hours' sleep, after instructing him to send men out to search for the new killing ground. He needed his deputy, but he wanted his mind fresh and sharp, not raw after too many hours of work. He should have been resting himself, but his brain wouldn't slow down.

His eyes were gritty as he rubbed them. Along with weariness, he felt self-doubt beginning to creep in. What if Carver was the killer, and he'd let him walk away to commit two more murders? He'd told Sedgwick he'd live with the guilt, but words were cheap. He'd been wrong before, and more than once. That had been over petty crimes, though, not murder. Murders, he corrected himself soberly. Murders.

Next door to the jail, the landlord of the White Swan was cleaning off the benches in a lacklustre fashion. The patrons were never too particular, so he didn't care too much, either. Quiet morning drinkers were scattered around the place as the Constable walked in. A few heads turned to glance at the newcomer, then returned to their mugs of ale or wine. The landlord nodded his head in greeting.

"Early for you, Mr Nottingham."

The Constable offered a thin, weary smile.

"If only drinking would get rid of all my problems, Michael."

"But you'll have something?"

Michael Harding moved behind the bar, wiping his hands on his apron. He was a carefree sort, at least until someone crossed him. Then his tongue and his fists erupted like a sudden storm on anyone who deserved it. As soon as he was done, the mild, easy manner returned. His way kept the tavern quiet and generally peaceful, but Nottingham often wondered just how far below the surface the temper really lurked.

"I don't imagine you've come in here for a restful hour," Harding said as the Constable sipped from the tankard.

"I think I last had one of those about twenty years ago, Michael." Nottingham laughed, but to his ears it sounded forced. "Seen much of George Carver lately?"

"What's the old bugger been up to now?" Harding drew himself some ale and leaned against the bar. "Heard you had him in yesterday."

Nottingham smiled again. Gossip spread like seeds on the wind in Leeds.

"We had a chat," he admitted, trying not to give anything away.

"Aye, he told me all about it. Came in here after you let him go. Said he needed a drink, but when does George not need one?" Harding winked.

"Did he stay long?"

The landlord cocked his head to think.

"Till ten, perhaps. He'd had a fair few by then."

"How was he?"

Harding shrugged. "Moaning a bit, got a little loud a couple of times. Didn't cause any trouble, though. You must have scared him."

"But not sobered him, obviously."

Harding gave a braying laugh.

"I doubt if God himself could do that, Mr Nottingham."

"Was he going anywhere else?" Nottingham tossed out the question.

Harding shrugged once more. "Not my business. He'd spent good money here, that's all I care about."

To his surprise, Nottingham discovered he'd almost drained the mug. He finished it in one long swallow and brushed back his fringe.

"Well, no rest for the wicked, or for those of us who have to try and stop them. Thank you for the drink, and the information."

"What's George done, then?" Harding asked as the Constable walked away.

"I'm not sure he's done anything. I hope not, anyway," Nottingham replied truthfully and let the door close behind him.

That accounted for some of Carver's movements, he thought, stopping on the corner to allow an overloaded farm cart to turn from Vicar Lane into Kirkgate. But he'd have gone on somewhere else. That was his way, to drink himself into insensibility every night. He assessed the options. There was the Old King's Head, the Ship, the New King's Head and even the Talbot, all within a distance Carver could stagger if necessary. And of course the Turk's Head. Nottingham sighed; he'd have to check them all.

It was a thankless business. For different reasons, most of the landlords had no great love of the law, and brought varying degrees of co-operation to their talks. But an hour later no one had admitted to seeing Carver the previous night and he was willing to believe them; it would be such a foolish thing to lie about.

One thing was certain; tonight they'd talk to George Carver again, and Nottingham dreaded the meeting.

15

John Sedgwick could rarely sleep during the day. He always went hopeful to his bed, but if it was light outside rest rarely came. Today was no different. Instead he watched his wife and baby across the room from his straw pallet on the floor. James was running across the floorboards, chasing dust motes that glistened in the light while Annie mended his shirt.

He closed his eyes and tried to will his brain to stop thinking, but the questions in it refused to go away. Why had the boss let Carver go? The man had to be guilty. He trusted Nottingham, but was certain he'd been wrong; the two new bodies proved it. But he couldn't gloat; he'd seen the Constable's face when he heard the news, the way it fell as he realised what it meant. There was no victory in that. At least finding Carver would be easy.

Finally he was able to drift away and doze for a few minutes until James began to cry and Annie swept him on to her lap to feed him from the breast.

They were luckier than many, he thought. Their room was a decent size and they didn't have to share it. Since he earned regular money they never went hungry. They had clothes that were more than rags, although he'd love to be able to afford a newer pair of breeches for himself and a better dress for Annie. Still, that would come. This was a long way from running wild on the streets as he'd been when he was a youngster.

Sedgwick sighed and rolled over. Sleep was a terrible thing when you needed it and you never got enough of it. His head ached and his body felt tight. Finally he admitted to himself that rest just wasn't going to happen and got up off the bed.

"I've finished your shirt," Annie said sullenly, handing it to him.

He put it on, thankful there was no longer a gap in the seam between sleeve and body. He wanted to say something to her, but wasn't sure what. These days every word he uttered seemed to incite a row, and at the moment he couldn't take that.

Annie had never been an easy girl to live with. But once, not so long ago, they'd enjoyed a few happy times among the fiery arguments. They'd laughed. Everything had changed after James was born. She seemed to sink into herself then, finding a little world that only had room for herself and the baby. Now Sedgwick could barely put a foot right by his own hearth. He remembered when he was twelve or thirteen, imagining how easy life must be for grown-ups, with none of the problems he'd had as a lad. Well, he was wrong there. Now he looked back he felt that childhood was carefree, full of days spent playing and laughing, even if he knew there were plenty of dark, hungry times in there too.

He looked at Annie, giving all her concentration to James as he sucked greedily on her nipple. He remembered the way she'd looked when they first met, glowing like a banked fire, the way she'd been willing to enjoy his bad jokes and find enough pleasure in simply being with him. Now James claimed all her time and affection.

He was a grand lad, there was no doubt about that, and Sedgwick was proud of him, strangely happy at what he'd created. From the time he was born, people had said he looked like his father, although Sedgwick could never see it himself in the chubby cheeks and thick chin. He looked like a baby, nothing more or less. But he'd started to take on some character, and at two and a half had a very real, cheeky personality. When the nipper was a bit older they'd be able to do lots of things together. He'd teach him how to fish in the Aire, how to kick a ball and all the other things boys did. And he'd send him to school so he came out with the education, with opportunities ahead of him. James would make something of himself.

Still holding the child to her breast, Annie stood and went to stir the pot that sat over the fire in the grate. A stew again tonight, the leftovers of yesterday's meal which he hadn't been home to eat. God only knew if he'd be back to help finish it. There was work that needed doing, and if he couldn't sleep he might as well do it.

She'd brushed most of the dirt off his breeches and coat, but they were both still in a sad state of repair. However, those were the only garments he had until he could afford more. Good clothes would only be wasted in his line of work, any-way. By the end of a day they were always dirty, sometimes torn. These were fine, and, to give Annie her due, she could work magic with a needle and make things last.

He tugged on his clothes, kissed James and Annie, then left. He was hungry, but there was little food in the house until he was paid and it seemed unfair to take any. He could scrounge a meal from an inn or a pie seller; it was one of the few perks of the job.

Yesterday's sun had given way to thick clouds and a feeling of rain. He made his way back to Turk's Head Yard to look at it in the light. There was little to be seen. With the bodies gone, everything existed more in his memory than in fact, illuminated by the torchlight of last night. Now there were only some stains on the flagstones of the yard that would fade with time. Everything else was in its place, exactly what you'd expect from somewhere that strove for respectability the way this did, with the hushed sound of voices from the inn.

He walked on, looking for the two men he'd detailed to search for the murder ground. He found them up Briggate in the Ship, supping ale.

"You'd better have a good reason for being here," he said sharply to one of them, a haggard, underfed youth named Johnson.

"We wanted somewhere to wait for you, Mr Sedgwick, seeing as you'd gone to get some sleep." He winked, and his companion, a brawny, older man called Portman, nodded agreement.

"Did you find the place?"

"Oh, aye, and a right bloody mess it is, too." Johnson laughed stupidly at his own wit, showing a mouth with most of the teeth missing.

"Then you'd better drink up and show me, hadn't you?" the deputy said testily.

The pair looked at each other, drained their mugs and stood. Eager to be moving, to find something, Sedgwick followed them.

It was in the old orchard just the other side of Lands Lane, perhaps a hundred yards from where the bodies had been left. The long grass under an ancient, gnarled tree was trodden down, the earth dark and still a little sticky with blood. Flecks of it were sprayed dully on some of the windfall fruit on the ground.

"Did you find anything else here?" he asked.

Each man shook his head in turn.

"Right. Well done, lads. You go on now."

Once he was alone, Sedgwick began combing through the undergrowth around the tree. He didn't expect that Carver would have left anything, but he still needed to search and be sure. After almost half an hour he gave up. Nothing. No buttons, scraps of cloth. Absolutely nothing that would help put the noose round the old drunk's neck.

He made his way back to the jail, stopping only for the gift of a warm meat pie from the seller at the corner of Kirkgate and Briggate. Nottingham was at his desk, deep in thought, only looking up after Sedgwick had collapsed into the other chair. He raised his eyebrows for a report.

"They were killed in that orchard by Lands Lane. Close enough to pull them to the yard easily."

"Anything there?"

Sedgwick shook his head. "I searched it myself. Was there anything on the bodies?"

"Nothing to tell us who they were," Nottingham replied in frustration. "I doubt we'll ever know her name unless some pimp comes to complain about a missing girl."

"Oh aye, and it'll snow in July next year." Sedgwick pushed the last piece of pie into his mouth and stretched.

"I want you to go out and start talking to the pimps and procurers," the Constable ordered. "Take a look at her, give them the description. One of them might say something. After all, someone's lost income with her gone."

"Are you going to bring Carver back in?" he asked. It came out as an accusation, but he didn't apologise.

Nottingham nodded very slowly. Sedgwick's rebuke was perfectly justified.

"I'll find him when he goes out this evening. I did some checking; he was next door until about ten. After that none of the inns remember seeing him."

"Yes, boss." Although he tried to remain grave, the deputy's face seemed to light up.

"I daresay I'll be getting another summons from his Worship today," the Constable observed. "He'll doubtless be concerned about the murders of respectable citizens going unsolved."

"And what about the whores?"

Nottingham smiled wryly.

"I suspect the Mayor and the corporation will only worry about them when they can't get one."

Carver, Nottingham thought when he was alone. Bloody Carver. Could he have been so wrong? Every sinew in his body had said the man wasn't capable of murder. Even now he found it hard to believe. So far there was nothing to connect him with these fresh killings. But if Carver had committed them... then perhaps it was time to quit this post, before the Mayor dismissed him for incompetence. He tried to blink the tiredness from his eyes. He'd love to be away in his bed now, but there wasn't going to be much sleep until all this was over.

The door of the jail opened tentatively and Nottingham looked up sharply, brought from his thoughts. A woman stepped in, glancing around nervously, as if unsure what evil she'd find inside and bracing herself to face it. He stood and bowed slightly to her.

"I'm looking for the Constable," she announced in a quavering voice.

"I'm the Constable," he said, moving to hold the chair for her. She was about thirty-five but worn by age and work, in a homespun dress of fair quality – her best, he guessed. She wore a woollen shawl around her shoulders, the fingers of one hand clutching it tightly at her neck. Her skin had the leathery look of someone who'd spent plenty of time out in the fields, lines radiating from the corners of her eyes and mouth in a plain face, her eyes flickering around the room, frightened. She'd tucked her hair into a cap, but he could see strands that had freed themselves, a mix of mousy brown and iron grey. He decided his farmer's wife had found him.

"I'm Richard Nottingham, the Constable of Leeds," he told her formally, settling into his own seat. "Might I ask your name, mistress?"

"Nell Winters." She blurted it out as her gaze took in the details of the room. He knew how forbidding it could look to innocent eyes: thick walls, the doors to the cells stout and dark. It was a place for those who'd broken the laws, not those who lived by them. From the Constable's office, spare and cramped, but at least warmed by a hearth, a corridor ran back long the building's single floor, past the heavy, locked oak doors of each of the five cells to the windowless mortuary room with its pair of stone slabs.

"I don't think you're a Leeds woman," Nottingham prodded gently. "I don't know your face."

"No." She tried to smile, but couldn't manage it. "We live in Alwoodley." He knew the area slightly, four or five miles to the north of the city on the road to Harrogate, with wooded hills and good grazing.

"You're looking for your husband, perhaps?"

"Yes," she admitted, and he saw she was glad at first that he'd understood without her having to explain. Then realisation flooded into her mind, and her hands were covering her face as she said, "Oh God, no."

Nottingham knew she needed comfort as tears and sobs racked her, but he didn't move. Propriety forbade it. Instead, the best he could do was offer his messy kerchief for her to dab her eyes and hide her face.

"Is he dead?" she asked finally, her eyes rimmed with red.

"How was he dressed when he came to town?"

She gave a brief description.

"I'm sorry," Nottingham told her gently, and she began to weep again. The minutes passed, until she seemed drained of tears for the present, and he began asking questions. It wasn't something he wanted to do, when she was struggling to keep afloat in her grief, but he had no choice.

"What was his name?"

"Noah." She barely whispered the word and tried to keep her face composed. "His mam called him that 'cause he was born when it had been raining for days and she thought they'd all end up living on an ark."

"He was a farmer?"

She nodded.

"Why did he come into Leeds?"

"He wanted a new suit." She shook her head at the stupidity and waste of it all, and her fingers pulled at the kerchief as if she was trying to tear it apart. "For years he'd wanted some clothes made in the city. He'd done well, the farm had made money the last few years, and he decided it was time to treat himself, so he could dress a bit more like a squire." She offered a faint, wan smile.

"Did he come in yesterday morning?" Nottingham asked, and she nodded in answer.

"Said he'd be home last night. When he wasn't back by this morning I had one of the lads drive me in on't cart." She hesitated, torn between wanting the truth and not wishing to hear a word. "How did he die?"

This was the part the Constable hated most.

"I'm sorry, Mrs Winters, but someone killed him."

"My Noah?" She couldn't believe it, couldn't understand, her eyes widening suddenly as she tried to draw a breath. "But why? He were a good man, he wouldn't get in a fight or owt like that."

"We don't know why yet," he told her, knowing there was at least a grain of truth in his words.

Her face had a stunned look, mouth hanging slightly open.

"We think he was in the wrong place at the wrong time.

I don't know how else to put it," he admitted.

"But you'll find whoever did it and see him swing."

He wasn't sure if it was a plea or a command.

"I will," he assured her, although at the moment it seemed as much hope as certainty.

"I want to take my man home and give him a proper burial," she insisted suddenly.

"Of course," he said. "Do you have your cart here? I'll have my men carry his body out."

She crumpled again at the mention of the word *body*.

"He's dead," she moaned in a voice that was little more than a croak. "He's *dead*. He's dead for a new bloody suit."

Nottingham helped Mrs Winters back outside, feeling the pull of her weight against his arms. Two farm lads waited by the cart, and he instructed them to look after their mistress, then went to round up two men to carry out the corpse. He couldn't have allowed her back to see him, not with the whore in the same room. She was a bright woman, that was obvious, and she'd easily have put two and two together; she deserved more dignity and a better memory of her husband than that.

By the time the wagon pulled away the day was well progressed. Nottingham felt the tiredness in his bones, an ache that crept from the inside out. He wanted this man who'd killed four people, wanted him in a way he couldn't remember wanting to find any criminal in the past. He wanted to see the man's face. More than that, he wanted to hurt him for what he'd done to Pamela. And if it was Carver, he'd find no mercy.

Before he could consider what to do next, a messenger from the Moot Hall walked in, summoning him to the Mayor's office. Nottingham drew a deep breath and wondered how to approach the interview. He didn't want to mention Carver yet, until he was certain, and the last thing his Worship would want to hear was that they had a madman targeting prostitutes and their clients. If that knowledge became public it would send a shock through the entire city. Too many men used whores, many of them gentlemen of influence. He pondered exactly what he might say.

He dusted off his coat, then ran fingers through his hair. It was another vain effort towards making himself presentable, but it would have to do. He had no looking glass in the jail. The man would just have to take him as he found him, exhausted in mind and body.

He was ushered directly into the Mayor's office without waiting; not a good sign, he decided. Kenion was at his desk, hunched over some papers with a quill in his hand. Absently he gestured Nottingham to a seat, then ignored him for several minutes as he pored over a document before fretfully adding his signature to it. After coming off worse in their last interview, he wanted to establish the pecking order, and make sure it was known before a word was said. Finally Kenion looked up.

"More murders, I hear," he said accusingly, skipping the pleasantries.

"Another prostitute and her client," the Constable responded.

"And what are you doing about catching the man responsible?" Kenion folded his hands across his chest, glaring at Nottingham.

"All we can. We know who the victim was, a farmer from Alwoodley, in town to buy a decent suit of clothes." Even as he said it, he knew it wouldn't divert Kenion.

"I don't give a tinker's cuss who *he* was." The Mayor's voice dripped venom. "It's whoever killed him that concerns me. We shipped that preacher's body back to Oxford yesterday. How do you think that sounds for the city? A man comes to

Leeds to preach the word of God and he's murdered. It's a wonderful advertisement for the good Christian folk of the city, don't you think, Constable?"

And less than a week ago that preacher was close to causing a riot with his bloody words. You wouldn't have loved him then, Nottingham thought, but kept his words inside.

"Things happen in every city."

"Well, I'll not tolerate them here." The Mayor's bluster left his face flushed.

"We're doing everything we can to find the culprit." Even as he said it the Constable knew the words sounded weak.

Kenion stood and leaned across the desk, his voice tight.

"Then your *everything* obviously isn't enough. You said the same bloody thing after the first murders. Now the man's been out and done it again, right under your noses and you still don't have a bloody clue who he is!"

"No, I don't," Nottingham let the lie slip off his tongue without guilt.

"So what are you going to do about it?" the Mayor exploded.

The Constable looked up calmly.

"Exactly the same as we've been doing," he responded evenly. "And I'd defy anyone else to be able to do better." As an attempt to muster his dignity it was hardly convincing, even to his own ears.

"Happen we'll see about that very soon," Kenion replied coldly.

"That's your decision, of course," the Constable acknowledged.

"It is, Mr Nottingham, and it's one I'll not be afraid to make if I don't see some progress very soon. I suggest you remember that."

This was where he paid for their last meeting, Nottingham

understood. He'd leave with no doubt as to who was in charge. But as long as Kenion restricted himself to words, not actions, the Constable had time. For now the new Mayor had no one who could replace him. Or so he hoped.

"I shall, sir."

The Constable stood and gave a short nod of his head as a bow before leaving. The Mayor had already returned to his paperwork as an attempt to show how important and busy he was. Busier than he expected to be, Nottingham warranted, and already beginning to wonder if the position was worth the time it took. But there was plenty of truth in his words. They needed progress and they needed it quickly. And right now George Carver was the key.

16

Sedgwick was always amazed at the way the pimps hid their wealth. If he had even half their money he'd own a good house with four or five hearths and live like a gentleman. Maybe they didn't want to draw attention to themselves, he thought, although what they did was no worse than the way some merchants and businessmen acted.

They all ran strings of girls. Sometimes one of the lasses would leave without a word, but there was never a shortage of new blood arriving from the country, thinking they might make their fortune in Leeds. But no girl was going to make money on her back for anyone but the man who ran her. Most of them would be lucky to survive to twenty-five.

After years in his job he knew all the pimps and procurers in the city. A few even seemed like decent folk, most treated their girls like objects, and some of the worst ones he could have happily killed – and would have, once or twice, if the Constable hadn't stopped him.

Whores were a fact of life. There was no more getting rid of them than fleas. But he could try to stop men openly murdering them.

Sedgwick walked down Briggate, beyond Boar Lane, following the gentle slope down to the Aire and across the stone bridge that spanned the river, its parapets old and wide. Someone had told him that at one time they used to hold the cloth market here, long before the Cloth Hall was built, and it had been designed for displaying the wares, bales of cloth spread out over the stone.

Around him carters were urging on their teams, the clack

of horseshoes and wheel rims sharp and loud on the cobbles. Men bowed by heavy packs on their backs negotiated the traffic with stoic looks on their faces, coming to sell or going home disappointed. A few smiled, hands jammed in their pockets to keep thieves from their profits.

That set him thinking. They'd heard nothing more about their cutpurse for a day or so now. Could he have moved on, deciding he'd tried his luck as far as it would go in Leeds? It was possible, but unlikely. Every thief he'd met liked to push it to the limit, and most ended up caught and hanged. It happened so often it almost seemed like a natural law.

At the south end of the bridge he turned into a warren of streets. Much of the area to the west, on Meadow Lane, was given over to grand houses built by the merchants as symbols of their success, with expensive brick fronts to illustrate their wealth. But back in these yards was someone who could give them a run, guinea for guinea.

Without even needing to find his bearings, he made his way through the tiny streets. Few people were around; they were mostly off at their work, or in their rooms, sleeping off labour or drink. It was a place without joy, without hope, like so many others he saw every day, where most people existed rather than lived.

Not Jane Farnham, though, Sedgwick thought as he stopped and knocked on a door. She was a woman who broke all the rules. She relished her life as a bawd and she'd made a small fortune pandering to the needs of others. No Amos Worthy, perhaps, but with plenty of money just the same.

A grille in the wood opened and a pair of eyes looked out. Sedgwick didn't bother to say anything. Whoever was looking would know his face. A thickset man let him in, a fearsome scar on a face that had been battered several times, the nose broken and awkwardly set.

"Henry." Sedgwick nodded. The servant wasn't wearing a waistcoat or jacket, and the muscles of his arms and chest bulged against the old linen of his shirt. He'd been a soldier once, at least that was the tale, and had killed his sergeant with his bare hands before deserting. Not that anyone, except perhaps Henry himself, knew the truth. And after all this time perhaps he'd chosen to believe the legend.

"What dost tha want?" The man's voice always sounded hoarse.

"Is she around? I need to talk to her."

Henry eyed him impassively before leaving him inside the door and going into another room, emerging a few seconds later and tilting his ugly head as invitation. Sedgwick followed. He'd been here a number of times, but on each occasion it took his breath away. Jane Farnham's morning room was the equal of any fine lady's residence, the furnishings expensive and exquisite, with a thick carpet of Oriental design like a cushion under his feet. From the outside of the building no one would have guessed at this interior.

But Sedgwick also knew that decorating her rooms in such a manner was as close as Mrs Farnham would ever come to society, for no procurer could ever be received by polite people. So she created her own rich world that would have intimidated most of the people she'd never be likely to entertain, and established her own superiority.

Farnham herself, wearing a fine jade silk gown of a fashionable London cut, her hair elegantly pinned up in an elaborate coif, looked up from the delicate chair where she sat. No one had ever seen Mr Farnham, if he even existed.

"Yes?" she drawled. She was a small woman, her head barely reaching Sedgwick's chest, and nearly as thin as a consumptive. There was a fine, moneyed air about her. She was used to her comforts. No one who didn't know would ever have guessed that she was a madam with a bawdy house and girls on the street. She strove to seem cultivated, always with a book open on the table. At times she seemed too genteel and tiny to be an effective pimp. But Sedgwick had seen her lose her temper with a whore. She'd beaten the lass so hard and long that the girl had to be carried away. The refined behaviour, he reflected later, was a very thin mask.

"We've got a dead prostitute in the jail," Segwick blurted. "Have you had a girl gone missing lately?"

Farnham exchanged a glance with Henry, who shook his head briefly.

"No, we haven't," Farnham informed him in a soft voice. "If we had, of course we'd have told the Constable's office."

Aye, if it suited you, Sedgwick thought to himself. With a slightly envious glance around the room, he bowed his head and left.

One down, he thought, crossing the bridge again, but so many more to go. He'd do as the Constable ordered and talk to a few more pimps, but he wasn't hopeful. He reckoned he might be better off chatting to some of the girls, describing the dead lass to them and see if anyone knew her. A few would certainly have seen her and might even know her name. Ultimately, though, it probably didn't matter. By tomorrow she was going to be just another dead body in a pauper's grave, mourned and missed by next to no one. There were dozens of them each year.

David Sheepshanks and Edward Paley didn't aspire to the same luxury as Farnham. Both were small time, with just four or five girls each. Neither of them had a girl missing and knew of no one who did. Two more brief visits revealed nothing, and Sedgwick began to believe it was going to be a waste of time.

So he followed his instinct and started canvassing the girls.

There were always plenty around, no matter the time, in the inns or on the streets, touting for trade. As they learned all too quickly, it wasn't a business for the shy, unless they had an inclination for starvation. Some of them were mean bitches, women he wouldn't dare cross for fear of his life, but most were simply trying to get by and live.

Lizzie Lane was like that. It had been her and her daughter since her man left – 'listed for a soldier when drunk, some people said, although no one seemed to know for sure. She was cheerful, brash and bawdy whenever Sedgwick saw her. For more than two years she'd been a fixture near the Old King's Head on Briggate. She kept her large breasts pushed high, almost out of the top of her dress, and she loved to trade lewd banter with passing men, usually getting a fair share of customers that she took to her dingy room down the grubby yard.

"Hello, John," she yelled as she saw him approach, a warmly lecherous smile crossing her face. "Come looking for the company of a real woman?"

"Now then, keep your voice down, you might put off trade, talking to the law," he told her, laughing, before adding in a quieter voice, "And my missus might hear about it."

"She didn't last time," Lizzie winked and folded the small fan so many whores carried.

"Aye, but if she found out she'd hurt me."

She rolled her eyes and sighed in mock frustration.

"You're not here for me, anyway, are you, luv?"

"Not today," he admitted.

"Well, you'd better not take long, then. Not that most do, anyway," she chuckled.

"You've heard a couple of girls have been murdered?"
Lizzie nodded.

"There's one, we don't know who she is, and the Constable

121

would like to find out. The pimps I've talked to aren't saying anything."

"You think those bastards would?" she interjected.

"Just ask around and see if anyone's gone missing, would you?"

"What did she look like?" Lizzie asked.

"Tiny thing, blonde hair, pox marks, scar on her chin, old blue dress," he said.

"That could be half of them around here," she pointed out wistfully.

"Can you ask a few questions and let me know if anyone says anything?"

Lizzie brightened. "Course I will. Can't have some prick killing us."

"You're a good lass," Sedgwick said with a grin.

"I bet you say that to all the girls."

"Only the ones who can help me." He winked and walked away.

Nottingham knew Carver wouldn't be too hard to find. He poked his head around the door of a couple of inns with no luck, then discovered him once more in the Ship, already on his third drink, according to the landlord.

"George," he said genially, standing over the figure on the bench who was contemplating his ale. The man looked up and answered mildly, "Am I to be harassed daily for the rest of my life then, Constable?"

"I hope not," the Constable said without a smile. "But I need to ask you a few more questions."

"Then pull up a seat and take a drink with me."

Nottingham shook his head.

"Not here. We'll talk at the jail, I think."

Carver shrugged, drained his tankard in a single swallow,

and stood with barely a hint of unsteadiness.

"I'm at your service," he announced with a small flourish.

They walked together in silence. The older man smelled especially ripe, his coat crusted with even more food stains, which didn't seem to concern him in the least.

At the jail he waited until Nottingham sat, then positioned himself on the chair opposite.

"Now, how may I help you Constable?" he asked, for all the world a gracious host relaxed in his own home.

"I'm wondering where you were last night."

Carver pondered the question for a minute.

"I woke in my own bed, so I can't have gone too far," he replied seriously. "Beyond that I'm not sure I can be too much help."

"You were at the White Swan until gone ten," Nottingham told him.

"Was I?" Carver asked. "Then you seem to have a better grasp of my whereabouts than I do."

"Where were you after that? Did you go to the Turk's Head?"

The merchant bit his lip as he thought, and shook his head.

"I don't know," he replied succinctly.

"Two more people were murdered last night," Nottingham informed him.

"I see." Carver considered the question gravely. "And what exactly does that mean, Constable?"

Nottingham shifted slightly in his chair and brushed the hair off his forehead. He was too exhausted to play any games, tired of answers that were no use at all.

"It means you need to recall where you were last night, and I need some witnesses who might have seen you."

Carver raised his hands, palms upwards.

"As I told you, I don't recall. I'm sorry."

"Then I'm afraid I have no choice but to arrest you," the

123

Constable snapped. He'd see if that made Carver remember.

A long silence filled the room. Nottingham impatiently studied the other man, who appeared to be thinking carefully.

"You must do your duty," Carver agreed finally. "I hope your cells aren't too uncomfortable." He stood, waiting to be escorted.

Nottingham unlocked the first cell and waited until Carver was inside before closing the door and turning the key. It was too easy, he thought with a twinge of guilt. Would a murderer, even a mad one, allow himself to be herded like a sheep? Maybe Carver really did have no memory of the events.

"I'll see you get some supper later. There's water in the jug."

"Bring me ale, too," Carver pleaded.

Nottingham smiled to himself. The man could probably survive for days without eating, but without drink he'd wither in a matter of hours.

"I will," he promised. "I need your address and the key to your room, too."

Carver gave both willingly.

He went next door to the White Swan and arranged for a potboy to take Carver food and drink. The city could pay; at least the man wouldn't cost too much. That done, he stood outside the inn and felt exhaustion hit him like a stone. Sedgwick had rested, but Nottingham had been working since the early hours and now it had caught up with him. He ached to go home and sleep without thought of waking. But first he had to go and search Carver's room, and do it now while he was still moving.

It was a filthy attic up three rickety flights of stairs, and he wondered how Carver managed to climb them each night. One small, dirty window gazed down on a rubbish-strewn court, its outlines blurred in the growing darkness. The Constable lit a stub of candle and looked around. The room was crammed with possessions, a stack of books climbing up the wall, some trinkets on the sill, piles of faded papers cluttering the floor. The bed was a bundle of straw covered with an old sheet; it smelt as though it hadn't been changed in years.

A flimsy table that looked like someone had thrown it out was covered with worn quills and paper filled with scribbles that made no sense. Carefully, the Constable moved them aside. Underneath, not even properly covered, was a knife. It hadn't been hidden, simply laid down and forgotten. It was not the one Carver had shown him before.

Nottingham picked it up and carefully studied the blade in the bleak candle flame. It was about the right size and length, the steel roughly cleaned. But as he examined it more closely, he noticed a series of dark flecks on the metal. He rubbed at them with a wetted finger, and watched the stains slowly smear, the deep rust colour lightening.

It was blood, beyond a doubt.

Christ. It felt like a blow on the head. Had he been as wrong as that? He bowed his head slowly and clenched his fists. Fuck.

His instinct had failed and he'd let himself be taken in. Carver had conveniently lied about a bloody knife. God alone knew how little of what he'd said was the truth. Walking back to the jail, he felt a bitter fire inside. He wanted to confront his prisoner, to find out what he'd really done. No, he decided after a pause, tomorrow was better, once he was rested and he'd had time to consider all of this. Tonight he was too tired to think properly, and for Carver he'd need to be sharp. He put the blade in his coat pocket and went home.

His legs carried him along the familiar route. He walked

past the turning to the White Cloth Hall, past Alderman Atkinson's grand mansion with its distinctive cupola, and the dark holy bulk of the parish church. Across the road an orchard stretched all the way to Sheep Scar Beck, its ground almost carpeted by windfall apples as the leaves began to turn and die.

There was a reassurance in the scenes. He'd lived through them all for so many years. They kept him anchored to this place he knew and loved so well.

At home the enticing smell of a lamb stew greeted him as he entered, and he followed his nose into the kitchen where Mary stood surrounded by the steam and heat of cooking. Sweat shimmered on her face, and he watched, smiling, as she wiped her forehead with her arm, a single lock of hair plastered to her skin. His heel banged against the floor and she turned with a shock.

"My God, Richard, you startled me."

"I'm sorry," he apologised, feeling a deep, loving tenderness for this woman.

"Are you back for the night?" she asked.

"God, I hope so," he said fervently. "I'm dead on my feet."

"Do you want something to eat? The stew's nearly done."

He shook his head, then beckoned her to him, folding her in his arms as she nestled against him. He could feel the warmth she gave off and let it soak into him like a hot bath.

"I think we've found him," Nottingham told her, but there was no sense of triumph in his voice. All he felt was his own failure of judgement as he spoke the name. "George Carver."

She pulled away from him slightly.

"The drunk?"

He nodded.

"But why?"

"I don't know yet. I'll find out tomorrow." Suddenly he

didn't want to discuss it any more, even with Mary. "I need to go to bed. When the girls get back, make sure they keep quiet. And if anyone wants me, it had better be life or death."

She looked up at him with an understanding smile. How many times over the years had he come home like this and said words like those, he wondered. And on each occasion she'd protected his sleep carefully, making sure he was able to rest until he woke refreshed.

It was some measure of his station that they had a house with two bedrooms, he thought, climbing the staircase and feeling the plaster of the wall rub against his coat. He stripped off his clothes, down to the linen shirt, pulled the covers over his body and felt peaceful oblivion overwhelm him.

17

It was dark when Nottingham woke, and for a moment he was disorientated. Mary was asleep beside him, the assured rhythm of her breathing comforting by his head. He had no idea what time it might be, and lay there, eyes open. Night thoughts drifted like ghosts in and out of his mind, insubstantial as spring mist.

He stretched slowly, taking care not to wake his wife, slipped out of bed and dressed silently before going downstairs. He didn't bother lighting a candle. After so many years he knew his way around the house by feel and sound. He poured a cup of small beer, cut bread and cheese and sat at the table.

He ate slowly, his stomach relishing the simple meal. Outside, the blackness was just beginning to fade on the eastern horizon as the first blue of Friday's dawn arrived. Somewhere between six and seven, Nottingham judged, a good time to wake and go to work. And to tease the truth out of Carver.

Outside he pulled his coat tight around himself as the cold morning air hit him, clouding his breath and sharpening his stride to the jail. Sedgwick was sitting at his desk, his brow furrowed, vainly trying to study a letter the Constable had written. A fire burned in the grate, and snoring came from Carver's cell.

"Morning, John, you're here early."

Sedgwick put down the paper with a look of relief and disappointment.

"I haven't been home, boss," he admitted sheepishly. "I fell asleep here." He paused, rolling his neck on his shoulders to work out the night's stiffness. "You did the right thing, you know, arresting him."

"I know," Nottingham agreed with a rueful nod. "I owe you an apology." He took out the knife. "That was in his room."

Sedgwick smiled with satisfaction and weighed the blade in his hand. The Constable watched his face, but there was no sign of smugness.

"Aye, you could certainly kill someone with that," the deputy acknowledged. "What did he have to say about it?"

"I haven't asked him yet. I wanted you there." He deserved that.

Sedgwick nodded his gratitude.

"Anything new overnight?" the Constable asked, glad to change the subject.

"A couple of fights, the lads handled them." He shrugged, then stopped. "But the cutpurse seems to be back again."

"Oh?" Nottingham raised an eyebrow warily. He wasn't sure he wanted to hear this.

"He got three more yesterday evening that we know of."

The Constable groaned. "Of course, no one saw anything?"

"Not a bloody thing." There was exasperation in the deputy's voice. "Whoever it is, he's like a ghost. And you haven't heard the worst yet," Sedgwick continued.

"Go on."

"Two of them were merchants. So you know he'll have got away with a pretty penny."

"That's not funny, John," Nottingham said with sad conviction. "It means there'll be another summons from the Mayor. That's the last thing we need on top of these murders. He roasted my arse yesterday."

"Want me to put more men on catching him, boss?"

"No," he answered, then stopped to weigh his resources in his head. With only a few men, he was always stretched.

But they'd caught their murderer, and that would ease the strain. "Yes, add another," he decided finally. "That way at least I can tell his Worship we're doing everything we can."

"And you can tell him we've arrested Carver," Sedgwick said with pride.

"Yes." Nottingham took a deep breath. "I can tell him that."

He unlocked the heavy cell door. The prisoner was half-asleep on his thin bed, staring at the ceiling.

"Well, Mr Carver," Nottingham began. He edged into the small stone room, Sedgwick close behind him. "How do you feel?" There was no sympathy in his voice.

"Bloody awful." He hacked and coughed, leaning to spit a plume of phlegm on to the stone floor. "This place of yours might be conducive to enforced rest, but you didn't build it for comfort."

"It's not meant to be a rooming house," the Constable told him sarcastically. "Or do you feel you don't belong here?"

Carver sat up creakily, arching his back in a stretch. He looked old and frail, his cheeks and nose a sagging network of broken red veins. But there was a strong twinkle of intelligence and character in his eyes.

"You tell me, Constable. After all, you're the one who invited me into this palace."

"How's your memory this morning?" Sedgwick leaned against the door, watching as the other man slowly struggled into full wakefulness.

"As good as ever." Carver shrugged and smiled, showing a line of rotted, dark teeth. "In other words, poor."

"So you still don't remember a girl helping you out of the Ship on Monday night? Or drinking with a preacher in the Talbot?" Nottingham prodded.

"No, I'm sorry," he said with genuine regret, shaking his

head slowly. "I get flashes of things. But when and where they happened, I couldn't tell you."

"Then what about the night before last? That's more recent. Do you have any more recollection of where you were?" Nottingham pushed harder, his gaze fixed on Carver's face. If there was a sign, he'd notice it this time.

"I'm a poor witness. I think I told you, I drink to find oblivion. Or perhaps it's to let it find me..." His voice tailed off momentarily. "Whichever way, it's usually successful," he mused. "So no, to answer you, I have no recollection at all. But what can you expect from a man who doesn't even know how he finds his own bed every night?"

"I can expect more than that," Nottingham informed him bluntly.

"Then I'm afraid you're going to be disappointed, Constable." Carver shrugged helplessly again. "I'd help you if it was in my power, truly I would. I don't want a madman on the streets any more than you do. And for what it's worth, I'm as certain as I can be that the madman isn't me."

"I'm not," the Constable informed him bluntly. He gestured to Sedgwick, who produced the knife. "You recognise it, Mr Carver?"

"Of course," he replied, blinking in astonishment. "It's mine, I've had it for years." He looked between the Constable and the deputy as understanding rose in his face. "You think I killed people with that?"

"Well?" Nottingham asked calmly. "Did you?" He saw the growing horror in Carver's eyes.

"Of course not." The old man shook his head slowly. "Don't be ridiculous. Why would I want to do something like that?"

"We don't know," Sedgwick interjected. "We were hoping you could tell us."

"But I can't." He sounded lost, adrift. "I can't."

131

"We're going to find out sooner or later," the deputy continued. "But it'll be easier if you tell us now."

"What if I don't tell you at all?" Carver asked forlornly. "What if I *can't* tell you?"

"Then you'd better remember, Mr Carver." Nottingham's voice was quiet but commanding.

"I've tried," Carver said with soft resignation. "I was thinking as you came in. But what I want and what the good Lord grants me are frequently two different things. I'm a weak man, Constable."

"So I'm told," the Constable agreed. "I've heard about your past."

Carver raised his eyebrows slightly.

"I'm sure you have. Most people here know about me. Or they think they do. And there's very little for me to be proud of in the telling."

"Or in the ending, at least the way it's going," Nottingham pointed out. "Hanging isn't a particularly auspicious death."

Carver was silent.

"So why did you kill them, George?" the Constable asked casually. "Four people. It's quite a total."

"Were you jealous because the women went with other men when you wanted them?" taunted Sedgwick, his voice insistent.

"What did you hate about them?"

"Or did they just ignore you?" said the deputy. "Was that it… George?"

Carver had lowered his head. Now he raised it again, and Nottingham could see the thin tracks of tears leaking down his cheeks.

"Stop it," he begged quietly. "Please. I don't know what I can tell you. I honestly don't know…"

The Constable glanced quickly at Sedgwick. He'd expected

132

a reaction to the quick barrage of questions, but not this. It left him nonplussed. Was Carver that good an actor? Or was he simply a man who really couldn't remember that he'd killed?

"I'm going to leave you to think," Nottingham said briskly.

"Thank you." The old drunk had become a small man, shrunken, like a corpse that hadn't died yet.

"But don't get too cosy," the Constable warned. He started to leave, then turned. "Remember, jail can also be a dangerous place. Especially for those with bad memories, Mr Carver. It can be a waystation to the gallows."

"I shall try," came the muffled promise through the door.

"What are you going to do with him, boss?"

Nottingham shook his head. He didn't know.

"Let him stew for a while. Maybe a little knowledge of the future might make him remember the past."

Shortly before noon, not long after they'd taken the anonymous young whore for a pauper's burial, Nottingham completed his report for the Mayor. It detailed Carver's arrest and the discovery of the knife in his room. That news, he hoped, should be enough to deflect attention from the cut-purse's antics. He put down the quill, reading over the words one final time.

He went to check on Carver, peering in through the iron grille. The prisoner sat on the bed, lost in thought. Nottingham folded the report and smiled. He'd take great delight in delivering this one personally and seeing the startled look on Kenion's face.

But instead he spent a frustrating half hour waiting to see his Worship before a clerk came along and plucked the paper from his hands, telling Nottingham that the Mayor was too busy to see him at the moment. He'd been quietly and firmly put in his place.

It began to drizzle as he left the Moot Hall, with darker clouds moving in from the west promising heavier rain. Nottingham drew his coat around himself and wished he'd worn a hat. Before he'd gone a hundred yards it started to pour, and the streets emptied as if God had swept folk away.

The water glued his hair to his scalp, rivulets running inside his collar and down his back, chilling him. It was a reminder that winter was around the corner with its bitter temperatures and driving wetness. At the jail he towelled his hair with a rough sheet from one of the cells, then took off his coat to dry in front of the fire. Carver was asleep, his snores and snorts loud.

Nottingham glanced out through the small, grimy window. Runnels of water sluiced down the street, washing away rubbish and shit like a biblical flood. Figures scurried through the rain. A horse across Kirkgate waited placidly, blinking its eyes slowly.

As he stared absently, the door opened and a tall figure blew in, enveloped in a heavy greatcoat and hat. He peeled them off and shook himself slowly before announcing, "I'm James Harwood," as if his name should be familiar.

"I'm Richard Nottingham, the Constable here."

Harwood stroked his chin, nodding for a moment, and preened his black wig. Sharp features and beady, almost black eyes gave him the air of a rook, alert for carrion.

"I believe you've been looking for me," he said airily, pulling his cuffs from his sleeves.

Nottingham leaned against the sill and looked the man up and down. The clothes had been very expensive once, and looked after carefully, but age was beginning to tell on the fabric, with wear on collars and cuffs and threadbare, shiny patches on the elbows. The style, with large buttons and cuffs and an expansive collar, was past the peak of fashion.

"Have I?" the Constable asked in mild surprise. God spare me another madman, he thought, then Harwood opened his eyes wide and said plainly,

"If you're searching for a murderer, then yes."

18

"So you've murdered someone?" the Constable asked sceptically.

"Not some*one*." Harwood relished the word, emphasising the last syllable. "Four people."

"Oh?" Nottingham pushed himself off the sill, eyeing the man more closely. He was perhaps thirty, his face streaked with dirt and stubble. "Four people in Leeds?" he asked in slight disbelief.

"I think you know who I mean." The man looked smug, even proud, the long fingers of his hands interlaced and pulling against each other.

"Maybe you'd better tell me." It was impossible to keep a touch of amusement from his tone. Just yesterday morning they'd had no one for the crime, and now there were two killers, one who claimed not to remember, the other falling over himself to confess. Quite the pretty pair, the Constable thought wryly. But if this one was telling the truth... He looked at the man more closely. "So? Mr...?"

"Harwood," the younger man reminded him with a defiant stare. "It was two men and two prostitutes."

"And why did you do it?"

"Because they wouldn't give me money," Harwood explained simply. He swept a hand over his clothes. "I used to have plenty. But I'm a disinherited son. I live on the charity of others."

"You could work," the Constable pointed out tartly. "There are jobs for those who look. You're not from around here."

"I grew up in York," Harwood answered with a casual, gentleman's manner. "My father grew tired of my gambling debts and put me out three months ago."

Nottingham sat in his chair and pushed the wet fringe back from his forehead.

"How long have you been in Leeds?"

"A week. I did come looking for work, or at least some Christian men who might help me." There was a weariness in his voice that seemed almost plausible, the Constable admitted.

"And where have you been staying?"

"I had a room on the Calls for the first three nights. Since my money ran out I've been sleeping outside." Harwood indicated the other chair. "Might I sit?"

Nottingham nodded and the other man eased himself gratefully on to the seat. Nottingham was willing to believe he'd told the truth about sleeping rough, and being from a good family. Beyond that...

"So you killed these people because they wouldn't give you money?" he inquired.

The man hung his head slightly. "Yes."

"But you didn't rob them." The Constable threw the words out carefully, like a fishing line, watching for a reaction.

"After I'd killed them, my conscience took hold of me."

He was quick, Nottingham acknowledged, allowing himself to relax slightly. Harwood hadn't been quite fast enough, though. There'd been a flicker of hesitation in his eyes before he answered, wondering what to say.

"On both occasions?" The Constable raised his eyebrows. "You obviously don't learn your lessons easily."

"Anger, sir... then remorse."

"And the prostitutes?"

Harwood shrugged.

"They were witnesses. They could have identified me." He shook his head. "And no one will count one or two more dead whores."

Nottingham smiled grimly, tilted his chair back slightly and put his hands behind his head.

"One of those prostitutes used to be a servant of mine," he said with slow relish. "So I'm a man who counts dead whores."

Harwood had the grace to redden slightly.

"Describe the girls to me," the Constable continued. "You killed them, you must remember what they looked like."

"Like young girls. Brazen as whores always are." He tried to emphasise the point by raising his voice.

"Blonde? Redhead? Brunette?" Nottingham kept his tone low and even.

"I didn't notice. It was dark."

"Of course you didn't." Nottingham bared his teeth slightly. "But it's hard to notice what you don't see, isn't it?"

Harwood jerked his head up.

"You didn't kill anyone." Before there was a protest, the Constable pushed ahead. "I'm sure you've wanted to, but I doubt you'd actually do it. I'm willing to believe some of your story, but not murder. There's no free bed and warmth for you."

Harwood shrugged.

"And being found out now is better than swinging on the gallows for something you didn't do," Nottingham continued.

"You'd have discovered the truth in a day or two," the man observed.

"I'd not deserve my job if it took me that long," the Constable countered. "So what made you come here?"

"Some men were talking about the murders, down by the bridge. I thought I might find some shelter if I confessed," Harwood admitted sheepishly.

Nottingham took a couple of coins from his pocket and tossed them at the other man, who caught them with a practised grab.

"No shelter here, but buy yourself something to eat," the Constable instructed, with a dark gleam of anger in his eyes. "Then you can get out of my city. I don't expect to see you in Leeds again. Wakefield isn't far; I hear they believe most things there."

Harwood settled the hat on his head and stood.

"Will you catch him?" he asked accusingly.

"Your news is behind the times, Mr Harwood," Nottingham said with a wry smile. "We arrested him last night."

The door closed loudly as Harwood left. Nottingham rubbed his hands over his face and let out a long, slow breath. He could feel a knot of rage inside. He needed a drink. Buttoning his heavy coat he ran next door to the White Swan. It was comfortably warm and smoky, the air thick with the powerful smells of wet wool and ale. He sat at the end of a bench, nodding at some of the faces he recognised and ordered some hot mulled wine from the girl. Her dress was cut low over the swell of her breasts, showing the darker curve of the top of her nipples, her smile inviting as she leaned forward to place the jug on the table. Another whore, he laughed to himself, tupping in her room or behind the building for a few extra pennies. As long as there were men there'd never be any shortage of them.

He was still sitting there, sipping the wine and letting its heat warm his body, when Sedgwick walked in, his height letting him peer over the crowd that had grown with the end of the workday. Spotting the Constable, he pushed his way through the people and sat on to the bench.

"How did his Worship react when you told him we'd arrested Carver?" he asked with a grin.

"I didn't have the chance. He was too busy to see me."

The smile slowly faded from Sedgwick's face.

"And I had someone else to confess to the murders."

"What?" The deputy looked up, dumbfounded.

Nottingham waved his hand.

"Don't worry yourself. It was just some con man looking for some free room and board for a day or two. Where were you, anyway?"

"I was trying to find a name for that second whore," Sedgwick explained. "Someone must have known her."

"Any luck?"

"Bugger all." He scratched his head. "If anyone knows owt, they're not saying."

"Get yourself a cup," the Constable said. "You've earned it."

Nottingham knew he should have gone home long before. But he was still at the tavern three hours later, sitting across from Sedgwick. He'd lost track of how much they'd drunk, and he didn't care. Usually he was temperate; tonight, though, he felt a need to lose himself. Mary would understand, he was certain.

Just before midnight Sedgwick pushed himself to his feet. His legs were a little unsteady, but his mind seemed clear enough.

"I'd better check the night men," he told the Constable in a thick voice.

Nottingham nodded. It was better to stop now, before they were too far in their cups. He rose too, wrapping the thick coat around himself and taking a final sip of wine.

"Let them manage by themselves for once," he said. "Go home."

Sedgwick's eyes shone bright and he shook his head briefly.

"Duty," he laughed. "That's what you taught me, boss." And he left.

By the time the Constable emerged, Sedgwick had vanished.

There was a raw, thin edge to the night air that made him shiver and pull up his collar. The cold sobered him slowly as he walked. The afternoon's rain and rushing wind had brought plenty of leaves off the trees, leaving them slippery and treacherous along the streets, and he trod carefully. The sky had cleared, leaving a bright rash of stars bright in the sky.

Nottingham tried to allow himself a small glow of satisfaction. After all, it looked as if they'd caught the murderer. But underneath, worrying away like a burr, was another fact: if that was true, he'd been wrong about Carver. His judgement, his instinct, had been faulty, and Sedgwick had been right. And two people had died because of it. Maybe his time had passed. Maybe he should quit his post.

What else could he do, though? This work had been his life for so many years. He'd kept the city safe. The citizens of Leeds – the ones who led blameless lives, at least on the out-side – feared that crime and murder might touch their houses at any time. No matter that many of them, especially the merchants, were involved in their own schemes that broke the law. Or, he laughed to himself as his thoughts wandered, maybe that was exactly why they feared things happening.

He'd been their Constable a long time, but few of them would miss him if he was replaced – as long as the next man kept them safe. Some might know his name, but most would be happily ignorant, recognising him only by face if they bothered to acknowledge him at all. Yet they'd still expect the Constable and his men to protect them from the sea of danger they imagined washing up against the walls of their impeccable houses and the driftwood of humanity that might touch them.

But at times it was all beyond his control. If a man spent his money on a prostitute, he took his risks. Sometimes it was a few minutes of satisfaction. Sometimes it meant a dose of mercury and a lot of prayer. And sometimes it meant robbery or death. Anyone who wanted to play a game with those odds couldn't complain at the outcome – but they did anyway, if they had the money and power enough to believe themselves untouchable. They thought money bought all the privilege in the world. On a few occasions he'd wanted to haul them down to Amos Worthy so they could see real power, the control of bodies and souls, and meet someone who'd end a life without a second thought. That made all the gold in the vaults seem like tin, and the protection of brick and glass crumble like sand.

Yet he knew he could never do that. To let them see that they didn't really run the city in the way they imagined, that the way they thought of themselves was an illusion, would be more than they could take. And more than his job was worth. So he'd bowed at the right times and to the right people and allowed it all to fall like rain off his back.

Nottingham was the first to admit he wasn't an educated man. He could add and subtract, he could write and read, but he'd never really had the chance to study anything. He was methodical, he had good intuition, but he understood he wasn't clever in the way most people used the word. He'd known and admired Ralph Thoresby, the local historian. Thoresby had been a truly clever man, his house full of artefacts and antiquities, the books he wrote about Leeds praised for their scholarship and erudition. He could never have done anything like that.

But what he did, he'd always done well. There'd been mistakes, of course, but never any that had cost lives – until now. With a heavy heart, he stopped on Timble Bridge and listened to Sheepscar Beck running loudly along its channel. His mind was drifting, dulled by the drink, so he didn't hear the running footsteps until they were almost upon him, and turned, unsure what was happening.

"Mr Nottingham!" The man careened to a stop, panting, his face flushed red, and he made out Joe Ashworth, one of the night men. "You'd better come quick. It's murder, sir. It's Mr Sedgwick."

19

He was pounding back up Kirkgate, immediately sober, feeling his heart thud in his chest. The night man was far behind now, unable to keep up Nottingham's brutal pace. He'd told the Constable where it had happened, another of the innumerable little yards that spidered off Briggate, and Nottingham had sprinted away.

Images came unbidden into his head as he ran, of Sedgwick dead on the ground, or dying slowly, and he shook them away. The sound of his footsteps echoed off the cobbles like rapid gunshot.

The city was dark, but he knew the place too well. He slipped into ginnels and through archways, bouncing off walls as he turned corners without slowing. He splashed through large puddles left by the rain, his feet and legs soaked, but he barely noticed. Finally he rounded into a small open space. The yard was filthy, and he trod through litter scattered over the mud, hearing voices around him.

"Someone get a bloody light here," Nottingham yelled urgently. In the corner a man struck a flint, but everything was too wet to catch.

"Boss?"

He turned sharply, following the direction of the word before kneeling in the dirt.

"John?" Nottingham touched Sedgwick on the chest and felt the ragged movement of his breathing. A sense of relief coursed hard through him, then a moment of doubt. He wanted to ask the question, but daren't.

"I'll be fine, boss," Sedgwick anticipated him. He was

sitting up, and Nottingham could faintly make out his grimace and shudder as he tried to move. "I put up my arm to defend myself, and he got me."

"Christ." The word whistled out of the Constable's mouth.

Someone finally managed to light a torch, and as it guttered into flame, Nottingham's could see the wide rent in the coat, and the thick, soft shininess of blood all over Sedgwick's forearm, and puddling on the ground. His face was almost white, and a sheen of chilled sweat glistened on his skin. As he struggled awkwardly to his feet, cradling his right arm, he turned to Nottingham, his eyes wide and contrite.

"I was wrong," he said quietly. "It wasn't Carver. Look over there." With his head he indicated a far, shadowed corner.

"Light over here," the Constable commanded.

The corpses lay at the foot of a wall, a man and woman. This time the murderer hadn't had the time to arrange them, and they lay sprawled on the ground, not touching. He dispatched someone for Brogden, so they could officially be pronounced dead, but by then he'd already felt their wrists; life had left them both a little while before. He glanced up at Sedgwick, standing very carefully still, clasping his arm against his body.

"What happened?" he asked, then ordered someone to bring a rag to tie around the wound.

"I'd met up with the night men, and I was down Briggate, on my way home, when I saw a couple coming in here," the deputy recalled slowly. His eyes were closed. "There was someone else right behind them. It looked wrong, so I came up to follow him in. I heard him kill them. It was so quick..." He paused, almost in awe of the act. "He must have heard me running down here. He came pelting out. I tried to stop him, he hit me and then the bastard cut me. He'd gone before

I could do anything." There was a sense of failure in his voice and the Constable could make out Sedgwick's mouth settling into a grim line. "I almost had the fucker."

Nottingham didn't wait for the coroner's arrival. He wasn't going to learn anything more about the bodies until he saw them in the light. Instead he accompanied a pale, shaky Sedgwick back to the jail, the rough bandage now bloody, and sent a boy to wake the apothecary.

"He took me by surprise," Sedgwick admitted guiltily as they walked slowly down Briggate. He shook his head in anger. "He must have heard me running towards him. Next thing I knew he'd cut me and he was gone.'

Nottingham knew that shock was making the deputy talk, but he encouraged him, while his memory was still fresh.

"Did you see his face?"

"No," he answered in frustration, but the Constable didn't give up.

"What was he like? Think. Was he big? Small? Broad?"

Sedgwick concentrated. After a moment he replied hesitantly, "I don't think he was as tall as me – closer to your size, maybe, boss. And he didn't seem particularly broad. But he barged through me like I was nothing."

"He was prepared for you," Nottingham pointed out.

"He was right-handed," Sedgwick recalled slowly, fleshing out the image in his head. "And he was wearing a cloak; I felt it brush against me. He moved very fast."

"Good," the Constable nodded. It all helped build a picture, and it kept Sedgwick's mind off his wound.

The apothecary was waiting at the jail, and he set to work immediately, exposing the gash. It was long and vivid, the length of the forearm, and although the cut was deep, he soon slowed the flow of the blood. Gently the apothecary cleaned the wound, then sprinkled a powder on it. Sedgwick drew in his breath sharply.

"Christ, that hurt," he complained through gritted teeth.

He waited patiently as his arm was swathed in a long linen bandage then secured in a sling. Nottingham watched with concern.

"Well?" the Constable asked finally.

"It's clean," the apothecary said, nodding his head with satisfaction. He glanced between the two men. "It should heal well, but it's going to take time. You won't have much strength in your arm for a while. Rest it," he instructed, and Sedgwick nodded. "You're going to have a scar, though."

The deputy shrugged. One more scar wouldn't make a difference.

"Any better?" Nottingham asked, once they were alone.

"It still hurts." He winced heavily as he tried to raise his arm. "But it could have been a lot worse."

In his cell, Carver began to snore. Sedgwick looked at the Constable.

"We'll have to let him go. I'm sorry, boss," he said quietly. "You told me he didn't do it."

"And then I decided you were right," Nottingham pointed out. "He had the knife. He was seen with both Pamela and Morton on Monday night. There was evidence against him."

But he was glad to have Carver's innocence proved all the same. His faith in himself had been rocked more than he wanted to admit by the old sot's apparent guilt. At least this meant he could still trust his instincts.

"So what now?" Sedgwick interrupted, crowding in on his thoughts. "Where do we go?"

"Back to the beginning." The Constable sighed, then gave a weak smile. "Well, almost. At least we now know Mr Carver isn't our murderer."

They stopped as the door opened, and men brought in the bodies, wrapped in their winding-sheets. Nottingham unlocked the mortuary and guided them in, then uncovered the dead.

The man had the undistinguished look and clothes of a clerk, worn and weary even in death. He was in his forties, as far as Nottingham could judge, cheeks sunk where most of his teeth had been removed. The cloth of his coat and breeches was cheap, third- or fourth-hand, the sewing uneven and ragged. The soles of his shoes had worn through in several places. His fingers were dark-stained with ink, the joints knotted by a lifetime of writing. It was a poor death after a poor life.

The girl was pretty enough, probably fourteen or fifteen, with fine blonde hair and blue eyes, but the bloom had already gone off the rose. Her young features were coarse, her skin reddened across the nose and cheeks. Her homespun dress looked reasonably new, maybe the gift of a pimp or merchant who'd been particularly pleased with her. Her wrists were thin and bony, and her unadorned fingers nearly as small as a child's.

Once again they'd each been stabbed with two precise strokes, and Nottingham wondered at this murderer. He didn't just slash, he truly cut to kill, and he knew what he was doing, even when he was rushed.

"John," he called into the office.

"What is it, boss?"

"Come and take a look at this."

Sedgwick walked in, his movements slow and a little unsteady.

"You see these wounds?" Nottingham pointed them out.

Sedgwick looked confused. "What about them?"

"If you were trying to kill someone with a knife, would you know where to put the blade to do it properly and efficiently?"

"Well…" he began, then realisation dawned. "So maybe someone with medical knowledge?"

"Maybe," Nottingham agreed. "Or someone who's been a soldier, or learned to fence… I don't know," he said with a frustrated shrug. "But it's one more thing we know about him."

"I should have seen more of him," the deputy said with embarrassment, and Nottingham shook his head.

"You were lucky, John," the Constable told him with heartfelt relief. "I'm just glad you're alive. I'm going to need you to help catch him. Now go home and rest. That's an order."

He woke Annie as he tried to undress. Raising his arm was painful and he cried out softly, enough to make James stir and start wailing. Sitting up sleepily, Annie cursed under her breath and reached for the child, starting suddenly as she sensed someone else in the room.

"John?" she whispered and she pulled the baby close.

"Help me," he said. "I can't get my bloody clothes off."

She lit the remains of a candle, gasping as she saw his arm.

"It's not as bad as it looks," he told her quickly, seeing the dried blood on the bandage.

"Work done that?" she asked without a trace of sympathy as she began to ease off the sling and his clothes. "I'll be up all night mending your coat. And I've only just sewn your shirt, now it's in rags."

"You don't care how I am?"

Annie rolled her eyes.

"You're here and moaning, so you can't be too bad. Take your son so I can get to work."

Sedgwick sat on the bed, cradling James in his left arm until the lad fell back to sleep. He lay the boy down tenderly and walked softly over to his wife, watching the needle move swiftly and surely in her hands.

"Is there any food?" he whispered.

She stopped and fixed him with a hard stare.

"No, there's no food, John." Before he could speak, she added, "We had the last of it tonight, and you haven't given me money to buy any more."

Guiltily, he reached into his pocket and brought out his wages.

"How much of it have you spent on drink and whores?"

"Nothing," he hissed, careful to keep his voice low. It was like this every time with her accusations and barbs. "I've been working." He felt his anger rising, the way it did whenever they talked. "What do you think I do?" He held out his bandaged arm. "The man who did that could have killed me."

"And where would I be then?" she retorted, putting down the sewing. "On my own with a babbie and no money. You think more of your Constable than you do of us."

"He's given me steady work!" Sedgwick protested. "More than I'd have found elsewhere."

"Work that keeps you out all hours." Anger flashed in her eyes. "Do you imagine I like it when people tell me they've seen you in the inns or talking to prostitutes?"

"I told you what the job involved when I started it." He'd explained it to her carefully, but she hadn't believed him. "You didn't say anything then."

"And how was I to know what it would really be like?" There was a vicious edge in Annie's voice. "You didn't tell me all the hours I'd be on my own, or how little you'd make." She let the coins fall through her fingers on to the table. "We're not going to get rich on your earnings. We're lucky we can eat on them."

"You don't mind spending my money – and I know it doesn't all go on food," Sedgwick accused, pushing his face close to hers. "You think people don't tell me things, too?"

"Believe what you want, John," she told him dully. "It doesn't matter to me."

He settled back on the bed, his body tense. That was the truth of it, he thought: it really didn't matter to her. And maybe it didn't to him either. Slowly the anger began to seep away, and he left her behind as he drifted into sleep.

There was nothing more to do in the brief hours before daylight. Nottingham needed sleep and to change out of his sodden clothes.

The rain had gone, but water from the deluge still lay everywhere. He skirted huge puddles, kept his senses alert for people throwing night soil from their windows, and soon crossed Timble Bridge. His house was dark, and he could hear the even sound of breathing as he made his way through the rooms. In the kitchen he stropped a razor and ran it over his cheeks and chin before sluicing his face with cold water.

He tried not to wake Mary as he crept into the bedroom, but as he draped his hose over the chair to dry, she stirred.

"Richard?"

"It's me."

She sat up, peering in the half-light to find him.

"You look like you've had a bad night," she said anxiously.

"Two more murders, and I'm soaked to the skin," he began to explain. "Which means Carver's not guilty, and — "

"It's Emily..." she interrupted, and he stopped.

"What about her?" he straightened up, suddenly alarmed. "Is she all right?"

"She's fine now," Mary assured him. "I looked in on her before I came to bed. But she went out, wouldn't tell me where, and she didn't come back until late."

Nottingham ran a hand over his hair. At this rate, if the job didn't kill him, that girl would.

"Tell me what happened." He sat on the end of the bed. There wasn't a chance of sleep now, he knew.

"After we'd eaten, Emily announced she was going out." Mary bunched the sheet in her small fingers. "I asked her where she was going, but she wouldn't tell me. She just ran out into the rain and over the bridge."

Damn the lass, he thought furiously, breathing hard and trying to contain his temper.

"How long was she gone?" he asked, his face set hard.

"A couple of hours."

"And when she got back? Did she seem hurt or upset?"

"No." Mary gave a small smile that was almost wistful. "In fact, she looked quite happy, even if she was all wet and bedraggled."

"She still wouldn't say where she'd been?"

Mary shook her head.

"You're going to have to do something about her," she told him.

"I know," he agreed, although, apart from beating some sense into the girl, he had no idea what. "As soon as I can."

"Not soon, Richard." There was a deep, hurting ache in her voice. "She won't listen to me."

"Do you think she'll take notice of me?" he asked in a fast whisper.

"You have to make her." Mary's eyes flashed. "You're the Constable of this city, you can't have your daughter running around like a wild girl. Make her." It was part demand, part plea.

He sighed. She was right. He needed to take Emily in hand, by reason or force. He just wasn't sure he had the energy or the will to handle her at the moment.

"Please, Richard," Mary said, reaching out and digging her fingers into his forearm, "wake her up. Find out where she was. We need to know."

He couldn't refuse her. He nodded his exhausted consent.

"Do you know what she told me yesterday?" Mary continued in slight amazement.

"What?"

"That if she could, she'd like to be a writer." She didn't sound amused or aggrieved; instead she seemed fascinated at the thought.

"A writer? Why?" Nottingham had no time to read. It was pleasant, he supposed, but a frivolous way of spending an evening when there were more important things to be done.

"Like Mrs Haywood, she said."

"Who's Mrs Haywood?" He didn't know the name.

"She writes novels," Mary explained. "And essays, too. Emily prefers those. She's married to a Reverend."

"And he makes no objection to his wife doing this?" the Constable wondered, shaking his head in surprise.

"No, he doesn't."

"Maybe you're encouraging her to read too much," he suggested sourly. "It's putting ideas in her head."

After dressing in dry clothes, he crossed into the room the girls shared. There was just one bed; Rose had always slept by the window, and Emily, the restless one, by the door. He watched them for a minute, marvelling that they'd come from him, that he'd helped make such perfect forms. Rose was curled on her side, hair neatly tucked under a cap. Emily lay on her back, hair all over the pillow, arms sprawled at her side. It summed up the difference between the sisters perfectly, he thought with a small smile.

He sat beside Emily, rubbing her shoulder gently until she began to stir. As she opened her eyes he put his finger to his lips and whispered, "Come on downstairs."

Nottingham had been sitting before the dead hearth for five full minutes before he heard her soft footfalls on the stair.

In the half-light he watched her come down, tousled and sleepy. She was ripening all too quickly into a woman, in the unconscious sway of her walk and the shape of her body. She gathered herself quietly on the settle, pulling bare feet under her, and looked at him.

"What time is it?" she asked, blinking slowly.

"Early. Or late, I don't know," he admitted.

"Why do you need to talk to me, Papa?" There was an undertone of defiance in her voice and she pushed her hair back in that gesture which reminded him terrifyingly of himself.

"You know the answer to that. Your mother told me you were out long after you should have been at home, and you wouldn't tell her where you'd been," he told her firmly.

"Mama thinks I should be just like Rose."

He was astonished as the withering contempt the girl summoned into such a short sentence, and considered his words before speaking.

"Rose is Rose, and you're you. We wouldn't have it any other way. But we do expect you to behave."

Emily turned her eyes to him.

"I've behaved with perfect propriety, father. No man's touched me yet." She paused to gauge his reaction, but Nottingham kept his silence, willing his face to remain calm. "Maybe some prudish people might consider some of the situations I've been in rather scandalous," she continued, "but I haven't been compromised."

"Fancy words for a young girl," he said after a while, angered by her attitude but not giving her the satisfaction of showing it.

"It's simply the truth," she shrugged sullenly.

"Shall I tell you what I've discovered over the years?" he asked, and continued without letting her reply. "Much as we'd like to think there's one truth, there isn't really. There's your truth, my truth, someone else's, and we each believe our own to be right. There are facts which are indisputable, but all too often they're not the same as truth."

He glanced at Emily. She was watching him intently.

"Go on," she said. "At least you're talking to me like an adult."

"When have I ever talked down to you?" Nottingham wondered, and she shook her head in answer.

"Never, Papa."

"And I never will," he told her seriously. "Your mother doesn't talk down to you either." He held up his hand as she opened her mouth. "We treat you with respect, which is more than most daughters get. Especially young ones who seem ungovernable."

Her face hardened.

"You might disagree, but we do," he continued before she could speak. "But if you want that from us, you have to give it, too."

Emily raised her head.

"I do."

"I thought we'd got somewhere the other night, but obviously I was wrong. Refusing to tell your mother where you'd been half the night doesn't sound like showing respect to me. I'd say you're lucky she didn't beat you."

"She wouldn't do that!"

"No," he agreed, "she wouldn't, although God knows there have been a few times lately when I've been tempted. But I haven't – yet." He gave the words as a threat, then smiled to take the sting from them. "We have a right to know where you are, Emily. More importantly, we need to know where you are. Do you really think the streets are safe after dark?"

"You're the Constable of the city."

He nodded. "I am, and that's why I know." Nottingham

leaned forward and took her hand. "Look, do you know what I've spent the last few days doing?"

"Trying to find the man who's committing those murders?"

"Yes. And there were two more tonight. The girl who died a few hours ago was no older than you, maybe a little younger."

"But she was a…" He was pleased to see she couldn't bring herself to pronounce the word.

"She was a whore, yes. But she was a girl, a human being. And I got to see her, and the others, broken and dead. I see them and I think of you and your sister. I don't want you ending up like them." He looked at her. "I'll do anything I have to in order to stop it."

"But we're not – " she protested.

"I know. Think on this, though. There but for the grace of God you go. If we didn't have any money, that might be your lot."

Emily lowered her eyes.

"Now, where were you last night, love?" he asked softly.

"I…" she started, then faltered before finding the words. "I was out walking with a young man, Papa."

He cocked his head.

"Oh? Who was he?" Inside, he was furious, wanting to know who would take advantage of his girl this way, but he tried to sound restrained and in control.

"Just someone I'd met at the market on my way home from school." She shrugged. "He seemed nice."

"He must have been very nice, if you were willing to stay out in the pouring rain. Does he have a name?"

"Robert." She spoke it as if it had a strange power. And to her, he thought, it probably did.

"If it's all so innocent, why couldn't you tell your mother?"

"Because she'd have made more of it than it was." Emily smiled. "You know how she wants to get Rosie married. She'd have been making plans for me, wanting to meet him."

"What's wrong with meeting him?" he wondered.

"Nothing," she admitted. "I like him, but he's not courting me." Little do you know, he thought. "I just wanted to be with him, and I knew Mama wouldn't have let me because she'd think it was wrong."

There was a finality to her words, and Nottingham realised he'd pushed her as far as he could for now. It was better to stop before the conversation moved from pleasant discussion to argument. He loved Emily dearly, but there was a great deal of his personality in her; when she chose, she could be every bit as stubborn as he was himself. He desperately wanted to know more, but Emily also had to feel he trusted her. Let that come gradually, he decided. Tomorrow or the next day he'd talk to her again. He gave her hand a squeeze.

"You go back to bed." She rose, gracefully stretching to her full height, and kissed the top of his head before vanishing up the stairs.

Nottingham rested his chin on his hand. Had he done the right thing? If it came to that, what exactly *was* the right thing? All he had to rely on was his feeling, and that was more tuned to questioning criminals than an errant daughter. Mary wouldn't be satisfied, of course; she'd want chapter and verse on the young man. So did he, but he was willing to draw it out a little at a time. However much she believed herself an adult, wise in the ways of the world, the innocence in his daughter shone through. For now, he believed, he hoped, she'd be fine. God help the young man if she wasn't. In a few days he'd learn the whole story, and then he could decide what to do.

He considered waking Mary, but light was coming through the shutters. There were places he needed to be.

20

The morning felt crisp, and yesterday's downpour was a memory, blown away by a brisk and bitter north wind. Nottingham's breath clouded lightly on the air. He felt as if weariness was tearing rabidly at the edges of his mind, fraying it with problems and questions, as he plodded back into town. His feet were heavy and his shoulders were stooped, but he had to do the work.

He didn't pause at the jail, but walked instead to the court where the couple had been murdered. Two men had been left to guard it and ensure nothing was taken, that the scene remained undisturbed. He dismissed them and they left eagerly for breakfast while he searched.

There was little left of the blood, most of it washed away by the rain, except for a single dark, red-brown pool in the depression of a flagstone. He tried to imagine the bodies as they lay last night, crumpled but still warm to the touch, the souls just departed from life. He walked around, shifting the rubbish with his shoe, looking for anything at all. But as before, there was nothing.

He made his way back, lost in thought, trying to puzzle together the few pieces he had into a coherent picture. But it was impossible. They were scattered fragments that didn't even form a shadow.

Sedgwick was sitting at the desk, his arm resting awkwardly in the sling. He was eating part of a warm, fragrant loaf and sipping from a cup of ale. Nottingham leaned over, tore off some of the bread and ate it hungrily.

"You should be at home, John. I told you to rest."

"Boss." The word, and the look in his eyes, was half-plea, half-explanation. He wanted this. Nottingham nodded slightly and asked,

"How's the arm?"

"You mean apart from being useless and still hurting?" Sedgwick grimaced.

"It's going to take a while. The apothecary said so."

"I can still walk and talk."

"Just don't push yourself too far," the Constable warned, although he knew it was pointless. The man would work hard no matter what he said. "What about our prisoner?"

"I apologised to Mr Carver and let him go."

"How was he?"

"Asked me for ale money so he could drink his way home."

Nottingham chuckled. "Give him credit, he has a right. We kept him here."

"I didn't have any money, so I told him to see if he could find his room if he wasn't pissed," Sedgwick grinned broadly. "It'll be an adventure for him." He paused and his eyes became serious. "I've thought of something else."

"Go on."

"I'm sure the murderer was wearing a hat."

"A hat?" the Constable asked.

"Yes." He rubbed some of the bread into pellets between his fingers. "I was thinking about it again this morning, and I remembered feeling the brim against my face."

"That's another thing we know about him, then." The Constable let his features relax into a momentary grin. "Bit by bit, it's all coming together." He started to allow himself the hope that they were going to solve this.

Nottingham chewed on a fingernail as he worried around an idea. It had come to him as he delayed writing his daily report, knowing exactly how the Mayor would react to another pair of murders. Was it possible the killer had come to Leeds from somewhere else? He hadn't fallen from the sky; he might have left bodies elsewhere before moving on. The Constable decided to send out letters to the surrounding areas; there was nothing to lose, and he might learn something useful. It had brought results before, helping to catch a murderer three years earlier. He gathered up paper and quill and began scribbling notes to other Constables in his rough, spidery scrawl.

He was sanding the fifth letter, drying the ink before applying his seal, when the door opened and Tom Williamson entered. The merchant's jacket was freshly cleaned, metal buttons sparkling, his neck stock a sparkling white, and shoes shining although he'd walked through the mud of the streets for the Saturday cloth market.

"Richard," he said, dipping his head. His face was grave, his voice dark.

"Morning, Tom," Nottingham replied. "You're just the man I need to see."

"Oh?"

"Do you know anyone in authority in Chapel Allerton? Pamela lived there, and I thought someone might have some information."

Williamson thought for a moment.

"Try Mr Bartlett," he suggested. "I've met him once or twice. He's the Justice of the Peace there, I believe."

"Thank you, I shall." He paused. "So what brings you here, Tom?"

The merchant looked embarrassed.

"I thought I'd better tell you – the Mayor's called an urgent meeting of the aldermen. He sent out a message first thing. He wants to dismiss you."

"Ah."

Nottingham sat back in his chair and let out a long breath. He'd expected this, but he'd thought it would be done summarily, with Kenion taking the authority into his own hands.

"I've been talking to some of the others on the Corporation," Williamson carried on, his voice still serious and intent. "We've decided to oppose him. I know you haven't caught the murderer yet, but I – well, we – believe you will if you're given time. You've always done an excellent job in the past."

The Constable looked up in astonishment. He could scarcely credit what he'd just heard. He listened to the words still echoing in his head and blinked. For a moment he didn't know what to say, then the words tumbled out. "You're really going to speak for me? Even though I was wrong about Carver and we haven't caught the killer?"

"Dear God, of course we are, Richard." The merchant appeared amused at his friend's confusion. "At least some of us know what you've done for this city. Kenion's a buffoon. He's champing at the bit to run roughshod over us, and we don't intend to let him, certainly not over this." He leant forward, his hands on the desk. "Look, I'm not saying we'll win. You could be out of a job when the meeting's over, but we'll fight for you."

Nottingham felt a glow of gratitude inside. He'd never expected support from the Corporation. But here were people who valued him, and who had faith he could find the answer to this.

"Thank you," he said simply, uncertain what to add. "Thank you."

Williamson smiled at him.

"I'll come back when we've finished and let you know. But if I have anything to do with it, you'll be Constable for years to come yet."

21

Briggate bustled with Saturday market folk, buyers and sellers crowding the street. At the lower end the cloth sellers were dismantling their stalls, some spending tuppence of their takings on a Brig Shot End breakfast of porridge, boiled meat and ale from one of the taverns.

Outside the King's Head, Tom Stookes was standing on his box auctioning off livestock the farmers had driven in from the surrounding villages. To Sedgwick, the man's braying voice, reeling off bids so quickly they became a blur of sound, was all part of the fabric of the city.

He spotted Lizzie, the prostitute, a little farther up the street, leaning dispiritedly against a corner, the fan dangling from her fingers. She saw him approaching, head bobbing above the crowd, smiled slightly and tilted her head before disappearing. Sedgwick followed her into the court, spying her in a deep patch of shadow by a wall.

"Why the secrecy?" he asked her as a greeting. She moved up to him, grinned, and rubbed against him.

"You've been in the wars," she said tenderly, stroking his bandaged arm in its sling lightly.

"I'll survive," he told her, enjoying the gentle touch of her fingertips. "Now, why do you need to see me out of the way like this?"

"Thought you might want to reward a girl for getting you some information," she giggled lightly.

"Oh aye?" In spite of himself, he laughed. "No fee, eh? On the house, is it?"

The whore glanced back over her shoulder at the wall and

winked. "More like against the house by the look of it. If you can manage with one arm, that is." Her laugh was hoarse, and she pulled up her skirts before wrapping her arms around his neck. "You know I've always liked you, John Sedgwick."

He knew it was stupid. He was working, he had a wife and bairn at home. But he was tired, his wife was a bloody shrew, and his pizzle was growing of his own accord. The girl's breasts were pushing hard against his chest, and she was looking up at him with the first real desire anyone had shown him in months – since the last time he'd been with her, in fact.

He freed himself from his breeches, and with practised ease Lizzie moved herself on to him. Sedgwick pushed his weight on her, rubbing the flesh of her shoulders raw against the stone, but she didn't care. Neither did he. He wasn't thinking with his brain now, just thrusting deep into her, feeling the world grow out from his groin. With a grunt and a muttered "Fuck," he came in her, faster than he'd wanted, but he couldn't hold back.

Lizzie's eyes were closed, her breathing shallow and fast. Finally she pushed him away gently and stood up.

"That's more like it, John." She laughed, the sound turning into a violent, liquid cough before it subsided, her face flushed. "You know how to pay a lass for talk, any road."

"Better be worth it, then," he said with a chuckle.

"That girl you wanted me to find out about?"

"Yes."

"She were called Molly. Nice girl, by all accounts, liked a laugh. Hardly been here three month."

"Who was pimping her?" Sedgwick asked her.

"Old Cedric, someone told me, but I don't know if it's true." She ran a hand through his hair, trying vainly to pull out some of the matts, then adjusted her dress over her breasts. She regarded him tenderly. "You're a good lad, John. Any time you decide to leave that wife of yours, come to me. I mean that."

For once, he didn't know what to say. He'd always liked Lizzie; she had a ready wit. They'd shared jokes, a few mugs of ale and a couple of tumbles, but he had no idea she felt that way about him. She'd said things, but he'd never taken them seriously. He tucked his prick, shrunk once more, back into his breeches, and kissed her on the forehead.

"Thank you, luv. I appreciate that. Now I'd better go and see a man about a girl."

He was back on Briggate before she could say anything, a grin splitting his face. Cedric was lucky; he was going to be in a good mood when he arrived.

The rumour was that Cedric Winthrop had once been rich, controlling most of the prostitutes in Leeds. If it had ever been true, those days were long gone. Now he was a broken old man who hung on by the skin of his teeth, with no more than three or four girls willing to work for him. Sedgwick hadn't even considered him when he was making his round of the pimps. Winthrop's cottage, a tiny, half-timbered dwelling by the bridge at the bottom of Lady Lane, was a rundown wreck, with slates missing from the roof and a musty, mildewed smell in its main room.

Cedric himself was a paunchy old man in clothes twenty years out of date, with the beaming face of someone's kindly grandfather, his blue eyes framed by grimy spectacles. A thick double chin rested on his collar, his skin so pale it was almost pearlescent. His wig sat on the table, leaving just a wisp of thin silver hair on his scalp.

"Morning, Cedric," Sedgwick said merrily as the pimp opened the door. "A little bird told me you've lost one of your girls." He pushed past Winthrop, ducking to avoid the low lintel.

Sedgwick sat at the table, carelessly wiping a layer of dust with his sleeve. "You ran a lass called Molly?"

"Ran?" Winthrop looked confused, as if he'd never heard the term before.

"Have you seen her in the last few days, Cedric?" he asked patiently.

"No." Winthrop took a handkerchief from his breeches pocket and wiped his spectacles. "I went looking for her yesterday."

"Well, she's in a pauper's grave now, poor girl."

"What? She's dead?" The spectacles tinkled on the bare floorboards. Sedgwick leaned over, picked them up and returned them gently to the man's hand. He was surprised to see so much emotion in a procurer.

"She was murdered. Her and a farmer."

"God," Winthrop said softly, and closed his eyes for a moment before tears could flow.

"What can you tell me about her?" Sedgwick asked him.

The old man half-smiled sadly, shook his head and shrugged.

"You've heard her story once, you've heard it a hundred times. She was nice enough, in from the country a few months ago. Most of the time I'd bring men from the taverns to her room. She was a bit shy. But I'd been down with a touch of rheum, so she must have gone out to work the streets."

"And got herself killed," Sedgwick pointed out. "How long were you in your bed?"

"I started feeling poorly Wednesday morning. Yesterday was the first day I went out," he answered slowly. "If..."

"*Ifs* don't work in life, Cedric," Sedgwick told him sympathetically. "You know that by now." He stood.

Winthrop nodded absently, not moving as the deputy let himself out.

Nottingham was staring at the corpses once more when he heard the door to the jail open. Wiping his hands on a rag, he left the cell. Amos Worthy, tall and straight in his threadbare coat, stood by the desk, a walking stick clenched in his hand. His face was deadly serious, eyes as cold as the Constable had ever seen them. He had two men flanking the door, muscled thugs who earned their bread being unleashed like dogs at his command.

"You won't need that pair, Amos," Nottingham said casually as he sat down. "No one's going to attack you here. What do you want?"

Worthy gestured at the cell. "You've got a girl in there."

"I've got a man in there, too." He leaned back. The procurer had only been in the jail once before that he could recall, and that was on a charge that had vanished along with the witnesses.

"The lass is mine," Worthy announced flatly. "A good little earner, as well." He looked down solemnly. "I don't like people taking what's mine."

"How do you know she's one of yours?" the Constable asked with contempt.

"She didn't come back last night. My girls know they'd better have a bloody good reason for not returning," he said matter-of-factly.

"What did she look like?"

"Little thing, blonde hair, blue eyes. Some daft bastard had given her a dress that was halfway decent and she always wore that," he spat out quickly, then looked up. "You need anything more?"

"What was her name, Amos?"

"Alice. Alice Fairbanks." He banged the stick on the stone flag. "These lads'll take her."

Nottingham nodded his agreement; he had no further need of the body.

Once they'd left, awkwardly carrying the shroud between them, Worthy rubbed a hand over his freshly-shaved chin.

"Six bodies now, Mr Nottingham."

"I can count, Amos," he replied testily, turning a quill in his fingers.

"I look after my own."

The Constable rose slowly, staring across the desk at Worthy.

"No," he corrected carefully, "you look after your own when they do what you tell them. I've seen what happens when they don't, remember?" He worked hard to keep his voice under control. "So don't come in here trying to sound concerned and bereaved, like you'd lost a daughter."

The pimp's face remained impassive. "Do you have any suspicion who's doing this?" he asked finally.

"No," Nottingham admitted.

Worthy stroked his chin again.

"If you want him, better pray you find him before I do, then."

"Are you threatening me, Amos?"

"I'm not threatening *you*, laddie," he answered with a brisk shake of his head. "You should know me by now; I never threaten. Consider it a promise."

"I don't think it's wise to make promises like that," Nottingham told him blandly.

The pimp cocked his head. "Are you threatening me now, Mr Nottingham?"

The Constable smiled, baring his teeth. "Consider it a promise, Amos."

"I'll still be looking," the pimp announced stonily. "I'm not going to let someone kill one of my girls."

"From what I've heard, you prefer to do that yourself." Nottingham waited as Worthy glared at him, knuckles tightening around the silver handle of the walking stick. "You're safe enough, I was never able to prove it. But I'll tell you something for nothing." He paused. "I wish to God I could have."

"Rumours have a habit of becoming exaggerated. You ought to know that by now," Worthy countered, relaxing his grip.

"True enough," Nottingham agreed with a small nod. "But others have a basis in fact."

"Maybe," he conceded grudgingly. "I'm more interested in the man who murdered Alice. I want to get my hands on him."

"No." Nottingham brought his hand down sharply on the desk, and the sound rang around the stone walls of the room. "I'm not going to say it again, Amos. This is my business, not yours. If you want to help me, I'll gladly take that. But so you understand me properly: I won't have your justice in this."

Worthy eyed him with no expression for a long time, then turned on his heel and left.

The Constable had no doubt that Worthy would be hunting the killer. He wasn't a man ever to back down from his words, and once he started, he'd be relentless. Nottingham was limited in what he could do, but the pimp's men would have no compunction about beating information out of people. He'd heard that Worthy himself had once tried to roast a widow over a fire when he suspected her of sheltering one of his runaway girls. The woman had refused to press charges, insisting it had never happened.

Worthy would also try to bribe information from men who worked for the Constable. He could trust John, he was certain of that, but beyond that, nobody. They'd have to be careful.

Of course, it might not even matter. If Kenion had been persuasive or forceful enough, Leeds might already have a new Constable. He glanced out of the window, hoping to spot Tom Williamson returning with a grin on his face, but all he saw were the heads of people going about their business, some grim, some happy.

It was impossible not to brood and worry. There were places he needed to go, but Nottingham couldn't stir until he heard the decision. Instead he tried to busy himself with small things, tasks he could finish easily and quickly, without too much concentration. He looked up, starting at every sound, in the end fidgeting between jobs, unable to concentrate on any of them.

Williamson returned when he was finally engrossed in a report. By the time he raised his head, Tom was already standing by the desk, hat in his hand. Nottingham tried to read the expression on his face.

"Well?" he asked. The word came out in a dry, nervous croak. He realised he didn't want to leave this job.

Williamson smiled broadly. "We won."

The Constable drew in a long breath and exhaled slowly. "Thank you."

"No need to thank me," Tom said merrily. "It was an embarrassment, really. The Mayor tabled his motion to dismiss you, and asked for the ayes. His was the only vote." He slapped his thigh and laughed. "He was almost purple with fury after the nays had been recorded. I don't believe I've ever seen anyone so humiliated. It was glorious, Richard. I wish you could have seen it."

"So do I," Nottingham agreed with conviction. He could imagine the colour rising from Kenion's neck, and his frustration at being thwarted. But from here the Mayor would be keeping a close watch on everything the Constable did, though, and trying to apply a tight rein. Still, there were ways around that, and after so many years he knew them all.

"The aldermen all believe in you, Richard," Williamson continued. "If ever a man had a vote of confidence, I'd say this was it."

"Please give the gentlemen my gratitude," Nottingham said formally, lost for words to express the relief and joy inside.

"I'll do that." The merchant grinned. "Now you can go on and find your killer."

"Oh, I will." He was really beginning to believe it. Things were moving. They'd find this bastard.

22

"What do you think?" Sedgwick asked in the White Swan, washing down the last of his stew with a long swig of ale. There was still the heel of a loaf on the table and he eyed it hungrily.

Nottingham filled their cups from the jug and leaned back against the wall. He'd related everything to his deputy.

"I think we're going to have to keep looking over our shoulders for Worthy's lot."

"Worried, boss?"

He shrugged. He was still feeling a surge of confidence after the decision of the aldermen. "Just be careful, and don't tell anyone anything."

"There's not a lot to tell," Sedgwick pointed out. He reached for the bread and took a large bite.

"We'll get there," the Constable reassured him, "and we'll do it first."

"Right, so what do you want me to do now?" Sedgwick asked, his mouth full.

"Question the whores again, see if they've seen anyone strange," Nottingham told him. "I doubt you'll get anything from Worthy's girls, but there are plenty more out there. Tell them what you remember about him and see if it rings any bells. Maybe someone's seen him."

"It sounds like a long shot, boss."

"Long shots have to pay off sometimes, John." He poured a little more ale and drank.

Sedgwick cradled his left hand around the mug, staring into the liquid.

"Why?" Nottingham wondered aloud suddenly, gazing intently at the deputy. "Why did he start this week? Why's he killing prostitutes and their men?"

"Does it really matter? The fact is that's what he's doing."

"Yes, but…" The Constable's words tailed off. Ultimately, he supposed, Sedgwick was right. The reasons were irrelevant. It was the act that mattered, the taking of lives, and trying to prevent him taking more. "So what do you suggest?" he asked.

"So far it's been every other night, right?" Sedgwick pointed out, and Nottingham nodded.

"Then tomorrow night we flood the streets," he continued eagerly. "Get twenty or thirty men out there. Stop everyone who looks suspicious."

The Constable listened carefully. "Go on," he said. "You've obviously been thinking about this."

"It puts the odds in our favour," Sedgwick said fervently, his eyes bright. "If he's out there, and we have twenty people around, then we have a much better chance of catching him. And even if we don't, it should scare him and stop him killing."

"For one night," Nottingham pointed out.

"Then we do it every night!"

The Constable smiled briefly, watching Sedgwick carried away by his enthusiasm.

"I think it could work," he agreed, before asking, "but where do we get the money to pay everyone?"

"Go to the Mayor and ask!" Sedgwick said heatedly. "It's his city. He doesn't want people killed."

"I can tell you right now that his Worship won't give me another penny," Nottingham said flatly. "After what happened with the aldermen this morning, he'll want nothing more than for me to fail. It would prove his point. So he's not going to do a bloody thing to help me succeed."

"Even at the cost of more lives?" the deputy asked in disbelief.

Nottingham ran a hand through his hair. "It's politics, John. Right now I think the Mayor would spend lives to make me look a fool."

Sedgwick spat on the floor in disgust. "So we're stuck?"

"Not necessarily," the Constable answered slowly. The kernel of an idea was growing in his mind. "How many people do you think owe us favours?"

Sedgwick glanced at him quizzically, uncertain of his meaning.

"People we've let off when we could have arrested them, little things we've let go," Nottingham explained.

"I don't know," the deputy assessed. "There must be quite a few."

"I think this might be a good time to start calling in some of those debts, don't you?" He grinned wickedly.

"They won't like it."

"I don't give a toss if they scream and cry like babies." The Constable's voice was firm and hard, the thought fixed in his mind now. "It won't hurt them to show a little public spirit for once."

"You think it can work, boss?" Sedgwick asked doubtfully. "Bringing in people like this?"

The Constable shrugged. "I don't know. But I'm certain it's the only way we'll be able to get anything like this done. We're not going to get the money to pay them, I know that." He grinned. "So we'll be creative instead."

"Maybe the Mayor will be impressed," Sedgwick laughed.

"I doubt it," Nottingham said. "I hope not. I'd much rather he was upset."

He could hear laughter as he approached the house, and picked out the voices of Mary, Rose and David, the young man who'd been courting Rose for months. As he opened the door, he was greeted by a wave of warmth. The fire glowed welcomingly, and the faces were happy. Nottingham could see Rose basking in the attention David was giving her. He wasn't a bad lad, a draper's apprentice who'd almost completed his time. Unlike most of the apprentices he didn't run wild, but was sober and serious with plans for the future. And Nottingham knew his daughter liked him.

"Richard," Mary said merrily, "come and sit down." She patted a space on the settle. "Have you eaten?"

He nodded, making himself comfortable as Rose went to fetch him a cup of ale. He sensed anticipation in the room and wondered what had happened before he arrived. Once he was comfortable, sipping his drink, he saw Mary nod at David.

"Sir," the young man began hesitantly, "I'd like... that is..." Nottingham could sense him struggling for words and began to understand, although he kept his silence. He'd suffered this once himself, and now the boy could do the same.

"I'd like your permission to marry Rose," the youth blurted out.

He put the cup down and rubbed his thighs slowly, turning to Mary, who was beaming. His daughter was blushing, her face flushed deep red as she held the boy's hand tightly.

"Then you'd better do right by the lass when she's your wife," he announced.

Suddenly Mary was hugging him, her eyes brimming with tears, as the young couple embraced tentatively. He pulled his wife close, savouring her smell and feeling her joy.

Rose was no longer his girl. Looking at her, seeing the adoration she had in her eyes for the man who'd be her husband, he knew that in the last few minutes she'd slipped away and given her allegiance to someone else. To his surprise, he found he didn't mind. It was the way of women to move from one home to another. He leaned across and shook David's hand, the lad grasping his firmly and looking him in the eye. He was reminded of himself at that age, when he'd wanted to marry Mary but had taken weeks to find the courage to ask her father.

"Where's Emily?" he asked his wife quietly.

"I sent her next door," she explained. "I didn't think Rose should have to share this with her sister."

"And how did you know I'd be home?" Nottingham wondered. She raised her eyebrow.

"If you hadn't come soon I was going to send a boy with a message. Some things are more important than work." She gave him a sly, womanly smile. "Rose and I have been trying to get him to do this for weeks. Neither of you stood a chance, Richard."

"What did you think, I'd have said no?" He gestured at the young couple. "Look at them. They think the moon's risen just for them."

"It has." Mary paused as the happy pair left for a walk. "You didn't come and tell me what you'd said to Emily," she resumed when they were alone.

"I had to get back to work. She has a young man too, it seems."

"What?" She raised her head quickly. "Who?"

"I don't know yet," Nottingham told her calmly, putting his hand on her wrist. "Don't worry, I'll find out. I didn't want to push her too much when she was willing to talk."

She looked up at him worriedly. "Promise me you will."

"I promise," he assured her.

"She's sixteen, Richard. She can't be going out at night on her own. I know she thinks she's clever, but she's still only a girl." Concern flickered in Mary's eyes.

"I know, and I've told her what can happen to girls," he

answered. "I'll go and get her now and we'll talk more. I'll find out about this boy and have her bring him here so we can meet him."

He rose wearily, feeling his tired muscles protest as he walked out into the darkness. There was light showing through the shutters next door and he tapped on the door.

Norman Earnshaw was a bluff man with a warm face. His weaving business kept his family busy, and Nottingham knew he employed others, too, working in their own cottages to turn out cloth. He'd come down to Leeds fifteen years before from a village outside Bradford and worked hard to build a fair, honest living. He and the Constable had been friends of a sort for over a decade now; their wives went to market together, and Rose often looked after Earnshaw's younger children.

"Eh up, Richard," he greeted him broadly, the smell of ale rising off his breath. "What can I do for tha?"

"I've come round for Emily," Nottingham replied easily. Sudden worry arrived when a frown creased the weaver's forehead.

"Isn't she back at your house? She left half an hour since, mebbe a bit less."

"Left? What do you mean?" He spun his head, looking up and down the empty street and feeling sharp pricks of fear on the back of his neck.

"Said she'd only popped round for a visit, and that she had to go home. What's wrong?"

"Probably nothing," Nottingham said reflexively, immediately thinking too many things at once as he walked away: she'd done it again, gone off without a word while someone out there was killing girls; wondering what he could tell Mary; and most of all how he was going to find her.

He could feel the fear rising up his spine and a cold, panicked sweat on his forehead. His hands were shaking.

Where could he begin to look for her? Unless he called out his men, he realised, he had as much chance as a cow in the Shambles. There were so many places she could have gone – in the city, into the country – that it was hopeless. He'd go and look, scouring the usual dark haunts of young lovers, but he wasn't hopeful. She had imagination, and a desire not to be found.

For a brief moment he considered going home and telling Mary, but stopped after a couple of paces. She'd be terrified, out of her mind with fear, and tonight, of all nights, she deserved her joy. He'd tell her later if he had to, and face the consequences then. But he prayed to God it wouldn't be necessary.

Nottingham had just crossed Timble Bridge, his mind racing as images came unbidden, when he spotted a pair of figures coming the other way. He paid them no real attention, just forms in the night. His thoughts were focused on finding Emily; where should he look first? How long before he called out the men to search for her?

It wasn't until the couple were upon him that he could make out his daughter, a sullen, bitter expression on her face. One of Worthy's guards was urging her along, a hand placed possessively against the small of her back. Emily moved reluctantly, almost staggering, but she was unable to resist the force propelling her.

"Mr Nottingham," the man said with a dip of his head that was acknowledgement rather than deference. "Mr Worthy's compliments. He didn't think you wanted your lass wandering round alone at night. I was ordered to return her to your house."

The Constable glanced at her, but all she did was stare back defiantly. Relief flooded through him, tempered by a cold fury.

"Thank you," he said civilly, his gratitude genuine. For the second time that day he was absurdly, stupidly grateful. "I'll take her from here." The man nodded curtly, removed his hand, and faded back into the gloom of the city. Emily tossed her head, saying nothing.

"Do you want to tell me what the bloody hell you were doing?" Nottingham rounded on her, satisfied to see her cower. "Well?"

"I wanted a walk." She tried to sound haughty, but her voice was tiny, a little girl's.

Nottingham took her by the shoulders and began to shake her. He was gentle at first, rocking her, then faster and harder until her head swayed wildly, long hair whipping across her face. Emily didn't complain and made no move to stop him.

"I should beat you," he said in a cold voice that made her look up at him fearfully. "I should beat you here and now until people come out to hear your cries. Maybe that would drive some bloody sense in you." He waited for her reaction, but she remained deliberately mute, although her eyes were wide. His fingers tightened on her skin until he knew he must be hurting her. "But I'm not going to," he told her finally. "The way I feel right now, it would be too easy." And it was true. If he hit her now, he might not be able to stop. She shuddered slightly under his hands, and he saw the moisture glistening in her eyes as she blinked to fight back tears. "Where were you? Were you going to meet him?"

Emily nodded, lowering her head.

"Who is he?"

"I told you, I met him at the market."

"And what does he do?"

"I don't know," she told him. But the words came too readily. He knew she was lying.

"He didn't tell you? You didn't even think to ask?" He asked the questions harshly, as if she was a suspect at the jail.

"It didn't matter." She raised her face to his. "You've always told us to judge people by who they are, not what they do."

"So you went to meet Robert." Nottingham ignored her statement and rolled the words around slowly, like a pair of dice before a throw. "Did he arrive?"

"No," she answered quietly, with a trace of disappointed sadness. "I waited and waited, but he didn't come. Then that man grabbed me and said I shouldn't be out on my own at night and that he was going to take me home. He scared me the way he touched me." She paused a second. "Was he one of your men?"

"No," he said, and stopped. In all likelihood Worthy had men in the shadows behind Rose and David, too. Returning Emily like that, bringing her home, was a quiet, powerful statement. Tonight Nottingham thanked God it had happened. Tomorrow he'd be filled with an icy rage towards the pimp.

"Come on," he said brusquely, grabbing her wrist and pulling her along so hard she almost fell. "We're going home. And as soon as we get in the door you're going to bed. Don't even think of answering me back or disobeying or I'll clout you into next week."

She followed meekly, her silence a tacit, frightened agreement.

Nottingham sat in the dark. The fire had died and the room was cold, but a nip in the air had never bothered him. Mary and the girls were all asleep. Emily had scuttled off to her room like a mouse, not saying more than two words while he deflected Mary's questions with vague, noncommittal answers. When he'd checked on her later, she had the blanket pulled up against her chin, her breathing even, as if the incident had never happened. He'd managed a couple of hours of broken sleep.

In bed blankness had come, but it was quickly tormented by dreams until he was sick of the tossing and constant waking. He rose and dressed, ran cold water round his mouth to flush away the night, and sat down to think.

Now, in the silence, he had time to reflect. He wasn't surprised Worthy had men behind himself and Sedgwick, but it scared him, too, to know his family was being followed. Tonight he'd been glad, but the menace in the message was eloquent. He sighed softly. These murders had brought work into his home. Violated it.

Elbows on knees, he put his hands together and rested his chin on them. He needed a shave. He needed rest, a wash. He needed this to be over. When it was done, he'd deal with Amos Worthy in his own way. He'd also find this Robert, whoever he might be, and teach him a lesson.

The hours passed slowly, but there was no chance of more sleep. His mind was crowded, thoughts pressing on his skull.

How could he solve the murders? He didn't even have any suspects. The only clues he possessed were faint and didn't point in any particular direction. At least he could be thankful that it looked as if the killer hadn't struck again as the city and its taverns were jammed in the respite of Saturday evening.

But tonight he'd have a small army of men around the city. Maybe the plan would work, and they'd catch this killer. If not, at least it might save a pair of lives. And that would be more than they'd managed so far.

When his brain finally rebelled against more hopeless thought, he wrapped himself in his greatcoat, closed the door quietly, and walked the silent streets back into Leeds. In the city, the evidence of people forgetting the working week just past was all around him in the rubbish and pools of vomit on the streets. A drunk had collapsed against a house, his hoarse snores ringing between the buildings. Saturday night was always a time filled with arguments and fights, something people needed to obliterate the days of work they'd completed for little money and the vision of the weeks and years that stretched ahead without hope of relief.

A man with a dazed expression, blood flowing from a cut on his cheek, wandered down the other side of the road. Nottingham made no move to stop him. He'd learned long ago that it was best to leave people be wherever possible. He had earned too many scars by trying to help.

Soon the bells would begin ringing for the first of the Sunday services, carillons from St Peter's, St John's and Holy Trinity bringing out the pious and the not so holy alike to fill the pews and pray for the redemption of heaven.

Ordinarily he'd have been there himself, wearing his best suit of clothes and leading Mary and the girls into the parish church. But this week he had too much to organise, too many people to contact; heaven would wait for another seven days.

At the jail, Sedgwick was kicking out the wounded drunks who'd been pulled in for their own protection and arranging for the worst offenders to be transferred to the cells under the Moot Hall to await trial. His sling was grubby, discoloured by soot and smeared with food.

"Is your arm any better?"

"It's not as bad as it was." He tried to raise it and the Constable saw the pain fly across his face.

"Busy night?"

Sedgwick shrugged casually. "No worse than usual, really. The only problem is the cutpurse. Someone tried to stop him and he pulled a knife."

The Constable raised an eyebrow, waiting for more information.

"No harm done," Sedgwick continued. "He just showed it then ran. But at least we know we're looking for a kid now. About twelve or thirteen, fair hair, grubby."

"That's about half the poor lads in Leeds." Nottingham snorted. "Anything more?"

The deputy shook his head. "The man who reported it was all shaken up, poor old bugger. Still, it's more than we had. I've put the word out."

"Good."

The room smelt like morning in a tavern, the sour, raw stench of stale beer and puke hanging in the air. He opened the door to let in some cleaner air and Sedgwick smiled wryly.

"Always like this on a Sunday, boss."

Nottingham remembered all too well; for many years, before he was Constable, he'd covered this duty himself.

"At least you don't have to sit through an hour's sermon," he pointed out.

"The way some of this lot go on it's not much better."

Nottingham rubbed his hands together. "Right, today we find people who owe us," he said. "You go west of Briggate, I'll go east. Don't take no for an answer. I want them out from ten tonight until three. And if anyone complains, remind them it's a lot better than a day in the stocks or a fine."

"You want them in the yards?"

"I want them everywhere, John," Nottingham said with a firmness that surprised himself. "Let's pray for some luck. If we can get twenty of them out there it should keep things quiet. More would be better."

"The killer's going to be on his guard after Friday." Without thinking, Sedgwick rubbed his arm.

"I know," Nottingham admitted, "but he still won't be expecting this. If he's planning on striking tonight, I want him stopped. Everywhere he turns he'll see someone. He isn't going to murder anyone else in Leeds."

There was a hardness to his tone that made Sedgwick take a long, appraising look at his face. The Constable looked gaunt, with smudged circles under his eyes. The lines around them seemed deeper than usual, but they held no laughter or gentleness. He'd never appeared more determined, or more weary.

"Well," Nottingham said finally. "Let's get going. We've got a lot to do today."

23

By now Sedgwick knew what to do. With no inns open on the Sabbath, the best time to find villains of any kind on Sunday was early in the morning. They'd be sleeping after a night of thieving or drinking, and the thumps and kicks on the door would rattle them into scared consciousness. He'd used it often before. It served to remind them who wielded the power in the city.

So far it had worked perfectly. Two of them had still been addled on ale, ready to agree to anything as long as they could return to their beds. Martin Grover had looked so guilty that he'd have said yes to carrying the devil around on his shoulders if only the Constable's man would leave. A couple had taken some persuasion, but reminders of the offences they'd committed, including the ones they thought no one knew about, had quickly convinced them.

He knew Nottingham was out too, using exactly the same methods, pressuring people to join him, with no refusals allowed. This was going to be the biggest thing they'd attempted, and he only hoped it happened. Extracting promises was one thing, getting the people out there tonight would be another matter. There'd be excuses and illnesses, sliding off from their posts and whatever else they could think of. He'd end up being a sheepdog as much as anything else.

But that was fine. Activity would keep the murderer away. He needed quiet places. The whores would grumble at the intrusion and loss of business, but it might keep another one of them alive. And the pimps would complain tomorrow, but they were the least of his worries.

Sedgwick saw Adam Suttler striding briskly up Briggate, a prayer book in his hand as he led his family to St John's. The little forger was another candidate for tonight; they'd certainly helped him enough in the past. He moved faster, catching up with Suttler by the Moot Hall.

"Morning, Adam." He nodded at the book. "Off to make amends for the week's bad deeds?"

Suttler grinned, showing a crooked row of chipped and missing teeth.

"Now, Mr Sedgwick, why would you be thinking that?"

"Happen because I've known you far too long."

"I'm keeping myself out of trouble," the man insisted, clasping the prayer book against his chest like a talisman. He tilted his head at the spire in the distance. "I go to church every Sunday, and I keep the commandments."

"Only because there's not one that says thou shalt not forge, Adam." He laughed at his own wit. "I've got a job for you."

Suttler raised his eyebrows high into his receding hairline.

"You're going to be patrolling Leeds tonight."

He stopped and turned towards the deputy.

"What?" he asked, his voice rising in astonishment. His head barely reached Sedgwick's shoulders and it would be generous to call his muscles puny.

"We're putting a load of men out on the streets tonight. We're trying to catch the man who's been killing the whores and their johns."

"What do you want me to do?" he asked nervously.

"Just be out there for a few hours. After ten, until about two or three." Sedgwick relaxed and let an easy smile slide across his face. "That's it, Adam. Nothing much." He put a hand on the other man's shoulder. "Look, we've saved you twice, haven't we?"

Suttler nodded warily.

"Well, think of this as your way of saying thank you." He

paused, hardening his voice a little. "And it's not meant as a choice."

The man's shoulders slumped in defeat.

"I'll be there," he said. "I promise, Mr Sedgwick. Can I go to service now?"

By mid-afternoon he'd collected promises from fifteen men to do their duty. He wandered home to sleep for a while before returning to work in the evening. The room was empty; Annie and James had gone somewhere, and the fire was burned down to nothing in the grate.

Sedgwick sighed. With the sling and his stiff arm he couldn't take off his clothes. Instead he settled down, fully dressed, the scratchy blanket pulled up high. He'd wake in plenty of time.

Nottingham had assembled his force, too. He'd persuaded gently where he could, and insisted where he had to. He knew that, at best, only two-thirds of them would appear, but that would be adequate.

He settled back at his desk, eating a slice of cold, greasy game pie that he'd regret later, and supping from a mug of small beer. He brushed the crumbs off his coat as he swallowed the last mouthful.

He'd done all he could for now; tonight would be the test. In his bones he knew that the killer would be out again, hungry for death. What he was doing to thwart him was extreme, maybe even ridiculous, but what choice did he have? He didn't have men enough to watch the whole city. So the volunteers were just performing their civic duty. That's how he'd explain it to the Mayor, if he ever bothered to ask. If their luck was good, they'd catch the murderer and that would be an end to it. But he knew all too well that luck was a capricious bitch.

He drank a little more, then sat back and let his thoughts wander. What was he going to do about Emily? He could beat her, the way most fathers did with errant children, but he knew his daughter; that would only make her more stubborn.

She was too clever for her own good, that was the problem, and trying to grow up too quickly. Another year and she could court and marry, if she wanted. Both he and Mary would be happy with that. And it might drive the ridiculous notion of writing from her head. He'd said little to his wife, but it disturbed him. He wrote because he had to, reports and figures. There wasn't any pleasure in it, and he didn't see how anyone could find the act enjoyable. He read the *Mercury*, but very rarely did he open a book. They reminded him too much of what he'd been long ago, a boy in a house with a library whose shelves reached close to heaven.

Above all it worried him because he understood that if Emily wrote, she'd fail. She wasn't aristocracy, or even well-connected. No London publisher would look twice at the scribbling of a Constable's daughter from Leeds. But he had no idea how to dissuade her.

That was the future; more immediately, he had to keep her away from the streets. When he finally had time, tomorrow he hoped, he'd find this boy of hers and he'd make him back away. He knew she was being canny and coy, telling him just enough, but not the information he needed to search for the lad. In that way she was her father's daughter again; she knew instinctively how to dole out facts.

The only thing he knew for certain was that an answer wouldn't come easily or quickly – if it even came at all. He wanted the best for her. But he had no idea what the best was in her case.

Nottingham must have drifted into sleep, for when he opened his eyes the first cast of dusk was spreading across the sky, above the chimney smoke of the city. His neck hurt and the muscles in his calves felt cramped from sitting at his desk. He stretched slowly, pushing out his arms and legs and revelling in the luxurious feel. A few more hours and it would all begin. Time to eat a good meal and make sure everything was ready.

By the time Sedgwick woke the smudges of darkness in the sky were thickening. He sat up in bed, shaking his head. The room was chilly and gloomy, deep shadows filling the corners. He realised that Annie and James hadn't returned while he slept.

He didn't bother building a fire; a few more minutes and he'd be gone, and there was no knowing when his wife and son might return. They were probably visiting her family so they could be hours yet. He looked around for food, but there was so little on the table that he couldn't bring himself to take it.

He locked the door as he left. It was going to be a long night.

24

By ten the men were out on the street. As Nottingham circulated, keeping quietly to the shadows, he counted around fifteen. Nowhere near as many as he'd hoped, but he'd remember the names of all those who hadn't come out, and deal with them later.

It was a good idea using men of dubious reputation, he decided. They knew how to be inconspicuous and quiet – at least the ones who hadn't drunk too much did. Yet the loud clumsiness of the others could be effective too, acting as a deterrent, funnelling the killer into the darker courts and alleys.

He was worried, but he tried to keep his feelings hidden. Everything hinged on the killer being out tonight, looking for his next victims. The weather was cloudy, an early autumn chill helping the leaves tumble, the moon well hidden. A perfect night for murder, he thought grimly.

Around eleven he found Sedgwick completing a circuit on Lower Briggate. They conferred in a doorway, away from prying eyes, talking in hushed voices.

"Not a wonderful turnout," the Constable said.

"Could have been better." Sedgwick shrugged in agreement. "I've given them all small areas. If they spot anyone in a dark cloak and hat, they're to challenge them loudly. Someone should always be close enough to help and raise the alarm."

"Good," Nottingham nodded. "We'll keep walking round."

"I'm surprised Worthy doesn't have men out. He must have heard about this."

"Don't underestimate him," the Constable warned. "He's a

sly old sod. If he's got his best lads out, they could be a dozen paces from here and we'd never know it. But if anyone catches a murderer tonight, it's going to be us. I want him sentenced in court, not left with his throat cut."

"And if some of our men are working for him?" queried Sedgwick.

"Some of them probably are," Nottingham admitted. "But if they fuck this up, they'll be moving to another city tomorrow, I can guarantee you that." There was a bitter iciness in his voice that made it a promise.

People were still out and about, visiting, walking, but the voices on the streets began to fade slowly. The slatterns and prostitutes were finishing their trade as men bade farewell to a day of rest and prepared for another week of drudgery. By midnight there'd been nothing to stir excitement and the Constable could tell the men were becoming bored and weary. He slipped between them warily, offering quiet words of encouragement, making sure their attention didn't lapse. Only one had left, after a short argument, and he'd been warned he'd pay the price for desertion.

Nottingham was nervous, the tension running through his body. The next two hours would be crucial. He brushed back his fringe and ran a hand through his hair, trying to breathe calmly and evenly. So much depended on him being right about the killer prowling tonight. He could feel his heart in his chest, the thick rhythm beating uncomfortably fast. After being alert for every sound for so long, he'd be completely drained by night's end.

He'd been parading the same streets for hours, until he felt he knew every crack and indentation of the paths. The night had quietened, broken only by the barking of stray dogs and the occasional blare of an argument or singing.

The minutes were passing too slowly, as if time itself was tired. He'd just completed another circuit, finishing at the top of Briggate near the Head Row, when he heard a confused bellow of cries from the yards behind the Shambles. Without thinking he began to run towards the sounds. The voices increased in number, shouting over each other in a babble of sound that grew more frenzied. Dear God, Nottingham prayed as he ran, let it be him. And let him be alive.

For a minute it seemed as if he could get no nearer; he was trapped in a maze of tiny streets. Then suddenly he was there, watching two men hold a struggling figure in the light of a pair of torches. A body lay on the edge of the shadows. Sedgwick was kneeling over it, then looked up and shook his head.

"What happened?" Nottingham asked breathlessly, and was immediately overwhelmed by several garbled accounts. "You!" He pointed into the crowd at a scrawny youth he didn't recognise. "Tell me!"

The lad ducked his head briefly.

"We, er, heard him coming, sir." He glanced around the other faces, seeing expressions ranging from agreement to anger. "We challenged him like you said, but he didn't want to stop. So Adam, he, er, started to fight with him, to stop him. We were shouting, and then some of the others came." He paused again. "Then he pulled a knife and started stabbing Adam. I didn't know what to do. Some of the others grabbed him."

Nottingham gazed around in horror. An innocent man was dead because of him. He walked up to the culprit, a man of about thirty, thin to the point of starvation, so cowed he didn't even fight against the men restraining him. He was dressed in tattered old clothes, hose ragged and breeches torn. The Constable had to resist the overwhelming impulse to hit him.

"Why did you kill him?" he asked.

"I thought he were trying to rob me," the man answered defensively, his eyes full of fear. "Then when t'others started coming, I thought it were a gang going to kill me."

Nottingham said nothing more. He turned and walked over to the body.

"Who was it?" he asked Sedgwick.

"Adam Suttler." The deputy sounded sombre. "I only asked him because I saw him going to church this morning." He kicked at a stone and heard it tumble away. "Who's that bugger?" He inclined his head at the man who stood with his head bowed.

"Just some poor man who got caught in the middle," Nottingham told him in sad blankness.

"He'll hang." There was satisfaction in his tone.

"Yes." He would. There was nothing more to say.

"Meanwhile our man's still out there," Sedgwick said passionately.

Nottingham shook his head.

"He's not a fool, John. He'll have heard all the noise and gone to his bed. Get Brogden here and the killer down to the jail. He won't give you any trouble."

"No, he won't." Sedgwick bunched his fist and Nottingham placed a hand lightly on his good arm.

"Don't take it out on him. He didn't know what was going on. Look at his face. That's not someone who killed for pleasure. He knows he's just waved farewell to his own life."

"So long as he doesn't expect any bloody sympathy from me." He began to issue orders as the Constable wandered away.

It was on his head, and Nottingham knew it. Another little piece of guilt to carry around piled up on all the others he'd accumulated over the years. It would worry at him for a while, itch like a wound, then fade to a scar he'd only notice in certain lights.

But at the moment it was digging deep, clawing raw at his mind and he needed to be alone. It was a mess, a deadly mess. If... that was a word he was going to be thinking often over the next few days.

Sedgwick would go and tell Suttler's wife. The city would pay for the funeral, he'd make sure of that. And he'd take responsibility for the death. At least the Mayor wouldn't worry too much about one poor man killing a forger.

He would, though. It was one more death to chalk up to this murderer. Yet he knew in his heart that he'd done the right thing in having so many men out. He had to be the hunter, to act and pursue. Inside, he truly believed the man had been out tonight. If it hadn't been for an accident...

Nottingham pulled the coat closer around himself and shivered in the air. It wasn't long until dawn; the sky was just beginning to lighten on the eastern horizon. He'd been walking for too long, his legs ached and his mind was reeling. There was a vicious thirst in his mouth, his head pounding along with his footsteps. He wanted to go home, but he couldn't face his house or the jail yet. He needed to be outside in the quiet, away from people. It wouldn't erase the horror he was feeling, but at least he'd have the time to push it down deep and keep his mind where it needed to be.

Down by the warehouses on the Aire the first workers were arriving to start loading cloth on to barges for Hull and the Continent. He stood and watched as the great doors above the river opened, ropes moving up and down over the pulleys, and the day straggled into its rhythm.

Early light spilled on to the water and Nottingham sighed, knowing he had to go back. He stopped at the Old King's

Head for ale and bread; swirling the liquid around his mouth took away the taste of the night.

Finally, when he could put it off no longer, he returned to the jail. Sedgwick was sitting at his desk, his long face ashen, half moons of shadow under his eyes.

"I'm sorry, John," Nottingham said gently. Sedgwick looked up without expression and shook his head.

"Not your fault, boss. I should never have asked him. Adam wasn't made for anything physical."

"Where's the body?"

"I had it sent home to his widow."

The Constable gave an inward sigh of relief; he hadn't wanted to view the corpse and confront his own failure.

"What about his killer?"

Sedgwick jerked his head towards a cell.

"Fast asleep." His tone softened a little. "I think it's the closest thing to a bed he's had in weeks." He sighed. "We've messed it up, and no mistake." He paused and handed Nottingham a piece of paper. "This came for you."

The Constable opened the plain seal. The note was terse, written in Worthy's surprisingly elegant hand: *A poor job, Mr Nottingham*. Baiting him like a chained bear on market day. He crumpled the paper slowly and tossed it on to the desk.

"Let's work out how to find our killer," he said darkly.

"We can't try the same thing again," Sedgwick pointed out. "After this, no one would come even if we threatened them with the Assizes."

"It was still a good idea." He thought for a moment. "Take two of the men off their usual duties."

The deputy looked at him quizzically. "What for, boss?"

"Amos Worthy's top men," Nottingham began. "You know them?"

"Of course I do." The deputy was astonished he even needed to ask.

"I want two of our lads on them. Have them try and stay out of sight. If Worthy's lot talk to someone, find out what they wanted and what the answers were. We know they're looking for this murderer, too. Maybe they can lead us to something." And it'll give Worthy a taste of being followed, he thought.

Sedgwick looked unhappy.

"Are you sure it's worthwhile?" he asked.

Nottingham pushed his fringe back wearily.

"No," he admitted with a slow shake of his head. "But what do we have to lose? The rest of us will still be looking. And it'll annoy Amos to be doing our work for us."

"I don't know…" Sedgwick began warily, but the Constable's dark look silenced him.

"Worthy's a pimp, he's a criminal. If half the members of the Corporation didn't use his whores, he'd have been hanged years ago." Nottingham slammed his hand down. "He thinks he's better than us, so let's use him. And if he knows we've done it, that's all to the good."

Sedgwick had seen this mood before. It brooked no argument, at least not until it had passed and turned to a brooding silence. Then, perhaps, he could talk some sense into the Constable. This wasn't going to bring them anything; the only thing it did was squander their precious resources, and all because Nottingham hated Worthy, and had for far too long. It had always been personal, as deep as the sailors said the oceans were, far beyond any desire to see the man simply pay for his crimes.

He left the jail to search for the two men he wanted. He couldn't read the note, but it was easy enough to guess that Worthy had sent it, a taunt following the night's failure.

Nottingham had responded to the goad, of course. Sedgwick could have predicted it. Now his job was to make sure his men stayed out of danger.

Johnson and Portman, the two men he'd use, were exactly where he expected, sitting next door in the White Swan. Sedgwick bought a jug of ale and carried it to their table, pouring himself a cup on the way.

"Got a job for you, boys," he said as he replenished their drinks. He explained the task, emphasising the fact that they should stay well back and report any contacts to him. They were good and honest, they'd do the job properly, but they weren't always the smartest. If there was anyone to talk to, he'd prefer to do it himself. That way he'd be certain the right questions were asked and he received all the information.

They left when the beer was finished, and Sedgwick sat alone, in no hurry to drain his mug. If he had any sense he'd go home and get more sleep. He knew he was exhausted, and a couple of hours away wouldn't matter. Annie would be home with James, and she'd probably have something cooking to warm his stomach. He left the tavern, striding purposefully back to his room.

The Constable sat back, fingers steepled in front of his face, and wondered if he'd done the right thing. The note had been the last straw. On top of having his family followed, it had been too much, and he'd let his anger boil over. He knew it was stupid. And yet… nothing else had worked. He'd let it go for a day and see what happened. As he'd told Sedgwick, at this point they had nothing to lose.

A messenger ducked in, bringing a letter. Nottingham saw the address, from Halifax, and as he opened the seal, his hopes rose. Surely such a quick reply to his request for information meant something? But as he read, he found nothing helpful;

they'd had no similar crimes.

His longing for a link, a connection of any kind, had come to nothing.

The clock on the parish church struck ten. He stood reluctantly, weighed down by a mixture of weariness and frustration, and set off up Kirkgate towards Briggate. Servants and housewives clogged the street, trying to keeping out of the path of carters and drovers and Nottingham walked gingerly among them. From the corner of his eye he sensed a small, sharp movement; his arm reacted instinctively, moving out to grab whoever was there.

Looking down, he saw he had hold of a boy of about twelve who was struggling against his hand, a small knife clenched in one fist. Nottingham tightened his grip and pushed the youth against the rough stone of the wall as a crowd suddenly gathered.

"You might as well put the knife down, laddie," he said. "It's not a good idea to rob the city's Constable."

The boy wilted, but Nottingham didn't let him fall.

"We're going to take a walk to the jail and you can tell me what you were trying to do" he continued, keeping a tight grip. "What's your name?"

"Joshua."

Nottingham pushed him harder against the wall.

"Joshua Forester, sir," he amended.

"Joshua Forester." The Constable could hear the tremor in the lad's voice. Glancing down, he saw wide, scared eyes and a pale, grimy face under unruly blond hair.

"I don't like cutpurses, Joshua Forester," he said grimly. "Especially not right now."

25

At the jail he pushed the lad into a chair and leaned menacingly against the main door.

"How old are you, Joshua Forester?" Nottingham asked.

Forester pursed his lips and concentrated as if he'd never been asked the question before. And, the Constable considered, maybe he hadn't. None of the other children would really care.

"Don't know," he answered eventually. "Me mam just always said I were her baby."

"Where's your mother now?"

He shrugged in a resigned gesture.

"I came home one day and she were gone. Me and me sister waited, but she never come back."

"What happened to your sister?"

"She died," the boy answered in a matter-of-fact tone.

"You've been making a living as a cutpurse?" Nottingham said.

Forester tried to keep a blank face, but even fear couldn't control the small smile of pride that crept across his mouth.

"You've been a busy lad," the Constable continued. "You've given us a lot of trouble. And you've taken a fair bit of money." His tone hardened. "What have you done with it all, Joshua?"

"Gave some to my mates." He cocked his head defiantly. "So we can eat and have somewhere to live."

The Constable nodded slowly. Scrawny and shaggy, dressed in coat and waistcoat a few sizes too big for his body, the lad looked an unlikely leader of a group of children. But he had quick hands and a special skill; doubtless there were others, larger and stronger, who would protect him in return for what he could provide. By rights he should have Forester up before the magistrate in the morning to be tried and off to begin serving his sentence. He eyed the boy, remembering his own youth and the struggle to survive each day.

"How long have you been fending for yourself?" he asked curiously.

"Four year, more or less," Forester replied in surprise. "Why?"

"Not easy to do," Nottingham commented. "How many do you look after?"

"Depends," the lad said warily, suspicious at the Constable's interest. "Five or six. Why do you want to know?"

"No real reason. I was just curious." He paused. "You're good at not being seen. You must be fast." When the boy didn't respond, the Constable continued. "You like being on the wrong side of the law?"

Forester shrugged. "I never really thought about it."

"You know a judge will probably transport you to America or the West Indies. That's seven years' hard labour in places so hot you'll fry – and that's if you even survive the journey there." He looked sternly at the lad. "You won't last."

The boy rounded on him. "Why would you care?"

"Because I think you could be more useful here." Nottingham paused to let the words sink in. "What would you say if I offered you a job?"

The lad raised his head, confused. "You what?"

"Work for me, be one of the Constable's men," Nottingham explained.

Forester stared, wide-eyed. "Are you having a joke before you lock me up?"

"No, I'm serious," the Constable told him. "Do you know your letters?"

"What do you think?" Forester asked derisively. "Course I don't. That mean I can't do it?"

"Not at all." Nottingham smiled. "But if you work for me, there's no more stealing purses, or anything else. You'll have a wage coming in every week. It's not a lot," he admitted, "but it'll keep body and soul together."

"What about what I've done?" the boy asked, unbelieving. The Constable studied him. He knew the lad was unsure what to make of the offer, whether it was genuine. "What you going to do about that?"

"The cutpurse will have left Leeds without being caught," Nottingham said guilelessly, with a wave of his hand. "An unsolved crime. They happen."

"Why should I believe you?"

"Because I've no reason to lie to you." He opened his palms. "Look, Joshua, I could put you in a cell and haul you off to court tomorrow without a word. Do you want to know why I haven't?"

The boy nodded dumbly.

"When I was your age I got by the best I could. I worked when there was work available. And when there wasn't, I stole. I thieved, I cut purses." He saw Forester's eyes widen more, trying to absorb this strange information. "So maybe I don't think you're beyond redemption. It's your choice. But if you turn me down, I can tell you right now that you probably won't live to see twenty."

Forester knitted his fingers together in his lap and bit his lip. Nottingham watched him carefully. He'd handed the boy a lifeline; the question was whether he was clever enough to recognise it.

"And nothing will happen to me for what I've done?" he asked, wanting to be certain on the point.

"Nothing," Nottingham assured him. "On my honour."

"I'll do it, then," he said after thinking for a long while. "And you promise I won't be punished?"

"I promise," the Constable told him. "You have any of that money left?"

The boy nodded tentatively.

"Make sure you eat well tonight, then. Be back here at six tomorrow morning and you can start learning the job. But I'll tell you this, Joshua – if you're not here I'll find you and you'll be convicted. Understand?"

Forester nodded vigorously, and Nottingham moved away from the door to let him leave. He ran up the street, as if he needed to put distance between himself and the jail. He'd be there with the dawn, Nottingham was convinced of that. He'd let Sedgwick teach him the ropes. They needed bright young talent, and who better than a thief to catch other thieves? What the lad lacked in size he obviously more than made up in cunning.

And it solved the problem of the cutpurse. Maybe no one would go to jail for the offence, but the crimes would mysteriously stop, and they could rule a line under the affair. It was no real consolation for everything else that had happened, but it was one thing fewer he had to think about – and one more person on the street to help find the killer. He'd managed to retrieve something from a bleak day.

Nottingham ran a hand through his hair and let out a slow breath. He knew he should send word to Sedgwick to call off his men. He'd do that tomorrow if they hadn't turned up anything useful.

For now, though, he was ready for home. Maybe the scare of the other night had jolted Emily; he hoped so, although deep inside he doubted it. He knew her too well; if she wanted something badly enough she'd find a way. And he was afraid she wanted her first young man.

He paused in front of the door, his fingers poised to turn the knob. The house seemed quiet and normal, a light shining through the shutters as if nothing had ever been wrong inside its walls. He walked in to see Mary darning hose, Rose embroidering, and Emily in the corner with a book. Inwardly he sighed with relief.

Mary stood gracefully and gave him a small kiss, and Rose smiled at her father. Emily hunkered down behind the pages of her book, never looking up or acknowledging him.

Nottingham sat by the fire as his wife brought him cold meat and bread. As he chewed hungrily, he relished the warmth of the blaze and the weight off his feet. It was as if the family sensed that he didn't want to discuss the day. Most likely a lot of the news had already reached them, he mused, laying the plate on the floor.

A hand rubbing his sleeve roused him slowly. Looking around he saw that the girls had gone and Mary was standing by his chair.

"You've been asleep for an hour, Richard," she told him with a soft laugh. "You dropped off almost as soon as you'd finished eating."

He shook his head, trying to clear it.

"It was bad," he explained, his voice thick and husky, as he reached for her hand.

"I heard."

"How's Emily been?" Nottingham asked.

"Quiet and helpful," Mary said with relief. "What did you say to her the other night?"

"Not a lot," he answered truthfully. "Maybe she just got a lesson in life."

"Why don't you come to bed? You look like you could sleep for weeks."

"I feel like it, too," he agreed, his eyelids like lead. "I just wish I had the time."

The evening had turned cold with a cruel wind blowing down from the north. Sedgwick listened as the men detailed everything Worthy's lieutenants had done for the last six hours. It had been a worthless enterprise, trailing them as they collected money from a number of girls, before vanishing into an inn where they drank and played hazard while the lawmen waited outside in the growing chill.

Sedgwick sent them home for the night. If there really was anything to be learned, it wouldn't be here or now. And he needed rest and some warmth himself, even if it was in Annie's unloving embrace.

He unlocked the room expecting to find a fire burning in the grate and the sound of voices. Instead it was in darkness, and when he lit the stub of a candle, it looked as if no one had been there since he'd left. That was strange, he thought, they should have been home hours before; James needed his sleep. Then, almost without thinking, he checked the chest that held their clothes. Both Annie's and James's were gone; his spare hose had been tossed into a corner. The spare money he kept in a tin by the fire had vanished too. It wasn't much, but he'd saved it carefully and conscientiously from his wages for emergencies.

Using only his good hand, Sedgwick clumsily built a fire in the hearth and sat quietly on an old joint stool as the flames took, letting the warmth slowly lick over him. His right arm ached constantly, with bright, shocking flickers of pain when-ever he tried to move it. So they've gone, he thought dully, watching as light from the blaze shimmered in the empty corners. But in spite of the evidence, he couldn't really believe it. Any minute she'd come through the door, James on her arm, a pack on her back, saying she'd made a mistake… he'd take the boy, then tell her to go and close the door behind her.

Except, of course, he knew it would never happen. If Annie had made up her mind to leave, then she wasn't returning.

He needed food, something cooked and hot, but it was too late and he was too tired. Searching around he found a carrot that hadn't gone soft and he chewed it. Tomorrow, perhaps, he'd buy a few things at the market. Better yet, he'd find a smaller, cheaper room since it was just him now.

It was funny, he mused. The only emotion running through him was relief. No hurt, no pain, no anger. If anything he was grateful to her for making the decision. It was a good end to something that had quite plainly gone bad.

There was old ale in a jug on the table, flat now but still drinkable, and he poured himself a cup. He knew why she'd gone, ultimately: she hated his job and the hours it took. When he'd been offered the work he'd told her and she'd agreed, yet within a year she was complaining. The baby crying when he was desperate for sleep didn't help either. It made both their tempers shorter.

Well, no more of that. He finished the drink and lay on the low straw pallet. He wanted to rest, and he closed his eyes and pulled the rough blanket around himself, but he couldn't drop off. Images kept replaying in his mind: Annie's smile, the throaty way she used to tell him she loved him, the feeling he had when he first saw James.

His feelings for her might have changed and died, but James…

He felt a surge of love in his heart for his son. She could go, but he'd be damned if he'd let her take the best part of him. He'd get him back and raise him properly.

He sat up, acknowledging that he was going to remain awake

all night. He poured more of the ale, leaning back against the wall and closing his eyes. Bloody woman, he laughed to himself. Even though she was gone, she still wouldn't leave him in peace.

26

Sedgwick reached the jail a little after six to discover a boy sitting on the doorstep, looking bitterly cold in his thin clothes but eyes shining and eager.

"So who are you, then?" he asked.

"I'm Joshua Forester." The lad introduced himself, gazing up high into Sedgwick's face. "The Constable told me to be here at six today."

"Oh aye?" The deputy smiled even as he stretched and yawned, his joints aching from lack of sleep. "Taken you on, has he?"

"Yes, sir."

Sedgwick eyed him with sudden respect. Nottingham rarely hired anyone new; he must have spotted something in Forester.

"Did he tell you what to do here?"

Forester shook his head.

"Probably wants me to train you, then. I tell you what, let's see if we can find you a coat. You must be perishing like that."

Inside the jail he rummaged in an old chest filled with tattered clothes taken from dead bodies. Some had mildewed, others had been eaten by moths, but he eventually found a heavy coat that was only a few sizes too big.

"Put that on," he ordered. "You're going to be doing a lot of walking and it's bloody parky out there."

Forester did as he was told, astonished at first by the weight of the cloth. Sedgwick walked around him.

"That'll do," he said approvingly. "Now, what do they call you? Joshua? Josh?"

"Josh."

"Then we'd better get you earning your pay, Josh."

They'd been criss-crossing the streets and courts for a full thirty minutes, the boy struggling to keep pace with the deputy's long legs, before Sedgwick casually asked, "How did the boss come to take you on?"

"He caught me," Forester answered slowly.

"Caught you?" His eyebrows rose slightly.

The boy wriggled with embarrassment in the coat.

"I tried to steal his purse."

Sedgwick began to laugh until tears trickled down his cheeks.

"Dear God," he said finally, gulping in breaths, his cheeks red. "Are you joking? You're the cutpurse? The one we've been after for weeks?"

"I was," Forester exclaimed in exasperation and with offended pride. "I was a cutpurse, I really was."

"And he hired you? That's rich. Still, it means you should do a good job."

"I'll try," Josh promised.

"Aye, I'm sure you will." He put an arm on the boy's shoulder. "Sorry, I wasn't laughing at you, lad. What alternative did he give you?"

"Prison, maybe transportation."

"That'd make a Constable's man of anyone pretty quick," Sedgwick agreed with a sharp nod.

"Is it true he was once a cutpurse himself?" Forester asked with a kind of wonder.

"Did he tell you that?"

"Yes."

"Well, maybe he was," Sedgwick told him. He had no idea if it was true, and realised he didn't really want to know. Instead he changed the subject. "You've heard about the murders?"

"Of the whores, you mean?"

"That's right. The bastard's got six people now – seven if you count Adam Suttler who got killed the other night." His face darkened. "Came close to eight." He indicated the sling.

"What does he look like?" Forester asked curiously.

"It was too dark to see properly. I know he had a hat and a cloak." The bell tolled the hour. "Come on, we'd better check the cloth market's under way properly."

Lower Briggate was filled with merchants and sellers, their cloth laid on trestles on either side of the street. There were perhaps two hundred people, but by tradition the market was conducted in near-silence. Only the whisper of transactions and muttered comments filled the street. Sedgwick and Forester stood at the top, staring down on the scene.

"That's Leeds for you," the deputy told him, waving a hand at the display. "That's what makes the money around here, and you'd better not forget it. You see him over there?" He pointed at a foppish merchant ambling from table to table.

"Yes."

"He made thousands last year exporting cloth. Spent a lot at the gaming tables and on whores, too. Probably only got a couple of coppers to rub together right now, but he walks about like he owns the place."

"You think he could have killed those girls?" Josh asked innocently.

"Him? No." Sedgwick dismissed the idea. "Not unless there was a profit in it for him. He's mercenary, that one."

"You said the killer had a cloak and hat?" the lad asked thoughtfully.

"Yes," the deputy said.

"What night was it?" Forester persisted.

"Friday."

"Where?" There was a sudden, alarmed urgency in his tone.

"Lamb's Yard, just after midnight." Sedgwick cocked his head. "Why?"

"I saw someone with a hat and cloak near there."

The deputy stopped walking.

"Go on," he ordered.

Forester shook his head. "But it was a woman."

He pushed hard on the door and it flew open. Nottingham started up from his desk as a worried Sedgwick rushed in, nursing his arm, with the boy running breathlessly to keep pace.

"Boss, you'd better hear this," he said urgently. "Tell him, Josh."

"Mr Sedgwick said he almost caught the murderer on Friday," Forester began, glancing nervously between the two men as he spoke hurriedly. "I was out then and I saw someone who looked like that near Lamb's Yard. But I'm sure it was a woman, sir."

"A woman?" Nottingham asked in astonishment.

"Yes, sir," the lad nodded his certainty. "I wasn't close enough to see her face or anything, but I could hear the swish of her skirts. And I saw them when she passed near a torch."

The Constable glanced anxiously at Sedgwick.

"What do you think, John? It could have been a different person."

"But she had a cloak and hat on," Forester insisted.

"A lot of people wear those at night," Nottingham answered evenly as his mind pushed through the things he knew about the case and the killer.

"No, you're right," the deputy declared flatly after some thought. He turned to Forester "I'm sorry, lad. I got carried away by what you said. But it wasn't a lass knifed me. And no woman could have killed like that."

"Are you sure?" the Constable wondered.

"As much as I can be, boss," Sedgwick said earnestly. "Whoever it was, they weren't as tall as me, but taller than a woman."

"I've seen tall women," Forester interrupted, but Nottingham shook his head softly.

"A woman doesn't cut like that," the deputy continued.

Nottingham ran a hand through his hair.

"Let's weigh what we've got," he told them, trying to piece reason from it all. "The boy saw a woman in a cloak and hat in the area. Do you remember how tall she was?"

Forester shook his head.

"And John – you said the murderer wore a cloak and hat."

"That's right."

"There was no shortage of people in cloaks and hats. It was a wet night." He paused and thought deeply. He didn't want to take away from the lad's intelligence, or his initiative in saying what he had, but it seemed impossible. A woman? "I'm inclined to agree with John," Nottingham announced finally. "It must have been a coincidence. I've never known a woman go out and stab in cold blood like this killer."

Forester looked crestfallen.

"Don't worry, lad, it was a good thought," the Constable offered as a consolation. "We need you to use your brain like that." To Sedgwick, he added, "You did right to come back here. Any luck last night following Worthy's men?"

"Nothing."

"Call them off, then," Nottingham decided, noting the relief in the deputy's eyes. "No point in wasting time, is there?"

"No, boss." Sedgwick kept his head lowered to cover his slow smile.

"You'd better get back out there. The cloth market must be nearly over by now. Make sure we've got most of the pickpockets out of the way. That's your job," he added to Forester. "You should be able to spot a pickpocket from a mile away."

"Yes sir," Josh answered, unsure whether the Constable was serious until Sedgwick cuffed him lightly on the head and laughed.

Once they'd gone, Nottingham sat again, slowly scratching his chin with his index finger. The information had left him uneasy. Suppose the killer really was a woman, a very strong, brutal woman. Jesus God, he didn't want to imagine it. He shook his head to dislodge the thought from his mind. It had to be a man.

He needed to go and check his informers again, and find out if any of them had heard even a faint whisper about this murderer. He didn't expect it. If there'd been anything, they'd have come forward. This killer was operating completely outside the criminal circle. Either that or he was exceptionally good at keeping quiet. Whoever he was, he was leaving precious few clues, and he was going to strike again soon.

The Constable pulled on his coat and left the jail. The days were beginning to get colder, he thought, turning up the collar against the breeze. Another year falling away with the leaves, although there were fewer trees each year as more and more buildings were erected.

Still, that was how it had to be. People kept pouring into Leeds and they needed places to live. Its shape and character kept growing and changing. When he'd begun working for the Constable, no one could have imagined murders like this. There were killings, but they came from arguments and drink. Most of the crime had been petty, easily solved.

And the penalties had increased. What had once merited a whipping or a day in the stocks now brought time in York jail picking oakum until the fingers bled, or transportation or hanging. Not that it seemed to stop anyone. In the last two years he'd arrested more people than ever before. It wasn't just the poor buggers, either; too often it was the well off just wanting to be richer. He had no qualms about handing them to the magistrate. For those without work or money – even for those with jobs – Leeds had become an expensive place to live. It scared him sometimes, wondering what he'd do once he retired. If he was lucky, and still had any friends left on the Corporation, there'd be a pension. But it would only be small, certainly not enough to live on. Then again, he told himself, he had to live that long first.

The clutter and clamour of market day on Briggate surrounded him and swept him along. The cries of the hawkers, offering five for threepence and a dozen for sixpence or fresh that morning, two for a penny, sounded like bird calls along the street. The clothes sellers had their wares ranged on tables, from the near-new that had recently graced the backs of the rich to the old rags of the poor. What do you need, what do you lack, they shouted, touting hopefully for trade. Nottingham knew the man he wanted would be along here, his stall set up, yelling for business with the rest.

William Farraday had been a tinker when Nottingham had first met him ten years before. He made a living going door-to-door in the city and surrounding villages mending saucepans and anything metal. It was a precarious trade, but one which took him into all manner of homes. Sometimes he heard things, and for a few coins would pass on information to the Constable.

Now he'd moved up in the world to a market stall, selling old pans he'd patched and working on those women brought him.

He spotted the old, worn canvas and piles of dulled metal. Farraday, with his shock of white hair and back stooped from years of carrying a heavy pack, was in deep conversation with a small woman, trying to sell her some of his wares.

Nottingham waited until she'd paid him and walked off, satisfied, before he approached.

"You're making money then, William."

"A little here and there, aye," Farraday agreed. Even after years in Leeds he'd never lost the more rounded vowels of his native Northumberland. "Need a saucepan for the missus, do you?"

"Information this time," Nottingham answered with a smile.

"If I can, you know me."

"Have you heard anything at all about this murderer?"

Farraday moved some pans around, trying to show them in their best light, changing the angles until he was happy.

"There's been nothing to hear, Mr Nottingham."

"No speculation?"

Farraday gave a hoarse laugh. "Always plenty of that, like. But if you mean is anyone giving names, then no, nowt like that. I'll tell you this, though – whoever's doing it is a canny mad bugger."

"I'd noticed that," the Constable commented dryly.

"Mr Worthy's people are asking around, you know."

"I know," Nottingham admitted.

"He's offering ten guineas to anyone who can name the killer and prove it."

"A sum like that can bring a lot of false accusations." Nottingham wasn't surprised by the reward. The pimp had said he wanted the name; the reward was an indication of how much he desired it.

"You know what Mr Worthy's like, sir," Farraday said uncomfortably. "I don't think anyone would dare lie to him. And if they did it once, they wouldn't again, like."

Nottingham nodded. Amos Worthy's sense of summary justice was well known.

"And no one's given him any names?"

"Not that I've heard."

That was something, he thought. Worthy was no further on than he was.

"I'll let you get back to business then, William. If you hear anything, and I mean anything at all, let me know. There's good money in it for you." But nowhere close to ten guineas, he admitted to himself.

"Aye," the man acknowledged, turning away towards a new customer.

Sedgwick and Forester were walking back up the Head Row from Burley Bar. To their right the city spread out in a jumble behind the old bulk of the Red House.

"He's somewhere out there," Sedgwick said, gazing into Leeds.

"Your murderer?"

"Our murderer now, lad, you're one of us. I'll tell you what, though, we'll get him."

"How can you be so sure?" the boy wondered.

"It's what we do, son. It's what we do, and if I say so myself, we do it bloody well."

27

A round of the other informers had yielded no more than he already knew, and Nottingham made his way back to the jail. He'd barely been sitting for five minutes before a boy came in, wide-eyed in fear and curiosity about the jail, holding a note.

"For me?" the Constable asked.

"I don't know, sir." The high voice trembled a little. "I was just told to give it to someone here."

He took the letter and gave the child a coin from his pocket before sending him on his way. Sliding a thumb under the wax of the seal, he opened the paper, glancing quickly at the writing.

Constable, it began, in a shaky script that was anything but neat, *you wrote wondering if there had been any instances of murder or disturbing incidents hereabouts. We had two such within a short space a little over a year ago. Although neither officially came to my attention as Justice of the Peace, I am familiar with the details. Should you wish to know more, please feel free to call on me at your convenience. Sincerely, Robert Bartlett.*

He could feel his heart beating faster. Bartlett's address was in Chapel Allerton, some three miles to the northeast, home of the horse and footraces, and the gallows where the hangman plied his trade. But far more importantly, where Pamela had moved when she married.

Nottingham put on his greatcoat and left immediately. His body was tense and his throat was dry. There had to be a connection. He walked swiftly along Swine Gate to the

215

stables. He was going to find answers, find a murderer.

Nottingham couldn't afford to keep a horse of his own, and the city wasn't about to pay for him to have a nag. Instead he hired one on the few occasions he needed to travel. To his relief, the ostler selected a gentle mare which was happiest at a canter, and that suited him; he'd never been much of a rider, uncomfortable and wary so high off the ground.

From Vicar Lane he headed north on the Newcastle Road, a rutted, pitted thing that needed attention like all the roads around Leeds. It ran parallel to Sheep Scar Beck, the fields running down to the water lush and green, with sheep cropping the grass. Around here the fleeces were more valuable than the meat; the demand for wool was insatiable as the cloth trade grew and grew. Cottages stood in small clumps at the roadside, and he could hear the insistent clack of looms from within as farming families worked to supplement their incomes by weaving. The children would card the wool, the wife and older girls would spin, and the husband wove. Come market day the man would weigh down a pack animal with the cloth and bring it into Leeds to sell. It had been the way throughout the West Riding for centuries, the only way for small tenants to survive the year. And the ones who couldn't earn enough here flocked into the city, hoping for jobs and money that all too often didn't exist. It was a bitter scrape along the knife-edge of existence.

The road began to rise on the long, slow climb and the horse slowed to an easy, manageable trot. Looking back, Nottingham could make out the city, the roofs and spires under a dark haze of smoke from thousands of chimneys burning Middleton coal. You're in there, he thought determinedly, and I'm going to find you. Soon.

The first sign of the village of Chapel Allerton was the Bowling Green Inn at the base of Chapeltown moor, a roughly

216

tamed wasteland that spread out to his left. He kept riding, past the gallows hole where the frame was erected for public hangings, following the road beyond the blast of heat and noise from the smithy, then taking a track at the top of the moor to the elegant facing of Clough House.

It was a new brick building in a lovingly symmetrical design, with the quiet taste only money could buy. The glass in the windows sparkled, and the garden was carefully tended. Nottingham tethered the horse and knocked on the door, to be greeted by a grave male servant in his late forties who escorted him into a small receiving room, its walls a duck-egg blue, with portraits and landscapes hanging from the walls above the dark wood wainscoting.

"I've come to see Mr Bartlett," the Constable explained. "He answered a note of mine."

"I'll fetch Sir Robert." The servant emphasised the title, chiding him gently.

Bartlett proved to be a large, rounded man who strode briskly into the room. There was an air of the country squire about him in his plain, tight-fitting clothes and thick hands. He wore a short periwig that seemed awkwardly settled on top of a large, rounded head with reddened cheeks.

"Constable," he said in a booming welcome. "I hadn't expected you to arrive so quickly. Thought you'd have too much to do." He seemed to fill the room with his bluff energy, pacing over to the window and looking out across the moor.

"Your information sounded important, Sir Robert," Nottingham said with careful deference.

Bartlett ducked his head a couple of times. "It may be. It's complicated, you see. Sit down, man," he offered, gesturing at the chairs that faced the empty fireplace.

"I'll stand if I may... I'm not used to riding."

Sir Robert chuckled lightly and shook his head. "Never mind, eh? We can get out and stretch our legs a bit if you prefer."

"I'd rather just hear your information, if you don't mind." Nottingham urgently needed to know what the man had to say, then return to the city to finish this business. Time was too important now.

"Of course, of course," Bartlett agreed readily. "You've seen Chapel Allerton, Constable. We're a small place, except when everyone comes up for the races or a hanging, of course. We have a few thefts, but never anything much." He glanced briefly at Nottingham who nodded his understanding. "About eighteen months ago a courting couple was attacked by a man." He gestured vaguely into the distance. "They were walking in the woods beyond the Black Swan, and someone tried to stab them. He wounded the man, then he ran off when the girl began screaming."

"Did you find him?"

Bartlett shook his head forcefully. "No, not a trace. But it happened twice more over the next six months. No one seriously injured, but it left everyone scared."

"And after that?" Nottingham wondered. "Were there any more attacks?"

"No, they just stopped. It was strange. We never did find out who did it. A few men were suspected, but it never came to anything."

"No one moved from the village?"

"Just one of the women who'd been attacked. She went back to Leeds, from what I heard." He dismissed her with a casual shrug.

The Constable's scalp tingled. "Do you remember her name?" he asked with urgency.

"No, I'm sorry," Sir Robert replied after a moment's deliberation. "Is it important?"

"The first of the girls to die in Leeds had moved back from

this area," Nottingham explained. "She'd also been a servant in my house before she came out here."

"I see." Bartlett focused his attention. "It could be a coincidence, I suppose."

"It's possible," Nottingham agreed cautiously, doubting it, "but I'd prefer to find out."

Sir Robert was already walking to the door. "Come on, man," he said, "let's go, then."

His broad pace soon carried him across the beautifully cut lawn in front of the house, through the gates and on to the moor. Nottingham, his thigh muscles already stiffening from being on the horse, had to walk fast to keep pace as they crossed the road and followed a track that led between houses and past hedged fields.

"Where are we going?" he asked, a little breathless.

Bartlett stopped suddenly, looking confused by the question. "You said you wanted to know the name of the girl who returned to Leeds."

"I do," Nottingham agreed.

"We're going to see the man who was her landlord," Bartlett explained. "We could have ridden over, but you looked as if you didn't want to spend more time in the saddle than necessary."

"Thank you," the Constable said, the sentiment heartfelt.

"It's not far," Sir Robert told him as they walked on. "Just over there."

Over there proved to be a long, winding driveway overhung with horse chestnut trees, their leaves in majestic autumn colours, conkers and shells shed all across the path and grass. Without hesitation Bartlett marched up to the front door and knocked heavily. Almost a minute passed before the handle turned with a creak and a weary, middle-aged woman with rheumy eyes peered up.

"Hello, Martha," Bartlett said warmly. "I haven't seen you in months. How are you?"

The woman perked at the sound of the voice, smiling and running fingers like a comb through her straggly grey hair.

"Getting by, Sir Robert," she nodded, "up and down. It's t'way o't world."

"Indeed, indeed." He sounded genuinely interested in her wellbeing, and in a small place like this, maybe he was, Nottingham thought.

"Is the master at home?" Bartlett asked.

"Gone off to York," the servant told him with a short chuckle. "Looking for a new wife, I shouldn't wonder, after the last one died in June."

"A man wants a woman around, Martha," Bartlett said seriously. "And he still needs an heir for the estate."

"Aye, although that weren't for lack of trying on his part," she observed with a cackle.

"Actually, we've come about a woman," Bartlett said, lowering his voice a little.

"Oh?" She cocked her head.

"You remember the girl who was attacked and then went back to Leeds?"

"Course I do. Lovely lass she were, until that madman attacked her and her husband."

"Her husband?" Nottingham asked sharply. Martha turned her head to gaze at him uncertainly.

"Aye," she continued. "They were walking up to the Black Swan one Saturday night when someone tried to stab them. The knife got him, but she started screaming so loud people said they could hear her on t'other side of Gledhow Valley and he ran off. You remember that, Sir Robert."

"Yes," he answered sadly, "yes, I do."

"She were with child," Martha told Nottingham, her face

crumpling at the memory. "Lost it two days later from t' shock. They'd been praying so hard for the bairn an' all. They'd lost two before."

"What about the husband?" the Constable said. He needed to know.

"He were hurt bad in t' chest, but she nursed him back," Martha recalled easily. "But he weren't same after. No strength," she explained with a sage nod. "Dead within six month. Couldn't even get out of bed towards the end."

"And his wife?"

"Poor lass." The servant dabbed at her eyes with the corner of her dirty, greasy apron. "I've never seen owt like it. She lost her faith. Said a real God wouldn't have let her man and her babies die like that. Ranted and raved. Refused to see the curate. When he called on her, she threw him out of the house. Finally the master had to turn her out. He didn't want to, mind," she added hastily, "but he needed the cottage for a couple to do the work. Last I heard, she went back to Leeds, a year back."

"What was her name?" Nottingham asked, holding his breath. He was certain he already knew the answer, but he wanted to hear the confirmation.

"Pamela Malham," Martha replied.

"Tell me," Nottingham asked, "did she wear something round her neck?"

"Aye, she did," the woman answered, her eyes widening. "I'd forgotten about that. Half a coin, a token she called it, although it didn't look much to me. Always had it on."

"Thank you," he said and turned away, walking slowly down the driveway. Before he'd reached the lane, Bartlett had caught up with him.

"That was your girl, wasn't it?"

"Yes," Nottingham answered simply. There didn't seem to

221

be more to say. Now he knew what had really happened to her before her return and why she'd changed. Not that the knowledge made anything easier, he reflected. It was an answer, but not the answer he needed.

"I'm sorry," Sir Robert said with the tentative tone of a man unused to expressing emotions. "Come and take a glass of wine with me before you go back. You look like you need one."

"I think you're right." The Constable felt shaken, his heart booming, a bitter, metallic taste in his mouth.

They strolled back along the track and through the village. After the constant noise and traffic of Leeds the empty streets seemed eerie, as if the people had simply vanished. But soon his ears picked out the sounds of voices and looms in the cottages and animals in the fields.

Bartlett left him in silence, and Nottingham was thankful. He needed some time where he didn't have to talk or be polite, where he could simply let his mind work. Was there a connection between the attack here and the one in Leeds? If not, then her killing was death's black joke, but he couldn't believe that. There had to be something.

But if he believed that, it raised more questions than it solved. Why had the murderer killed others too? Was he trying to cover his crime with more deaths, or had he found a taste for corpses?

Most importantly, who could he be? In his bones Nottingham could feel that the answer was here among these cottages.

Before he realised it, they were back at Bartlett's house, with the scrawny manservant bringing wine. Once they were alone, Bartlett stared thoughtfully at the Constable before shrewdly saying, "You believe her attacker here was her murderer in Leeds."

Nottingham swirled the wine, watching the deep red

colour move and shimmer in the glass.

"I do," he answered finally. "Which means her killer either lived here and moved to Leeds or still lives here and comes into town."

Bartlett shook his head.

"As I told you before, no one's moved except your girl. A few casual labourers, I'm sure," he said dismissively, "but you can't keep track of them."

The Constable knew how true that was. People arrived for harvests and drifted off after. Some stayed a few months then disappeared suddenly, often just ahead of due rents or creditors. He felt the surge of hope dying in him. He knew more, but it did him no good.

"It gives me a start, anyway."

"Oh?" Bartlett asked, raising his eyebrows.

"We can ask around and look for people who might have arrived in Leeds from this area," Nottingham explained. "We'll find some, talk to them. Even if one of them's not the murderer, they might be able to offer some ideas."

"Do you think that can work?" Sir Robert asked sceptically.

"It's the best we've got for now," the Constable replied with a small, helpless shrug. "To tell you the truth, it's the best we've had at all."

He finished the wine and placed the glass on the delicate, elegant table at the side of the chair.

"You've been very helpful, and very gracious, Sir Robert," Nottingham said, bowing courteously. "I'd better get back and start my men on this."

Bartlett rose and offered his hand.

"It's been an education, Constable. I'm just sorry your girl suffered so much."

"Thank you," Nottingham told him sincerely. He liked the man. Unlike so many gentlemen he'd met, this one didn't affect airs and demand respect. He wore his title and his power quite casually. Escorting him to the waiting horse, Bartlett offered,

"I'll keep asking. If I learn anything more I'll send you a note."

"I'd appreciate that."

The Constable mounted in his clumsy fashion, aware of his awkwardness on display, and leaned down to make his farewell.

"I hope you solve this soon, Mr Nottingham," Bartlett said sincerely. "I'm sure it'll be in the *Mercury* when you do."

The journey back to the city seemed to go faster, but his mind was racing, paying little attention to the road. It wasn't much, not what he'd hoped, but he knew a little more than he had this morning, and now he could push the attention of his men in the right direction.

People moved into Leeds all the time. Some arrived from local villages like Chapel Allerton, others from much farther afield, settlements and hamlets across Yorkshire, up into the Pennines and the Dales. To all of them, it was a large city, beckoning with its chance to become rich – or at least not as poor. It drew workers and beggars, the hopeful and the hopeless, and from them his men could find names.

But time was crucial. They had to work fast, and find this man before he killed again. Nottingham hoped Sunday night had made the murderer wary, but it wasn't something that would last forever.

And once they'd caught him, when he was finally sitting in the cells, the Constable would be able to discover just why Pamela and the others had to die. Because, for the life of him, he didn't understand it.

It was late afternoon when he reached the jail, to find Sedgwick at his desk, a preoccupied look on his face. As Nottingham

224

walked in, he started, as if surprised at having his thoughts interrupted.

"What did you do with the lad?"

"I sent him back to his lodgings for a while. I thought I'd take him out tonight, so I told him to get his head down for a few hours."

Nottingham nodded. "Good. I'm going to want everyone out this evening." He outlined what he'd learned in Chapel Allerton.

"So what do you want us to do, boss?"

"Talk to people. He's here, he has to be. Ask around, find out who's moved to Leeds in the last fortnight or so."

"That's going take a long time," Sedgwick demurred.

"For Christ's sake, John, I know that." Nottingham had expected enthusiasm, not reluctance, and a note of exasperation crept into his voice. "Why do you think I want all the men on it immediately? I need the information as fast as you can."

"I'll get them working." Sedgwick stood slowly, pushing himself out of the chair with his good arm. As he opened the door of the jail, the Constable asked, "How's the boy working out?"

"Josh'll be fine. He's smart and he doesn't mind grafting."

"Push people hard," Nottingham instructed. "Leeds isn't that big. Follow up on the names you find. Come back later and tell me how you're getting on."

The deputy gave a curt nod and left, and Nottingham stared after him for a few seconds. Maybe the injury had left Sedgwick exhausted. Normally he was so eager to work, willing to put in every hour God made if need be. Here they finally had something definite to pursue and he seemed like he'd rather sit on his arse and do nothing. But at least he knew that Sedgwick would follow orders, and once he started he'd

225

do his best.

Now he could only wait and hope they discovered something. They needed some luck on their side, and a fast result. For the moment they had the edge on Worthy's men, but he knew that couldn't last. It wouldn't be long before people began talking, so they had to make use of their advantage.

He paced the floor, feeling a terrible mixture of fear and anticipation. They were getting closer, almost breathing over the killer's shoulder. He could feel it now. Nottingham rarely used one, but it was an occasion when he wished he had a pipe and some tobacco to calm his nerves. He wouldn't be going home for a few hours yet, until it was certain they'd have no name tonight.

Instead he decided to write the reports for the Mayor that he'd deliberately neglected, and work on the other papers that littered his desk. He'd begun reading desultorily when the door opened and Williamson walked in.

"Am I disturbing your work, Richard?" he asked with a friendly smile.

"Nothing I wouldn't rather put off until later," Nottingham admitted with a rueful grin.

"I was wondering about your progress," Williamson said, sitting cautiously on the hard wooden chair.

"Did your friends ask you to find out?" He held up his hands to stop the merchant's protest. "It's fine, Tom, I don't mind. They supported me, so they have a right to ask."

Williamson reddened with embarrassment. "It's not that we don't trust you, Richard, it's just that…"

"You want to check on your investment."

"That's a very crude way of putting it," Williamson said.

"But true," Nottingham told him with a smile. "And I have a little good news." He recounted his visit to Bartlett. As he finished, the merchant sat with pursed lips. "What's wrong, Tom?

You're not convinced."

"No, no, it's not that," Williamson replied slowly. "It seems to me I remember hearing about someone coming from there recently. I was trying to think who it might be." He shook his head. "For the life of me I can't bring it to mind."

"Try, please," the Constable said desperately. He was clenching his fists, nails digging into his palms. He'd sent his men out into the taverns and inns, believing the criminal was probably a labourer. But what if it was someone of a higher class? "Can you ask? It's vital."

"Of course," Williamson agreed and stood up. "I'll go to Garroway's. Someone's bound to remember. I'll send a boy down with a note as soon as I know."

"Thank you," Nottingham said gratefully.

What if it was a gentleman or a merchant of some sort, he wondered when he was alone? It made sense, the pieces fell into place. A man like that would probably have learned to fence; he'd know how to handle a knife. He might even have been a soldier. And his station in life could put him above immediate suspicion. But to charge someone like that he'd need very strong proof.

He rubbed the rough bristles on his chin. And what proof did he have? He could search a man's rooms and pray to find a bloody knife, just as he had at Carver's, and maybe a cloak and hat. But no man who could afford a good lawyer would worry about things as trivial as that. They could be convincingly explained away in the blink of an eye and at the cost of a large purse.

Think, he told himself, think.

The truth was, there was nothing. With vigorous denials, a well-connected killer could walk away from his crimes. But he'd face that possibility after an arrest; at least he'd have that satisfaction first. He sat, drumming his fingers anxiously, hoping that Williamson might send word soon. Outside, evening had come, the long twilight of autumn when the city began to close its doors.

He listened as the sound of traffic slowed and the voices outside lowered to a muted buzz. The colour of the sky deepened, casting thick shadows in the room. And he waited.

But when it arrived, the note wasn't one he'd expected.

28

The boy wasn't one of the town lads who earned money delivering messages. Nottingham recognised him as one from his own street, clutching the paper tightly in his fist as he entered nervously. The jail always had that effect on them.

He snatched at the offered coin, and the door had closed behind him before the Constable could unfold the paper.

Richard – Emily hasn't returned from school. I sent Rose to look for her, and the teacher said she never arrived this morning. For God's sake, please bring her home.

He could hear the desperation and fear in Mary's words. Fuck, he thought. The stupid bloody girl. She'd done it yet again, run off to be with the boy and damn the consequences. This time he really would give her a leathering she'd never forget. But first he had to find her. And he knew he couldn't. Not now. There wasn't a single person he could spare to search for her.

He pressed the back of his knuckles against his eyes. His throat was dry and his heart was knocking hard inside his chest. God damn the girl and her imagination.

Nottingham stood looking out of the window, but saw nothing of the street and people beyond the filthy glass. Instead, the images in his head were of Emily, when she was young and fragile, still needing his care. Now she thought she was too old for that, old enough to blithely go her own way while her parents grew frantic. He could feel the anger and the fear welling up inside him, filling his mind and pounding in his blood. He wanted to go and search for his little girl, but he couldn't move. The name he was waiting to learn was too important. He was as trapped and helpless as if he'd been locked in a cell. He could serve the city or he could help his family. And he knew what he'd chosen damned him.

Nottingham walked out into Kirkgate, and signalled for one of the urchins lurking outside the White Swan.

"Do you know Mr Worthy on Swinegate?" he asked, and gave quick directions when the boy shook his head. "Tell him the Constable asks if he could come to the jail as soon as possible."

He hated himself for doing it. It was an admission that he couldn't control his own daughter and couldn't find her in his own city. But it was necessary – and for Emily he'd even dance with the devil to his own tune. The Constable went back into the jail to sit and brood. He didn't have long to wait. Within twenty minutes Worthy had thrown open the door, his back straight, eyes glowing, to stand menacingly by the desk.

"You asked to see me, Constable?" His voice was deep, resonating from his chest.

"Thank you for coming."

Worthy's two bodyguards stayed unmoving in the door-way, their faces deliberately impassive.

"Something must be urgent."

"Do you still have men following my family?" Nottingham asked quietly, feeling defeated inside.

"What makes you think I ever did?" he wondered with a sly smirk. "You mean when my man brought your lass home?"

"Yes." He knew Worthy was toying with him, relishing his advantage, and that he'd press it for all he could.

"That was sheer luck, Mr Nottingham. He recognised her and he didn't think a girl like that should be out so late."

"I'm grateful."

The pimp gave a short nod.

"I'll tell him. But what's the problem now?" He paused and

cocked his head. "Not gone again, has she?"

He already knows, Nottingham thought as he leaned back in his chair. The bastard knows exactly where she is. He knew he should be furious, but instead he felt only relief. Worthy was going to make him sweat and pay, he was sure of that. He stood and stared at the man.

"Yes, she has," he was forced to admit. "And I need her found."

"What makes you think I can help you?" Worthy asked bluntly. "Or why I should?"

Nottingham lifted his head. "You can probably find her in minutes if you want."

"Ah." Worthy smiled wolfishly, showing a mouth of rotted teeth and gaps. "But you made it quite clear in the past that you didn't want my help, Constable. What about your own lads?"

"Working." He knew he wasn't giving any information the pimp wouldn't already have.

"A little bird told me you were looking for someone from Chapel Allerton." Worthy's tone hardened a little. "That would be our murderer, I take it?"

"It might be."

"And what else do you know about him?"

This was where he'd tighten the hold, Nottingham knew. He prayed no one came with information while the pimp was still here.

"Do you think I'd be casting my net so wide if I knew anything more?" he asked.

Worthy considered the idea for a moment. "No, I suppose you wouldn't," he agreed reluctantly. "What do I get if I find your Emily?"

Directly to the nub, Nottingham thought. "My gratitude."

The pimp spat on the flagstones. "That doesn't buy me anything."

"You want money? I'll pay you," Nottingham offered. It was part of the game; he knew he'd be refused, and then Worthy would reveal the real price.

"I've already got money, more than you'll see in your life," Worthy said flatly. "I want the one who killed my girl."

He'd expected nothing less. The Constable took a deep breath. "So do I. And we can't both have him."

Worthy held the Constable's gaze and waited a long time before speaking.

"Then maybe you'd better consider the value of things, Constable." He held out his hands like scales on a beam. "Your lass." One hand went down. "The murderer." The balance returned to even. "It's your decision."

From the moment he sent Worthy the note he'd known it would come to this. He'd been waiting for it. He closed his eyes. "You can have him," he said softly.

"I know where the courting girl is. I'll have her here in half an hour," Worthy promised with a grim smile. "Unhappy, but unspoilt."

Nottingham nodded his agreement, keeping a blank face. As soon as he discovered the identity of the killer, he'd arrest him and damn his promises. But for now he needed Worthy. Once he'd left the Constable sent a boy to bring Mary to the jail. She could take Emily home.

Time ticked away too slowly. He kept expecting something to happen – word from Tom, Sedgwick with information, even his wife – but there was nothing.

It was Emily who arrived first, escorted by a man of Worthy's that Nottingham had never seen before. He was tall and heavy, but surprisingly well-dressed, wearing a deep brown wig that appeared almost new. His big hand gripped the girl's arm tightly and there was a sly, vicious smile on his face. Less than twenty minutes had passed since Worthy had left.

"Sit down," Nottingham commanded his daughter in a hard voice that dared her to disobedience or hesitation. "Now." He turned to the man. "Who was she with?"

"I don't know," he answered with a careless shrug. "They just told me to bring her here." He began to leave, then turned back in the doorway. "Oh, Mr Worthy said to tell you something. Look at her neck." The door slammed closed behind him.

He gazed down at Emily, shut in on herself on the chair. With slow tenderness he put a finger under her chin and tilted her head back. Her eyes were wide with fear, and tracks of grimy tears ran down her cheeks, but he only noticed them in passing.

Instead, his eyes fastened on her throat.

"Oh Christ," he whispered, the bile rising suddenly. "Christ."

The broken token that had belonged to his mother, that he'd given to Pamela, lay against Emily's skin, held in place by a new blue ribbon.

For a long moment he stared at it in horror.

Then, before she could react, before he could even stop himself, he grasped it in his fingers and in a single violent motion tore it off her. She gasped with pain as he held it in front of her face, the half-token swaying gently.

"Who gave it to you?" Nottingham asked with deceptive softness. The tears were welling over in her wide eyes, hands clutched so tightly together in her lap that her knuckles were white. She wouldn't look at him. He tried to keep his voice steady and hide the urgency of the question. "Who gave it to you, Emily? I need his name."

Emily shook her head mutely. He breathed slowly, trying to calm himself. The token was the key, and Worthy already knew what it meant. Emily knew the answer. He had to find out, and quickly.

He looked down at his daughter. She was bent over, sobbing silently into her hands. There was a vivid red mark on the back of her neck where he'd ripped off the ribbon. He'd always tried to keep his family safe from his work, but now, here, it all came together. He loved the girl so much, he ached to protect her from everything bad, but he needed her answers.

"You see this, Emily?" Nottingham asked, hoping she'd raise her head, but she kept still, curled away from him. For a moment he wanted to grab her by the hair and pull her up so she couldn't hide from him. "I need to know who gave you this," he insisted. "It belonged to your grandmother. I gave it to Pamela. Whoever gave it to you murdered her."

"No!" In one quick, furious movement she sat up straight, mouth firm, her eyes alive with anger. "He couldn't have!" She stared at him defiantly, then lowered her gaze. "He wouldn't," she added softly.

"Then where did he get it?" Nottingham asked in exasperation. His patience was raw, on a knife-edge. He could feel himself shaking. "Come on, you want to be treated like an adult. You say he hasn't killed anyone. Tell me who he is. I'll talk to him. If he's innocent he'll be able to tell me the truth."

"You're already calling him a killer," she hissed. "Why would you believe anything he says?"

He gazed into her eyes, trying to quell the bitterness he saw there. "Because it's my job to find the truth and separate the guilty from the innocent." He sighed. "Emily, you know what I do, what I am." He held up the ribbon, seeing his hand tremble a little and feeling the chill of cooling sweat on his face. "I need you to help me. Please."

She hesitated before answering and he could hear the first sign of weakening in her voice.

"I promised him I wouldn't tell anyone."

"Why?" He ran a hand through his hair. It was better than hitting her.

"Because he asked me to. He asked me to trust him and I said I would."

"I need your trust, too. That man who brought you here is employed by someone who also wants to find the killer," he explained urgently. "I don't know how, but he knows what this token means." Nottingham took hold of her shoulders and forced her to look into his face. "He's not going to arrest the lad who gave this to you. He's going to make him suffer and then he's going to make sure he dies very slowly and in a lot of pain."

"Why should I believe you?" she asked warily, but now he could see fear flicker in her eyes. "You could be lying to me just to get his name. That could have been one of your men."

"You heard what he said to me. He wasn't one of mine." He kept hold of her. "You care about this man. Right now he has one chance of still being alive tomorrow morning, and that chance is me."

She was torn, he knew it. He wanted to push her harder, but if he did, she might back away. He waited, watching the young emotions conflicting on her face.

"I can't," she said finally, with a sad shake of her head. "I promised him I wouldn't."

The slap resounded round the small room, lifting her off the chair and sending her sprawling on the flagstones. He saw the sharp redness burn her cheek, hating himself for what he'd done, lashing out at his daughter. He knew he'd had to do it, to jolt her, but he still wanted to gather her close, to apologise, to stroke her hair and tell her that everything would be all right.

"Please, Emily, tell me his name," he begged softly. Gazing

up at him, she pushed herself away quickly on her hands and feet, moving awkwardly like a crab until she was backed against the wall. He walked towards her and she drew her knees up against her chest. The outline of his hand was clear on her pale skin; he saw the tears brimming in her eyes and the agony of fear on her face.

Squatting, Nottingham held out his hand. She watched it as though he was going to hit her again.

"I don't have the time to fence with you," he explained sadly. "I have to get his name, lúv."

The door opened and he glanced up hopefully. But it was Mary standing there, hands on her hips.

"What's going on?" she asked, her voice rising sharply.

"Mama..." Emily began, struggling to her feet.

"Dear God, child, what happened to you?" She pulled the girl to her, examining her face and neck. Nottingham rose slowly, feeling the ache in his knees, and a growing sense of something lost.

"What did you do to her, Richard?" Her tone demanded the truth from him. He held up the ribbon with its dangling token, still clenched in his fist.

"She was wearing this," he told her. "Do you remember it?"

Mary's mouth widened in astonishment, and her eyes moved to her daughter.

"I believe the man who gave it to her is a killer, and she won't tell me his name," he continued.

"Tell your father," Mary ordered. She held Emily fast as the girl tried to pull away.

Before Nottingham could speak, the door opened once more, and Williamson entered. As soon as he saw the women, he removed his hat and bowed in an automatic gesture.

"I'm sorry," he said with embarrassment. "Richard, it took

me longer than I expected."

"Do you have the name?"

"Robert Crandall. He's the new curate at the parish church."

Nottingham glanced at Emily. Her face had fallen, and he knew he had his man.

"Mary, take her home now," he said, before turning back to the merchant. "Tom, thank you."

He dashed past them, out on to Kirkgate and the sprawling Vicar's Croft where Dr Cookson lived. It was no more than two hundred yards, but he was panting by the time he arrived. He banged hard on the thick front door, and kept knocking until an exasperated servant finally opened it. If only Bartlett had remembered this, he thought.

"Where's the Reverend?" Nottingham asked, forcing his way past the woman.

"He's in the library, sir," she replied, polite but terrified by his manner. The Constable moved quickly down the hall, turning latches as he went until he found the right room.

Cookson was seated comfortably by the fire, a book on his lap, and three more stacked on a small table at his side, next to a half-drunk glass of wine. As he glanced up at the intrusion, Nottingham said, "I need to know where Crandall is."

Coolly, Cookson closed the book.

"Barging into my house and making demands isn't the best way to find things out, Constable," the Reverend announced.

"Where is he… sir?" He spat out the word with deliberate insolence.

"And why do you need to know so urgently?" He crossed one leg over the other, smoothing his breeches over his ample thighs.

"Because he's murdered six people." Nottingham kept his eyes on the Reverend's disbelieving face.

"Another of your wild theories?" Cookson laughed. "It was

George Carver last time, wasn't it? Don't be so stupid, man. Mr Crandall is from a good family in the county. Why would he do something like that?"

"I'll tell you after I've talked to him," the Constable replied grimly. "But he used to be in Chapel Allerton, didn't he?" He didn't wait for an answer. "There were people attacked there. One of them came back to Leeds and was killed just after your curate arrived."

Cookson pursed his lips.

"Coincidence is hardly damning evidence, is it?"

"I'll give him the chance to clear himself, if he can." He chose not to mention the broken token or Worthy. Keep it straightforward, he thought. "But I need to find him, and I need to do it now."

"He lodges with Widow Cliffe on Briggate. But she's a good Christian woman. She keeps early hours. I don't want you disturbing her."

Nottingham said nothing, just walked past the servant and out of the house. He knew Widow Cliffe all too well, a prissy woman who'd plagued his office for years with ridiculous, petty complaints about her neighbours.

A merchant's widow, she lived in an old house with a wide frontage, the plaster limewashed a crisp white every year. She spent her days peering out from the small mullioned windows and making carping comments about the people she saw.

He knew of at least five servants she'd turned out for their behaviour, and pitied those who stayed even more. She liked to think of herself as the city's moral judge, and was constantly disappointed with everything she saw.

No lights showed through the shutters as his fist hit the door, but he didn't care if he woke the entire street. When no answer came, he hammered on the wood again until a downtrodden girl pulled it open, her eyes puffy with sleep, clothes bundled quickly over her shift.

"Is Mr Crandall here?" Nottingham asked without introduction.

"No, sir," the girl answered with lazy sleepiness, stifling a yawn. "He left this afternoon. He was all in a hurry. Said his father was ill and he needed to go home for a few days."

"And where's his home, do you know?"

"Harrogate, sir."

"Thank you."

The door closed quietly. His mind was churning as he strode back to the jail. Maybe Crandall really had run away and gone home. Not this afternoon, though; he'd been with Emily since then. He might have planned to leave, but the curate was still in Leeds; he knew it as surely as he knew his own name.

The jail was crowded with Sedgwick and the other men, all milling around in loud conversation that ended raggedly as he entered.

"They've had no luck yet, boss," Sedgwick told him.

"I have," Nottingham said. "It's Crandall, the new curate at the parish church." He heard a crescendo of sound around him and raised his hand. "I want you to go out and find him. He lodges with Mrs Cliffe, but he's not there. I want two men on the place, front and back, in case he tries to return. He claimed he was going back to Harrogate, where his family lives. Check the coach inns and the stables, let me know if they've seen him. The rest of you get out there and start looking."

Sedgwick rose, but Nottingham held him back as the others left.

"I want you with me." He explained briefly about Emily and the token. "Worthy knew what it meant. I don't know how, but he's ahead of us. I don't think he's got Crandall yet;

if he had he'd be crowing."

"Where do you want to start?" the deputy asked, rubbing his arm in the sling.

"Crandall hasn't been here long," Nottingham considered. "He'll want somewhere he feels safe."

"The church?" Sedgwick suggested.

"It's a good bet." He reached into one of the desk drawers and removed two pistols.

"How's your arm now?" Nottingham asked.

"Getting by," Sedgwick answered, although it was far from the truth. The Constable loaded and primed the guns, and handed one to his deputy.

"Just in case," he said. "Don't be afraid to use it."

29

They walked together down Kirkgate. Apart from pockets of noise outside a pair of taverns, the city was quiet. A few torches gave out moments of light in the darkness.

Sedgwick breathed softly and glanced at the Constable. There was a hard, determined cast to his face, and his hand kept straying to his coat to rub the pistol. God help Crandall when they found him, he thought.

His mind slipped back to the thing it hadn't been able to shake. If there was one person he could tell, it was the boss.

"Annie's left," he said casually, as if the news wasn't so important. "Took James with her."

"Are you going to bring her back?" Nottingham didn't break his stride, although now he understood why the deputy had been so quiet. "You'd be within your rights, if you wanted."

He didn't even need to consider the question.

"No. She was always nagging and arguing."

"What about James?"

Sedgwick straightened his back and chewed his bottom lip. They walked a few more yards before he answered with determination,

"I'm not letting him go. She can go to hell, but I'm having my son."

"The law's on your side," Nottingham told him with certainty. "You can claim him and keep him."

"Thanks, boss," he answered sincerely.

"Just remember, though, you'll need someone to look after him. It won't be easy."

"Aye, I know that," Sedgwick said. He'd been giving a lot of thought to the responsibility of raising a child, and the way his own parents had been. "But he's worth it. And I can see he's brought up right."

Nottingham touched his arm lightly. "I'm sorry, John."

"It's fine," he lied glibly. "Everything'll sort itself out."

At St Peter's they separated. Sedgwick lit a candle and explored the deep, shadowy nave while Nottingham searched in the vestry. Nottingham knew that Cookson wouldn't be happy if he ever heard that the law had gone through his church, but it had to be done. There was no sign of Crandall, but one chest lay open, a surplice crumpled on the floor beside it, with books and a pile of papers roughly strewn over the stone floor. Crandall had been here, he was certain of it. He looked in the tall cupboards, pulling the doors open in a sharp motion, but they only held elaborate vestments. Holding a lantern, the Constable entered the body of the church and called, "Anything?"

His voice echoed around the high emptiness of the building.

"I don't think so," Sedgwick answered with caution. His light flickered around the font at the far end of the building. "But there are a hundred places someone could hide in here."

"He's been in the vestry. The question is, how long ago?"

Nottingham felt awkward as he walked around the altar and the chancel, as if he had no right to be there and was doing something sacrilegious. He pushed the light into dark corners, finding nothing more than a family of mice.

From the corner of his eye he could see the flame of Sedgwick's candle moving around. Methodically he checked each of the elaborately carved family pews, kneeling to be sure Crandall hadn't tried to tuck himself under the wooden benches.

242

Pigeons nesting in the rafters gave soft coos, their sleep disturbed by the noise below. Nottingham edged around pillars, feeling the prickly chill of holiness on his skin.

Finally they met in the middle of the nave. Sedgwick shook his head.

"We can come back when it's light," Nottingham decided. "Let's go."

Outside, the wind had picked up, and thick clouds scudded from the west to obscure the stars and bring a promise of fresh rain soon.

"Where now?" Sedgwick asked as they walked through the graveyard. He craned his head around, hoping to see a sudden movement behind the stones.

"I don't know." Nottingham was thinking hard. Crandall must have panicked when Worthy's men grabbed Emily, not knowing what was happening, thinking that somehow they'd come for him. If he'd fled the city, where would he have gone? Not Harrogate, he was certain of that. There were plenty of places in England where a man could change his name and hide, but he didn't have Crandall pegged as someone with the endurance for that. He was a son of privilege who'd probably taken to the church only because he had an older brother who'd inherit the estate and the wealth. But his father would still grant him an allowance; curates made less than Constables. Abroad, though, a man could live handsomely off very little money...

"We'll take a walk down by the river," the Constable announced suddenly. "There'll be barges loading early for Hull. He might try and get on one of those."

Sedgwick glanced at him speculatively but said nothing, simply loping along beside him. With his arm close against his chest in the sling he looked like an awkward, wounded bird. It was quiet along the Calls; only a few lights shone in the windows of rooming houses and somewhere a drunk vainly tried to remember the verse of a broadside ballad.

They followed the path past the water engine, its pumps pulling liquid from the Aire along pipes to feed the reservoir up by St John's Church. At the riverside the bridge loomed above them, the roar of the current through the arches achingly loud.

"Keep your eyes open for Worthy's men," Nottingham warned, taking the pistol from his coat pocket.

They tried the doors to the new brick warehouses, checking they were locked and secure, moving cautiously and quietly.

"I can hear something," Sedgwick whispered. They stopped to listen, taking shallow breaths, ears and minds alert. "Over there," he said finally, pointing to the undergrowth that rose from the quay up to Low Holland.

"An animal?" Nottingham whispered.

Sedgwick shook his head.

"No idea."

"We'll wait here for a while and see what happens."

They remained tense, muscles cramping from standing still, hidden by the deep shadow of the buildings.

"It's there again. It's too big for an animal."

The Constable had heard nothing, but trusted him. He leaned against Sedgwick, speaking softly into this ear,

"Give it some more time."

He'd never hunted, although he had very faint memories of his father riding off with the hounds as he watched with his mother. Or perhaps that was simply his imagination. Here, though, there were no horses and hounds, no trampling of crops and spills over hedges. This game involved stealth and patience, and not even the certainty he had the right quarry. It could be just someone sleeping rough in the grass; he'd done that often enough in his youth.

Finally, after the dampness of the night air had leeched into his skin, he signalled for them to move. He went one way, Sedgwick the other, moving slowly over the gravel path and into the grass.

But they'd barely taken ten paces when the sound of footsteps and muttered curses filled the air at the top of the hill. The Constable froze, tightening his grip on the pistol.

"Right, you two go down there, see if he's hiding," a voice ordered, and Nottingham heard three men push their way down the hill. Worthy's men. He stood still, safe and invisible in the faint moonlight. As long as John kept out of sight, everything would be fine. The pimp's thugs could do their work for them.

It was only a couple of minutes before they discovered the man in the undergrowth, pulling him to his feet as he howled and protested. Very likely thought he was going to be robbed and beaten, the Constable imagined, and probably he would be. But he couldn't stay and stop it; the voice wasn't Crandall's. Cautiously, he retraced his steps to the doorway, relieved to see Sedgwick had done exactly the same.

"Looks like they haven't found him yet," Sedgwick said in a low voice.

"If he was round here, that'll have scared him off." Nottingham pushed the fringe off his forehead.

"Pushed him deeper, maybe."

"What do you mean?"

"No one came out past me," Sedgwick explained. "If he's here, he's still here. If." He emphasised the word.

"And if I knew where he was, we'd have him in custody now," Nottingham retorted sharply. "All we can do is play the odds. The men are out searching, Worthy's lads are looking. You and I are taking the likeliest places. The bastard's somewhere."

Worthy's men had moved off, crossing the bridge noisily

while their victim lay moaning in the grass. To the east, there was the faintest smudge of light on the clouds against the horizon. My God, Nottingham thought in surprise, have we been looking all night?

"You go along the path, I'll cover the water side."

It was awkward, laborious going. The banks were sheer and slippery, and he found himself grabbing thick tufts of grass to try and keep his balance as time and again he slid perilously close to the river. The warehouses rose tall, their walls sheer, broken only by doors and pulleys for moving bales on to the barges. A couple of flatboats were tied up, ready for loading, but as he approached the warning growls and bark of a dog kept him away.

Where was Crandall? He climbed back to the path by Dyer's Garth, where men and women spent their days colouring finished cloth. The stink of the dyes they used hung in the air and he wrinkled his nose, his eyes watering. Maybe they didn't notice it after a while.

"Boss!" Sedgwick's loud, hoarse whisper pulled him back.

He ran quickly back along the path to the deputy. Sedgwick was squatting, eyes searching the ground. He held up a large piece of expensive black material in a good, tight weave.

"It could be a cassock," Nottingham speculated, running his fingers across it, and suddenly the memories clicked in his brain. "Dear God. Do you remember young Forester saying he'd seen a woman the night of the second murders?"

Sedgwick nodded slowly.

"A curate in a cassock," the Constable explained. "In the dark that would look like a woman in a dress."

"Looks like he was here, then."

"Maybe. But where's he gone?" Nottingham wondered. "And how did the cassock get torn?"

"Do you want me to go and get the men and have them

comb down here?" Sedgwick asked.

"No," he decided after a moment. "He can't have got inside the warehouses and he's not down by the river. If he's still anywhere around here, he's on the hillside." He scanned the trees and the undergrowth.

"There could have been a struggle here," Sedgwick observed marks in the wet dirt. "It's difficult to tell."

"Over there, too." Nottingham pointed at the grass on the hillside. "You see where it looks trampled?"

He waded through the tall stalks, the dew on the cattails soaking his breeches. There was a space, about five yards by three, where the stems were broken in thick patches too rough to be someone's camp. Two trails ran to it, one from the hill top, another from the path below. Squatting, he ran his fingers lightly over the ground, feeling for anything that might have dropped. It seemed a hopeless task with so much to cover. He tugged at roots and the short young stems of trees poking from the ground, looking for something that might yield to his touch and give a clue. But there was nothing to proclaim beyond doubt that Crandall had been here.

Back on the towpath he joined Sedgwick. It was close to dawn now, and Nottingham could see the signs of strain and weariness on the deputy's face. They were probably on his own, too, seamed and magnified by age. But they'd have to continue until they found the curate or were certain he'd left Leeds.

"Nothing up there," he said in a voice edged heavily with frustration.

"You think Worthy's men got him?" Sedgwick asked, echoing his own thoughts.

"I don't know," he replied, shaking his head. "It's beginning to look as if they might." He gave a dark, forbidding frown. "For Mr Crandall's sake, let's hope they don't."

"So where now, boss?"

He had no idea, he realised. The church had seemed obvious, the riverside an inspiration. But they'd missed him at the first, and Nottingham had a growing fear that they'd also arrived too late at the second. They could go to Worthy's and tear the place apart, but he had so many rooms and rat's nests around the city it would be impossible to find and check them all.

"Back to the jail. See if any of the others turned anything up."

Inside, he was raging, the anger boiling, as if he'd been cheated but unable to prove it. Crandall was around somewhere, he felt it, but in a place just beyond his reach. If Emily had said something immediately, if Bartlett had recalled the curate leaving, if Tom Williamson had found his information sooner... but none of that was worth a damn now.

He knew no one could have put together the threads any earlier; there was too little to make any kind of pattern. But he blamed himself anyway. It was his responsibility; he was the Constable, in charge of the investigation. And if Crandall had found his way out of the city, Nottingham's career was over. Even a squawking gaggle of aldermen wouldn't be able to save him.

"Maybe the lads got him and he's waiting in a cell," Sedgwick offered with a small, hopeful smile.

It was possible, but he doubted it. Still, maybe one of the men had discovered something useful. He'd keep them looking all day and all night if he had to, but for the moment he simply didn't know where to send them. And, as if to crown his despair, the first fat drops of rain began to fall from a heavy sky.

He trudged on, his mind churning, eyes on the ground, until Sedgwick nudged him.

"Under the bridge, boss." The words were a bare whisper.

The tunnel was long, and dark as thick velvet. Water surged along the bank, the sound echoing loud. Nottingham stared into the gloom, his heart thudding loud, until he was slowly able to make out a shape. Gradually the features took form. At last. The figure was cowering, trying hard to stay small, hidden as deep in the blackness as he could burrow. Crouching, he looked lost, too broken to even run any more. It had to be Crandall.

"Let's take him," Nottingham hissed, feeling a fast surge of satisfaction in his veins.

They approached patiently, carefully hugging the shadows. It seemed to take an age to draw close, holding their breath with each step in case the man heard them. Nottingham kept his eyes on him; he didn't move. The Constable edged nearer, so close he could smell the pure terror in the man's sweat. Behind him Sedgwick's shoe caught a pebble, kicking it along the path. The figure started suddenly. He began to rise, his eyes panicked. It was Crandall. The Constable leapt, pinning him against the dank stone of the bridge.

"You're not bloody going anywhere," he said through gritted teeth, staring into the curate's blank eyes.

There was nothing left of the Crandall's smugness or elegance. His face was carved with fear, his mouth a thin, pale line. A night of trying to hide in the open had left him filthy, a pathetic figure with a battered leather satchel slung over his shoulder.

Together, Nottingham and Sedgwick hauled him out into the growing light. He was past resistance, moving like a doll in their grasp. Finally, the Constable thought with relief, finally. Now they could put an end to this.

But as they started up the track from the riverbank to Briggate, three figures appeared at the top of the hill.

Worthy was standing there, and next to him the man who'd

brought Emily to the jail. He was dressed in fresh clothes, a foppish coat and breeches of pale turquoise silk cut to hide his muscles. The third had a face the Constable recognised, Harwood, who'd come to the jail and confessed to the crime. Nottingham felt Crandall stiffen with terror.

"Bringing me my prize, Mr Nottingham?" Worthy asked with a slow, vicious smile.

Sedgwick glanced at the Constable, confused. Nottingham shook his head.

"He's mine now, Amos, and I'm keeping him until he hangs."

"That wasn't the bargain you made when you wanted your lass found." The pimp gazed down on them, his voice flat, his eyes showing nothing at all.

"That was last night."

The Constable pulled the pistol from his coat and let it dangle in his hand.

"You'd best get out of the way, Amos," he said slowly, and began to raise his arm.

For a long moment Worthy stood his ground, challenging the Constable. Then he spat on the grass, and in a quick movement turned away, his men following close behind.

"Mr. Harwood."

The third man halted.

"I believe I told you to leave Leeds."

Harwood tilted his head.

"Mr. Worthy was good enough to offer me employment."

"Don't consider it a permanent position. What I said still stands."

The man saluted, grinned and scrambled after the others. Sometime, somewhere, there'd be trouble with that one, Nottingham thought.

He let out a long, slow breath. As he'd levelled the pistol

he'd realised suddenly that he didn't want to kill the pimp. The revelation astonished and worried him, but he had no time to think about it now. He replaced the gun and felt his hand shaking; with the other he tightened his grip on the prisoner's sleeve.

"Let's get this bastard to the jail. I want to hear everything he has to say."

"What did he mean by bargain, boss?" Sedgwick asked warily.

"It doesn't matter any more," the Constable replied firmly.

Nottingham stripped the satchel from Crandall and watched as Sedgwick threw him into an empty cell, the door closing with a heavy, final thud. The two men looked at each other across the desk and the Constable said, "Go home and get some sleep, John. You deserve it."

"What about him?" Sedgwick inclined his head towards the cell.

"I'll deal with him."

The deputy hesitated.

"What was the bargain with Worthy?" he asked again.

"Just words." Nottingham sat down heavily and leaned back in the chair, trying to rub the throbbing from his temples. "If he chose to believe me, that's his misfortune."

Once Sedgwick had gone, Nottingham wearily opened the satchel, emptying the contents before him. There was a clean shirt, the linen white and almost new, and a pair of expensive silk hose. Tucked into a corner was a purse full of glistening gold guineas, enough to establish a man in a new place and keep him in comfort for a few months.

But it was Crandall's letters that really interested him, however, and he laid them out, pressing the paper down carefully. The first was to his father, written in a smooth, educated hand:

Sir, I've sinned most grievously again, even more than I have in the past. Now I have no choice but to leave this wicked place quickly. Its temptations proved too strong for my weaknesses after my many months of prayer and repentance. I think it best if my destination now is outside the kingdom, where no one knows me, and I have the chance to redeem myself with a more Godly life. I have money for the present, and I shall keep you informed about my progress. Please continue to pay my allowance to the bankers, and I will be in contact with them to draw upon it wherever I might be. I'm sorry to have brought disrepute on a good name, and beg your forgiveness. Your loving son, Robert.

So, he thought, he'd guessed right; Crandall was running abroad. But the letter also made it plain that the man's family knew what he'd done in the past, and had colluded to keep it hidden. They might not have wielded the knife, but they were as guilty as he was. He threw it to one side, to send on to the curate's father later with the hanged body and a few words of his own, then skimmed through the rest of the correspondence. One note was addressed to his banker in London, another to the Bishop, announcing that he was forced to quit his position immediately due to problems within his family. The last was for Emily. He read it with trepidation, knowing he'd be furious after.

My dearest Emily, although we've only known each other a very short time, you've given me more joy than any man can expect in this life. Because of that, my heart is heavy as I write this. There are men in Leeds who believe I've committed crimes, but they don't see the world clearly. All I've done is to try to cleanse this world, to make it a place for the virtuous, like you. Your father is one of those men, so I have no choice but to leave and go abroad where I can find peace. Leaving this city is easy – it hasn't been a friendly place to me. But leaving you is the hardest thing I've ever had to do. Once I'm settled I'll write again, with enough money for your passage to join me, if you're willing, and all the words you've said still mean something. Please trust in the power of love. Your Robert.

30

Crandall looked like a man in torment. He sat on the rough bed, legs drawn up to his chest, displaying a pair of thin, pale calves. His cassock was torn, a piece missing at the hem. The back of his hands, clasped around his knees, were bloodied with cuts. The tracks of tears had cut through the grime on his face. How could Emily have loved a creature like this, Nottingham wondered.

He'd barely glanced up when the Constable entered. Was he lost in his guilt, Nottingham wondered. Was he penitent? Or was he just fearful of the death that lay ahead?

"Stand up," the Constable ordered briskly, but the prisoner didn't move. He didn't even flinch as Nottingham reached down and yanked him to his feet, pulling him so close that their faces almost touched.

"You're going to talk to me, Mr Crandall," he said with menacing slowness, the anger of the curate's words to Emily still boiling within him. "You're going to make me understand why you killed those people, and you're going to tell me why you went after my daughter." Nottingham twisted his hand in the material of the cassock. He could feel the quick hammering of the curate's heart against his fist. "And if you lie to me, I'll give you to Amos Worthy."

"He had me." The voice was little more than a dry whisper. Nottingham slackened his grip and the curate raised his head, his eyes slowly focusing. "He had me last night, but I managed to escape."

That would explain the fear, the Constable decided. Worthy would have relished telling the man what he planned to do to him, and his justice would be the lingering kind.

"I thought I might be able to find passage on a barge to the coast."

"But I came along." Nottingham paused. "You're still going to die, Mr Crandall," he said with satisfaction.

"I know." There was resignation in his voice.

The Constable let go of him altogether and the curate remained shakily on his feet.

"Why did you kill them? What had they done to you?"

"I…" he began, then halted and shook his head. "I need something to drink." When Nottingham made no move, Crandall looked beseechingly at him. "Please," he asked hoarsely.

Finally the Constable nodded, locking the cell door behind him, and returning a few minutes later with a jug of small beer and two cups. He watched the other man drain his mug eagerly and pour a second before he said softly, "Now, Mr Crandall, I want the truth."

The curate stared at the corner of the cell for a long time. Just as Nottingham began to believe he'd say nothing more and that the moment had passed, he began to speak.

"I didn't want to come to Leeds. There's so much evil here. I'd go walking at night and see them, all the fornicators and drunkards."

"They're the people of the city, Mr Crandall."

"Someone had to stop them," the curate said plaintively. "Someone had to teach them."

A lunatic, Nottingham thought. A man with a twisted mind. He brushed the fringe off his forehead in a quick movement.

"Why Morton?" he asked, and a moment later, "Why Pamela?"

"The Reverend had told me all about Mr Morton," Crandall

explained. "I was out one night and I saw him." He looked up sadly. "I wanted to talk to him and find out what he believed. But before I could get close enough he'd gone off with a whore. He was as weak as all the rest."

"So you killed them."

"He was supposed to be a man of God," the curate said earnestly, his eyes wide. "I followed him. When I saw what they were going to do, I had to kill them. I couldn't allow him to do that."

Nottingham closed his eyes briefly.

"What about the girl?"

"She had to die, too," Crandall said with straightforward honesty. "She tempted him, she made him fall."

"Did you know who she was?"

"I remembered her," the curate admitted. "I wanted to arrange them so everyone would know and understand their sin. When I saw her face I thought it had to be God's judgement on her."

Nottingham bunched his fists but forced himself to remain calm.

"You'd stabbed her husband in Chapel Allerton. He died because of you. When she was turned out of her house, she came back here and did the only thing she could to survive."

"They were fornicating in the woods," Crandall answered plainly, as if it was justification. "I saw them all, rutting everywhere like animals. I had to make them understand they were above that."

"She was with her husband. She was carrying his baby." Nottingham stared at the curate.

"Then there was no need for the evil they were doing. It was Godless rutting." He took a timid sip from the mug.

"And what about the others you murdered here?" the Constable asked.

"They didn't learn." He looked up, his eyes sharp and clear. "I tried to teach you, but none of you learnt a thing. So I had to keep on with the lessons."

"Is that why you left the corpses the way you did?" Nottingham asked suddenly. "To teach us?"

"To *tell* you," Crandall answered, as if it was the most obvious thing in the world. "So they could die with their shame and you'd know what they'd been doing."

"Where did you learn to use a knife like that?"

The question seemed to take the curate by surprise.

"My fencing master," he answered. "I had lessons when I was younger. He thought I'd have made a good soldier." Crandall smiled vaguely. "But I felt a calling to serve the Lord instead."

Nottingham leaned back against the wall. So many dead to feed the battle of good and evil in a madman's head, the war only a madman could hope to understand. But the God he'd tried to please would judge him soon enough, after man was done with him. How forgiving would He be?

"And what about my daughter? What about Emily?" He tried to keep his voice even and unemotional.

"I met her in the market," Crandall explained, and Nottingham could hear his small pleasure at the memory. "We talked about life and hope." He glanced up to face the Constable. "I'd never found anyone like that before. She listened to me. She's not afraid of life. It felt as if we'd been looking for each other. She talked to me about her dreams." He seemed to drift away briefly before saying, "I really would have sent for her. And I'd have prayed she'd come."

"You were leaving," Nottingham said, pushing ahead. "If you cared so much for her, why didn't you want to stay?"

"I wanted to." Crandall gave a weak smile. "But I knew you were close. I saw your men out on Sunday night. I still have work to do. If you won't let me do it here, there are other cities that need me."

He sounded so sincere, Nottingham thought. He truly believed all this, God help him.

"Why did you tell Emily to keep your name secret?" he asked.

"Would you have approved of the match?" The curate shook his head to answer his own question before the Constable could respond. "You'd have thought the worst of me. And later..." He shrugged. "She kept faith with me."

"And you never imagined bedding her?"

"Of course not," he said dismissively. Nottingham waited for more, but Crandall was quiet.

"Why did you give her the token you took from Pamela?"

The curate replied as if the explanation was obvious.

"Because a whore didn't deserve the promise of love; Emily does. I knew I'd have to go before you caught me. I wanted to give her a keepsake."

"That token belonged to my mother," Nottingham told him coldly. "She was a whore. I gave it to Pamela as a birthday gift when she was our servant."

The curate was silent for a long time.

"Ask Emily not to think too badly of me," he said eventually.

"No, Mr Crandall. I'll keep telling her the truth about you until she believes me."

Nottingham let the door close loudly and finally, locking the madness behind him.

Nottingham found Mary kneading dough, forearms deep in the big glazed bowl, punching down firmly and continuously. He came up behind her softly, putting his arms around her waist and burying his head against her neck.

"How is she?" he asked softly.

"At school. I took her myself." She turned and held him at arms' length. "Did you really have to hit her like that? Her cheek's all bruised and swollen."

He was silent for a moment before he spoke.

"Yes," he answered honestly. He'd thought about it as he walked home. He'd thought about a lot of things, both good and bad, scared of what he might find if he let his thoughts stay anywhere for too long. But he knew he had needed that information from Emily, and he'd needed it immediately. "I had to have that name. She wouldn't trust me enough to tell me."

"You terrified her."

"I had to," he began. "That young man she was protecting had killed Pamela and five other people. For what's it's worth, I didn't do it out of anger. I'd begged her. It was desperation, the only way to save him from someone who'd have taken delight in killing him very slowly."

She began working on the dough again, pushing at it hard. He stood and watched in silence. Finally she stopped and asked, "Did you catch him?"

"Yes."

Mary looked at him, wanting to know more. He tried to explain. "We found him first thing. He seemed to believe he was teaching all of us about sin by killing."

Nottingham sighed. The deaths had all been so futile. "He's mad. But he'll hang soon enough." He poured himself a mug of ale from the jug on the table and produced a piece of paper from his pocket. "He wouldn't have hurt Emily. He left a letter for her."

She took her hands from the bowl and wiped them on an old piece of cloth.

"What does it say?" she asked him.

"That he has to leave her, he'll never forget her, and he'll send for her," he answered with disgust. "All the words to tear a young girl's heart apart. It'll be bad enough when I tell her he's to die, without her seeing this."

Mary raised an eyebrow.

"Are you going to give it to her?"

He shook his head quietly.

"I can't. She might believe him." He walked over to the fire and tossed the paper into the flame, waiting until it all turned to ash. Emily need never know about Crandall's letter, thank God. And she'd learn all about his evil.

"Richard?" she said softly, reaching out her hands. He took them, rubbing his fingers over the skin of her palms. "She's going to hate you, but give her time, please. She's never been in love before and her world's just been turned upside down."

He wanted to smile and reassure her, but he couldn't. Instead he gently kissed the backs of her hands and said, "I need to sleep."

31

Crandall was committed to the Quarter Sessions. Nottingham gave his evidence, then sat at the front of the court. He watched the curate's pale, almost lifeless face throughout, and supervised as he was led away to the secure jail under the Moot Hall. There was no doubt as to the end; Crandall was already a dead man in everything but fact.

On his way back he stopped to see Meg, to tell her that justice had been done, and repeat what he'd heard in Chapel Allerton. It was cold comfort, he knew, but at least now she could begin to understand. As much as anyone could understand lunacy. The logic of it was like dew, Nottingham thought; it evaporated in the light.

Sir Robert Bartlett had sent a note filled with apologies. Such a long time had passed since Pamela left, and although he knew the curate had gone to Leeds, he'd never suspected a man of the cloth of murder. He felt a fool. But he was no more a fool than anyone else, thought the Constable.

After a few days, life began to fall into its old patterns. Crime continued; cutpurses and pickpockets struck, men fought after drinking. It was all simple stuff, nothing his men couldn't handle. After finishing his work, Nottingham began going next door to the White Swan for a couple of mugs of ale before walking home. His house had become a tense place. Emily, the bruise on her cheek just beginning to fade, wouldn't speak to him. He wanted to talk to her, but Mary kept counselling him to be patient.

He was ruminating, sipping idly from the cup, when

Sedgwick sat down heavily across the table, wearing his first smile in a week.

"Good news?"

"I've got James back," Sedgwick beamed. "Turns out Annie was happy to give him up. Got hersen a soldier and she's off with him."

"You'll see he's brought up right." Nottingham raised the mug in a toast.

"Aye, boss, I will."

"Who's going to look after him, though?" he wondered. As far as he knew, Sedgwick had no family to call on.

"There's a lass I know. She's going to move in." A faint blush of embarrassment crossed his cheeks.

"Good luck to you." He felt genuinely happy for the deputy.

"She's a prostitute," Sedgwick admitted.

"As long as she's not one of Worthy's girls," Nottingham warned him with a wink.

Sedgwick smiled, glancing around the inn, then brought his head closer to the Constable's, speaking in a quiet, secretive voice.

"I was wondering, boss…" he began, then drew a breath and continued. "You said I'd need to learn to read and write to get on."

"You do."

"And now it's me and James – "

" – and your new girl," the Constable added, smiling.

"Her, too," he agreed readily. "Well, would you teach me? You were right, I've seen that."

Nottingham leaned back. For the first time since this business had begun, his heart felt lighter.

"I'd be glad to, John."

He left Sedgwick to drink to a happier future. Instead of walking over Timble Bridge back to Marsh Lane, he headed down Briggate, past the bellowing laughter and voices from the taverns and the whores touting for business. On Swine Gate he walked into Worthy's house. The woman sat sleeping in the front room, a glass of gin on the table beside her, but the children had gone.

The pimp was holding court in the kitchen, perched on a high stool close to the blazing fire. Two girls and three of his men stood in the room, off guard until Nottingham entered, when the men began to reach for knives and cudgels. Worthy waved them back casually as he turned to the Constable with a wintery smile.

"I'll give you this, laddie – you've got balls showing yourself here." He dismissed the others with terse words: "You useless lot have work to do, so you'd better get doing it," and waited until the room was empty.

"Sit down," Worthy said, indicating a battered wooden chair across the small, overheated room. "So you think it's polite to welsh on a deal to give me the curate and still walk into my house, Constable?"

"From what he told me, you had him and he escaped again," Nottingham answered mildly, watching the other man. "You knew I could never keep the bargain, Amos."

Worthy gave a curt nod.

"I wanted to know how desperate you were, Mr Nottingham."

"And you found out." The Constable sat back.

"That's not why you're here, though," the pimp told him.

"Isn't it?" Nottingham asked.

Worthy's face relaxed into a rictus grin.

"Of course not, laddie. You have things you need to ask me."

Nottingham let the statement hang between them. Finally

he said, "Since you seem to know the answers, why don't you save me the trouble of questions?"

"But it's your job to ask questions, Mr Nottingham," the pimp smirked. "I wouldn't deprive you of that."

Sod it, Nottingham thought. He wasn't in the mood to play these games this evening. He didn't want to be here. He didn't want to think about why he hadn't shot Worthy on the river-bank. But the pimp was right, he had questions that needed answers.

"The token, Amos," he started. "You knew what it meant when you saw Emily wearing it. How? How did you know?"

"Straight to the crux, laddie?" Worthy taunted.

Nottingham nodded. It was the real question, one he'd gone over so many times since Crandall's arrest. How could Worthy have known about the token?

"And tell me the truth."

The pimp appraised him warily and raised an eyebrow.

"If you're sure that's what you want."

"I am," the Constable said decisively.

Worthy shrugged, then gathered his thoughts for a moment. Finally he reached into his deep waistcoat pocket, feeling around before drawing something out and tossing it on the table between them.

"Look at it," he commanded.

It took Nottingham a few seconds to realise exactly what he was seeing. At first he thought it was the token, that somehow Worthy had picked his pocket. His hand went to his breeches… and then he understood. It was the other half, the metal rubbed shiny by the years, a hole neatly drilled through the metal. When he was younger he'd dreamed of this time. Now the moment left him defenceless. In shock he raised his eyes to Worthy.

"Does that explain anything to you?" the pimp asked coldly.

He didn't know how to answer. A chill filled him. He stared at the other half of the token again.

"No," he replied thickly. He reached out, picked it up and polished it with his fingers before putting it back on the table. Like this it explained nothing at all.

"Now, are you sure still want the whole truth?"

Nottingham nodded.

"Please," he said, knowing he was begging and not caring. He had to hear the tale.

Worthy raised a thick eyebrow. "Right, then. You remember what happened when you were a lad?" he asked, searching for confirmation in Nottingham's eyes. "You know your mother took a lover? Well, that lover was me. I don't suppose it matters any more how it happened, save that we didn't meet until after you were born – you were three, in fact. But your father found out eventually, and convinced himself that you couldn't be his son. So he turned the pair of you out, never mind that the house was a place she'd inherited from her father." Worthy coughed, picked up a glass of gin from the table and swallowed it in one swoop. "You remember leaving?"

The Constable nodded. He'd tried to put it from his mind, but he'd never been able to completely.

"She turned to me. I'd have helped her if I could. But your father had decided to destroy me, too." For a minute he appeared lost in his reflections, but Nottingham stayed silent, scarcely breathing. "He was a powerful man in this city, was your father. I was in trade, not a merchant, not that class, although they were my main customers. Your father made sure they all knew who was responsible for the downfall of his wife. Within two months I didn't have a business any more. He'd succeeded."

"What about my mother?" Nottingham's voice was dry, his throat suddenly parched.

A wan smile crossed Worthy's face.

"I had no money left to support her, lad. I had no reputation, I had nothing. I tried thieving for a while, but I wasn't any good at it. I wanted my revenge on them all, though. Your mother had been forced to whore, just to make ends meet." His words tailed off. "She hated it, you know," he said, looking at Nottingham. "There just wasn't anything else she could do, she had no skills, no one would take her as a servant with a child, especially a fallen woman. So she did the only thing she could. When I started running girls just to get by she started to despise me. I was making money, but she wouldn't take any when I tried to give it to her. Then she refused to take any comfort in me." He shrugged. "So finally I stopped coming around where I wasn't wanted any more. She wouldn't even let me near."

When he finished, the only sounds were muffled, only half-heard from other parts of the house.

"The token?" Nottingham prompted him.

"I made it when she was still with your father. Cut the coin and drilled the holes myself. It was our secret, our bond." He began to cough again, then spat phlegm on the flagstone floor before nodding at the coin. "Take it."

The Constable hesitated.

"Take it, laddie. I've told you the story now."

Abruptly, Worthy turned and left the room.

Nottingham stood slowly. The muscles in his back ached and he took time to stretch. He wasn't sure what he'd expected to hear when he arrived, but it hadn't been this. He reached out and closed his fingers around the token, weighing it lightly, looking at the way time had eroded the design. Worthy had carried it around all the time. His mind felt as if it was tumbling around him, bringing to light things he'd locked away for years. Then he slipped it into his pocket, where it could finally join its mate after so long. He made his way down the hall. Worthy was in the front room, standing over the old woman in the chair.

"Think on, lad. The past is past. You'll get nowt for dwelling on it. The present is the only thing that counts."

Afterword

Very little of 1731 Leeds remains nowadays. There are two churches (St John's and Holy Trinity – the present parish church dates from the 1800s), the Ship Inn, and Turk's Head Yard. The old street names are still there, however – although you'll never find Queen Charlotte's Court, which is my invention – in very much the same layout. Richard Nottingham and John Sedgwick might gaze in stupefaction and horror at many of the modern buildings, but they'd still be able to navigate from place to place.

I've tried to be as accurate as possible with my history, and I owe a debt to several wonderful books, notably *The Illustrated History of Leeds*, by Steven Burt and Kevin Grady (Breedon, 1994), *The Municipal History of Leeds*, by James Wardell (Longman, Brown, 1846), *Leeds*, by Ivan Broadhead (Smith Settle, 1990), *The Merchants' Golden Age: Leeds 1700-1790*, by Steven Burt and Kevin Grady (Grady and Burt, 1987), *Chapel Allerton: From Village to Suburb*, by R Faulker (Chapel Allerton Residents' Association, no date), and a number of publications from the excellent and helpful Thoresby Society, as well the seminal work on Leeds, *Ducatus Leodiensis*, by Ralph Thoresby (handily available on CD-ROM). Any historical failings are purely my own.

I was born and raised in Leeds, but the real genesis of *The Broken Token* happened far away, when I lived in Seattle. I'd go back to Leeds regularly, but it was the advent of eBay that brought a number of the above works into my possession.

Although this book has my name on the cover, several others have played important roles in bringing it to publication. Lynne Patrick of Crème de la Crime believed in the novel, Thom Atkinson (a superb writer) offered his insightful and constructive criticism, ideas, and above all, friendship. Linda Hornberg gave her skills to draw the wonderful map. Shonaleigh gave graceful lessons in the art of storytelling, and Emma performed an initial edit. Without all of you, this would never have come to fruition, and I'm hugely grateful to you.

Meet Richard Nottingham again in

CRIMINAL TENDENCIES

**a diverse and wholly engrossing collection of short
stories from some of the best of the UK's crime writers.**

**£1 from every copy sold of this
first-rate collection will go to support the
NATIONAL HEREDITARY
BREAST CANCER HELPLINE**

*She lay on her face, as if asleep. I turned her over and saw the deep
wound on her brow...*
– Reginald Hill, *John Brown's Body*

*...she was shaking badly. Terror was gripping her; the same terror she
previously experienced only in her dreams...*
– Peter James, *12 Bolinbroke Avenue*

*His lips were thin and pale. "She must be following us. She's some sort
of stalker."*
– Sophie Hannah, *The Octopus Nest*

*When he thought he was alone, he squatted down and opened the
briefcase. I was interested to see that it contained an automatic pistol
and piles and piles of banknotes.*
– Andrew Taylor, *Waiting for Mr Right*

*Avengers, that's what we are. We're there to avenge the punters who pay
our wages.*
– Val McDermid, *Sneeze for Danger*

The job was a real peach. Soft, juicy, ripe for plucking.
– Simon Brett, *Work Experience*

ISBN: 978-09557078-5-8   **£7.99**

DEBT OF DISHONOUR   Mary Andrea Clarke

Even a highwayman has friends –
sometimes in unexpected places

London society is outraged when charming, popular Boyce Polp is murdered on his way to an evening party, apparently by one of the highwaymen who make travelling even a few miles such a perilous business.

But Miss Georgiana Grey, herself no stranger to peril, has her own reasons for doubting the version of the tragedy which is soon the talk of the town.

She uncovers a darker side to Polp, and though her probing makes her as unpopular as the Bow Street Runner who is investigating the case, Georgiana is determined that justice will prevail.

Third adventure for the Crimson Cavalier.

Published August 2010   **£7.99**
ISBN: 9780956056641

The Crimson Cavalier also rides in:
The Crimson Cavalier   ISBN: 9780955158957
Love Not Poison   ISBN: 9780956056603

ALSO COMING FROM
CRÈME DE LA CRIME:

**A brand new case for Birmingham's finest from
one of Crème de la Crime's most popular authors**

DEATH LINE   **Maureen Carter**

*When a child is murdered
everyone gets a life sentence...*

When ten-year-old Josh Banks's body is discovered dumped on
waste ground, Detective Sergeant Bev Morriss wants justice. She's not
alone. Everyone hates child killers – even hardened criminals.

Tip-offs trickle in, and the new press liaison officer has his work cut
out when the squad springs a leak. Trial by redtop is the least of the
cops' worries.

If Bev's under pressure, her guv faces more: as if nightmare
memories of an earlier case weren't enough, he's facing an internal
enquiry.

Even if he's cleared he's no longer convinced he wants the job.

And if the guv goes – where does that leave Bev?

Published July 2010   **£7.99**
ISBN: 9780956056634

More witty, gritty Bev Morriss mysteries:
Working Girls   ISBN: 9780954763408
Dead Old   ISBN: 9780954763467
Baby Love   ISBN: 9780955158907
Hard Time   ISBN: 9780955158964
Bad Press   ISBN: 9780955707834
Blood Money   ISBN: 9780955707872